“Lynn Downey has captured and cultivated a very enticing time and place. She gives us characters with flesh and blood; plots with intriguing twists and turns. You want a reservation at the H Double Bar Dude Ranch! That’s why I predict this second book in her series will fill her walls with even more awards!”—Jana Bommersbach, author of *Cattle Kate* and co-author with Bob Boze Bell of *Hellraisers and Trailblazers, The Real Women of the Wild West.*

“The wonderful Phoebe Kelley—fledgling author and accidental investigator—returns in Lynn Downey’s delightful sophomore outing. *Dude or Die* is a leisurely love letter to 1950s dude ranches, suffused with fascinating characters, stunning mid-century fashions, and dashes of suspense and romance. It’s sure to captivate readers hungry for a smart story about a strong, independent woman.”—Theresa Kaminski, author of *Queen of the West: The Life and Times of Dale Evans.*

“Dude or Die captures idyllic cowboy life, and the H Double Bar dude ranch brings the thrill and excitement of rodeo by holding the first ‘dudeo.’ What’s more, the book introduces a character who represents a story of the American West not often told: the story of Americans with Japanese heritage who endured a shameful injustice of forced internment during WWII.

“I’m a fourth-generation Japanese American who grew up hearing my family’s stories of internment. Their sacrifices shaped the lives of the generations who followed and their stories will always be honored. I’m also a former professional trick rider and was delighted that this beloved rodeo artform is featured in *Dude or Die.* The partnership between rider and horse is truly special and Lynn Downey really captures this deep connection with her characters. This unique intersection of Japanese American identity and rodeo trick riding brings to light the prevailing strength shared by both worlds. That strength is resiliency or, as the cowboys would say, *grit.*" —Miko McFarland, global educator and professional trick rider.

"Give me a book about horses, dude ranching, and trick riding, and I'm one happy reader. But I was especially happy while reading Lynn Downey's book, *Dude or Die,* which weaves together all three subjects in an intriguing, fun story. A sequel to her first novel, *Dudes Rush In,* the book again features Phoebe, whose investigative skills are put to new test when a trick rider with a mysterious past comes to the ranch. And then there's the romance that lingers in the air. Downey's love and knowledge of dude ranching shines through the story. I believe the correct term for *Dude or Die* is a 'page turner.' Here's hoping a third book is in the works."—H. Alan Day, author of *Lazy B, The Horse Lover* and *Cowboy Up,* and co-host of *The Cowboy Up Podcast.*

"From the changing cast of characters—two with a malicious agenda—to a colorful description of a 'dudeo,' to a tender love story, Lynn Downey writes with a knowledge and passion for the American dude ranch. Whether you're a seasoned rider, a dude, or a dudine, *Dude or Die* will leave you ready to saddle up for your own dude ranch vacation. I look forward to the next novel in the H Double Bar Dude Ranch series."—Sandra V. McGee, Co-author of *The Divorce Seekers—A Photo Memoir of a Nevada Dude Wrangler.*

"Dude or Die reads like the author, Lynn Downey, had a ball writing it. Like the first novel in her dude ranch series, the story centers on Phoebe, a can-do heroine drawn to the magic of Tribulation, Arizona. The author's deep knowledge of 1950s dude ranching is evident in the rich details. I was utterly charmed by the Double H Ranch—from the people who run it, to the food they eat and the clothes they wear. That's not to say it's all happy trails—serious mishaps are plaguing the H Double Bar, and Phoebe is driven to investigate. But while she boldly dives into the mystery at the ranch, she avoids investigating the longings of her heart. This creates a wonderful tension for the reader—and a rewarding ending when Phoebe's able to solve both. Warning: This book may compel you to drink whisky and Google 'dude ranches.'"—Kate Anger, author of *The Shinnery*

"This novel took me right back to the days of my first stay on a dude ranch in Arizona. The plot is a page turner, the history the author includes is surprising, and the characters are realistic and very lovable. *Dude or Die* helped me relive some of the happiest days, and gave me a much-needed break to return to those heartwarming memories. I hope there will be a sequel."—Manuela Schneider, award-winning novelist, author of *Arma del Diablo,* and filmmaker of *Miner's Candle.*

Praise for Dudes Rush In

Winner

Will Rogers Medallion Award
2021 First Place for Arizona Historical Fiction,
New Mexico/Arizona Book Awards

"*Dudes Rush In* is the touching story of two bereft women, separated by decades, whose lives cross in the most unexpected manner. Set against the expansive landscape of the Arizona desert, Downey has created a compelling story of love, betrayal, greed, and redemption."—Donis Casey, author of *The Wrong Girl*, starring Bianca LaBelle, star of the silent screen action serial *The Adventures of Bianca Dangereuse*.

"This page turner of a novel truly captures and illustrates the hospitality and ambiance of an Arizona dude ranch in the 1950s and even today."—Bryce Albright, Executive Director of The Dude Ranchers' Association.

"In *Dudes Rush In* Lynn Downey demonstrates a novelist's imagination for plot twists and believable characters and a historian's grasp of realistic locales and events. Downey's female characters are relatable, colorful, and smart—like friends I want to hang around with myself. As fast-paced as a beach read but smarter, *Dudes Rush In* is a book for both a sunshiny day and a rainstorm that sends you to your favorite reading chair. Even without visiting the H Double Bar Dude Ranch in person, I could almost smell the spicy sagebrush and piney, citrusy creosote bushes. I hope to meet the independent-minded Phoebe McFarland again in future books."—Jill Hunting, author of *Finding Pete: Rediscovering the Brother I Lost in Vietnam.*

"*Dudes Rush In* was a pure joy to read! Compelling characters inhabit these pages and Downey's knowledge of the Arizona desert and its history, with excellent writing, have combined to make a real page turner. Dude ranches; mines; western life; and intrigue are cloaked in a great story from start to finish. Her first novel? No way! More Ms. Downey, more!" —Dr. Jay Cravath, scholar, musician and writer of humanities and indigenous studies. His latest album is *Songs for Ancient Days*.

Lynn Downey

ISBN# 978-1-941052-69-3Trade Paper
ISBN# 978-1-941052-70-9 Ebook
Library of Congress Control Number: 2023945868

Cover Design: Antelope Design
After a photograph of the Monte Vista Dude Ranch, Wickenburg, Arizona. Courtesy Desert Caballeros Western Museum, Wickenburg.

Pronghorn Press
pronghornpress.org

This book is for my father,
Harvey O. Downey, Jr.
(1925-2005)

And for the friends he lost
to prejudice and war
from
Analy High School
Sebastopol, California
Class of 1943

1

June 1954

AS THE APPLAUSE washed over her, Phoebe looked again at the front row of chairs, even though she knew the man with the roadrunner bola tie wasn't there. This was San Francisco, not Phoenix. She smiled as the audience members started raising their hands to ask questions, and called on a college-age brunette whose hat was starting to slide off her head.

"Can you please explain again how the diary you found got to the dude ranch where you were staying?" She managed to catch her hat before it fell on the floor.

"Sure. I went out to the H Double Bar dude ranch in Tribulation, Arizona, two years ago to help my late husband's sister Mary and her husband, who own the place. I stayed in a little house on the ranch, which Mary furnished with a few pieces of furniture she bought at a church rummage sale. One of them was an old desk. I discovered a hidden panel in it one day, and out popped the diary, written by Ellender Shepherd starting in 1910."

A man who was probably in his fifties, wearing a salt-and-pepper tweed jacket that was too small for him, raised his hand next.

"Why did you turn the diary into a novel? Why didn't you use it as the basis for a history book, perhaps something that could be used for a college class?"

"Well, I did consider that, but the diary had so many exciting elements I thought it was better suited for fiction."

The man obviously didn't like this answer, but Phoebe moved on, answering a few more questions before Dorothy, the bookstore's manager, got her attention and announced that it was time for the book signing. Phoebe stepped away from the podium and sat at a table covered with copies of *Lady in the Desert.* She smiled again as the first customer approached, picked up a copy, handed money to Dorothy and gave the book to Phoebe to sign. After everyone had walked away happy with her book under their arms, Phoebe turned to Dorothy.

"Thanks again for setting this up for me."

"Are you kidding? I've been bugging the owner for weeks to get you in here. I finally convinced him that a book about a woman who helps find some lost gold in the Arizona desert would bring in the crowds. And I was right."

Phoebe smiled. "Even I wasn't sure about the story at first. I thought it was just something that was interesting to me. But the response has been amazing."

"I think when people learn that Ellender Shepherd was a real person, and that the plot of your novel came from a diary that had been hidden away for forty years, they're hooked."

The two women gathered up extra books as they chatted. Phoebe asked if she needed any help putting the chairs away, but Dorothy thanked her and said she would take care of it. They shook hands, and Phoebe picked up the well-worn copy of her novel, her purse, and the small briefcase where she kept Ellender's diary.

Written with a strong hand in still-dark ink, the old accounting ledger with its deep-red leather cover and gold-edged pages was in good shape, and Phoebe wanted to keep it that way. She stored it inside a linen pillowcase that her mother had embroidered with pastel-colored flowers. When she took the diary to book talks, she kept it inside the case she'd splurged on at Gump's.

Books, Inc. was only three blocks from Phoebe's apartment at the corner of Sutter and Jones, near San Francisco's vibrant downtown. Her family's former business, an equally busy corner grocery, was now owned by Bob and Sue, a young couple from Nevada. It took up the ground floor of the building where her apartment was; the place where she'd grown up and to where she had retreated when her husband Jack died during the war. With her parents gone, it now belonged to her.

She walked up a flight of stairs and once inside her home, she put the briefcase on a shelf in her bedroom closet, changed into a pair of slacks and a white cotton shirt, and made a cup of coffee.

Her talk had started at 2:30 p.m. on this first Saturday in June, and it was now just 4:15. Too early for cocktails, but not too early to call Katie and see if she wanted to get together for dinner and a movie. She sat at the telephone table and dialed her friend.

"Hi Katie, I'm back."

"How did it go?"

"Thirty people! I couldn't believe it. The book has only been out for two months."

"Well, I believe it. I've seen you in action, and your publisher certainly has faith in you. Sorry I couldn't make it this time."

"You've already come to two of my book signings. I think you've earned the right to do what you want with your time."

Katie chuckled, and Phoebe asked, "How did finals go?"

"The usual horrors, but I had a few standouts in my western history class. Graduation is next Saturday, thank goodness."

"I miss being on campus, but I don't miss finals."

"I wish I could miss them."

Phoebe knew Katie didn't mean it. She loved teaching at San Francisco State College, even with exams.

"So, shall we go out to celebrate?" asked Katie.

"I'd love to."

"Let's get dinner and then see *Dial M for Murder*. I've been waiting for the latest Hitchcock to hit theaters."

Phoebe agreed. They decided to eat at John's Grill, so Katie drove over from her apartment near State, found a parking place on Jones, and the two friends took a cab to the restaurant. They both liked to walk, but not in the pumps they wore for evening. June nights could also be chilly in San Francisco, especially for women in thin nylon stockings.

Once they were seated, they ordered cocktails, and after the drinks arrived Katie asked Phoebe about her date the previous night.

"Richard just isn't giving up on you, is he?"

"I like him, and we had a good time. He took me to the St. Francis for drinks after dinner."

"So, is anything else happening? Do you have another date planned?"

"Not really. I managed to not commit to anything at the moment."

"Why not? He's a great guy. He's got a job with that big accounting firm. He's a...what do they call that? A rising young executive."

"Yep, that's it. He's nice, he's well-dressed, and actually reads books. But he's not..."

Katie jumped into the void.

"Exciting?"

Phoebe shrugged.

"Well, I'm not surprised," said Katie.

"Really?"

"Of course not. You went to Arizona and met cowboys, a cop, and a murderer. How can an accountant possibly compare?"

"I didn't think of that."

"Phoebe, you've never been truly conventional."

"High praise from the woman who takes a movie camera with her wherever she goes."

"Why do you think you were so intrigued by Ellender's diary? She was an independent thinker, too, and that was in 1910 when women were supposed to be compliant and not have opinions."

"True. Well, I'm not going to worry about Richard, or anyone else at the moment. I'm still doing some clearing out at the apartment. I've been looking for a job in the Help Wanted ads too, but there hasn't been anything very...um....exciting."

"Maybe you aren't interested in Richard because you've got your eye on someone else."

Phoebe blushed a bit and stammered, "Uh...who do you mean?"

"There are a couple of men you've been talking

about for the last year and a half. Who live in another state, for god's sake." When Phoebe didn't respond, Katie sighed. "You're really trying to make this difficult, aren't you?"

"No. I just don't want to make a mistake like I did with Jack."

"That wasn't a mistake, Phoebe."

"Okay, maybe not. Anyway, I don't want to rush into anything. And what about you? When was the last time you went on a date?"

"The only men I meet are academics, and they do not approve of women wanting to become filmmakers. If I ever find someone who does, then maybe I'll have dinner with him. But until then, I'm happy on my own."

"I thought I was, too, but it would be nice to have someone in my life again."

"Of course it would. For you, I mean. You have a lot to give to someone. Someone who lives in Arizona."

Phoebe rolled her eyes, and Katie got serious.

"Are you still having nightmares?"

"You know, I haven't had a nightmare for maybe six months now. I guess I'm finally getting over what happened out at the ranch."

"Well, you're too level-headed to let something bother you forever."

Phoebe smiled her thanks. They finished their dinner and took the short stroll to the St. Francis Theater.

They cabbed back to Phoebe's place for a nightcap after the movie, talking all the while about its twists and turns.

Katie thought Hitchcock was a genius.

Phoebe was still thinking about the film the next evening, and just as she mentally replayed the pivotal phone call scene, her own phone rang, and she jumped. She chuckled and picked up the receiver.

“Hi, Phoebe.”

“Virgil! How are you?”

“I’m good, thanks. How did your book talk go?”

“What? Do you keep my schedule on your desk or something?”

“Well, yes.”

Phoebe smiled, and Virgil heard it in her voice when she spoke.

“It went well, the people really loved Ellender’s story. But you know that already.”

“I do. What are your plans for the summer?”

“I was actually going to write you a letter tonight and tell you the latest. I have one more book signing this month, but I’m also looking for work.”

“Are you having money trouble? Oh, sorry, that’s none of my business.”

“It’s not a big deal. You know I have a very long lease on my apartment, my family’s apartment, and I sold our grocery store. So, I’ve got a nice nest egg, but I can’t really be a lady of leisure. Besides, I like working, being out in the world with people. I also want to write another book, though I don’t have any ideas at the moment.”

“Have you…uh…considered coming back to Tribulation, to work with Mary and Sam at the ranch again this fall?”

“I love it out there, you know I do. It was great helping Mary for a couple of seasons. I had such fun with the guests...well, *most* of them.”

There was a moment’s silence on both ends of the line. One guest in particular almost cost Phoebe her life.

She took a breath and went on. “I think Mary asked me to help her at the ranch because she thought I needed a change of scenery. And I really did. I confess that I miss the desert and the ranch. And…well, I miss our talks.”

"I do, too."

"I thought about asking Mary if she wanted my help again when the season opens this October, but I don't want to impose. I'm not sure I was that useful."

"Did you tell her that?"

"No. When I left the ranch in April, I said I didn't think I'd be able to return this year. I didn't want to presume she wanted me there, knowing she'd feel awkward about telling me to stay home if she planned to hire more people."

Virgil heard the note of disappointment in her voice. "Well, I'm sorry to hear that."

"I was thinking about coming out over the holidays, though. I'll ask Mary if I can stay in the *casa*. Will you come to visit?"

"Of course I will. I'll always come to town if you're there."Phoebe's face grew warm, but her response was a change of subject."Did you get a new car? You were having trouble with your truck. You told me it couldn't even make it out of your driveway, much less get to Tribulation."

"Yes, I bought a good, used Buick from a buddy here in Phoenix. It runs like a top, and just needed a new set of tires. I put them on myself. I was glad to see that this old man can still do a few things on his own."

"Oh, Virgil. You're not old."

"Spoken like a true whippersnapper. You may think thirty-two is getting up there, but just wait thirty more years to catch up with me."

"Well, I've seen you ride horses, sling hay, and crawl under trucks to fix what's broken. And you weren't a basket case the next day."

"That's just helping out a friend, I don't do it all the time."

"You'll never convince me you're an old-timer."

He just laughed.

"And what does Hunter think of the new car?" she asked. Hunter was Virgil's energetic, mottled-fur cattle dog.

"He doesn't care what he rides in as long as he gets to keep moving."

Phoebe wanted to keep on chatting, but she was mindful of the cost for a long-distance call, even though it was Sunday night and the rates were cheaper. Virgil seemed to have the same idea, as they talked for only a few more minutes and then hung up, promising to write to each other soon.

As she got ready for bed that night, Phoebe thought about how much she really did miss the desert town of Tribulation, and the busy but peaceful life on Mary and Sam's dude ranch. Mary was Jack's sister and she and Phoebe were still close. She and her husband Sam Watts had turned the old McFarland family ranch into a dude outfit during the war. It was thriving, and when Phoebe was at a turning point in her life (her thirtieth birthday) Mary had asked her to come out for the six-month season to help with the paperwork and some guest wrangling.

Phoebe loved it, not just for the place but the people she met, like Virgil. And police officer Steve Magly, who was both handsome and partly responsible for rescuing her when her life was threatened. She and Steve had gone on a few dinner dates before she left Tribulation, and kept in touch with the occasional letter or postcard.

Phoebe also spent time with Virgil before coming back to San Francisco. He drove out to Tribulation from his little house in Phoenix to visit a few times. Being with Virgil was like settling into a favorite coat that held important memories. She avoided examining her feelings too closely, but she knew they were there.

The following Thursday Phoebe got a phone call from the Thomas Cook travel agency, which did big business from their office near Union Square. A woman named Sharon, who was the office manager's secretary, asked her if she could come in to discuss a possible job with the firm, and they set a meeting for the next day at two. Phoebe was intrigued, though Sharon wouldn't tell her what the job was.

She dressed carefully for the interview in a belted, navy blue linen dress with matching heels, and a smart little blue-and-white hat which she perched on the side of the wavy light-brown hair that brushed her shoulders. She started to put on her mother's pearl earrings, but at the last minute decided to clip on the little turquoise roadrunners instead, which Mary had given her for Christmas two years ago. She tied a silk scarf around the handle of her purse, artfully arranging the two ends together. The bright white fabric was decorated with scenes of horses, riders, and cacti, and was last year's Christmas gift from Virgil. She noticed that the hem was frayed on one of her white gloves, and she made a mental note to repair it. Or maybe she would just buy a new pair.

Phoebe walked down to the office, holding on to her hat in the breeze that always came with the summer fogs. She was a few minutes early, and waited by the spacious reception desk, enjoying the collection of colorful booklets and brochures on display.

Right on time, a middle-aged man in a pin-striped blue suit and yellow silk tie walked up to her and introduced himself.

"Miss Kelley? I'm Marshall Flagg, the manager here. Thank you for coming in."

"Hello, it's very nice to meet you."

"You, too. Let's go into my office. Would you like a cup of coffee?"

Phoebe declined with thanks, and they walked into a small, but comfortable office at the back of the room. Flagg gestured to a chair in front of a chrome and glass desk, and sat in a larger chair on the other side.

"Well, first I want to tell you that I loved your book, *Lady in the Desert*."

"Well, thank you, I'm so glad to hear that."

"I run this travel agency and I send people all over the world, but my passion is the West, so your story kept me fascinated for hours. Did you really find that old diary?"

Pleased, Phoebe briefly told him about finding Ellender's diary, a story she never got tired of repeating. She noticed him glancing at her earrings as she spoke.

"That's just astonishing, and I'm envious!" Flagg said. Then he put on a more professional face, cleared his throat, and said, "I asked you to come here today because we need someone to write promotional material for a new series of brochures we will be introducing during the holidays this year. You can certainly write exciting stories, and we could use your skills for these products."

It took a moment for Phoebe to take this in, and then she said, "That sounds very interesting, and I'm flattered that you asked. Can you tell me a bit more about the job?"

Flagg talked about the kind of clients they had and what they expected from the agency, what information the brochures would have, how the office operated, the hours, and the salary. It was lower than she anticipated, given the opulence of the place, and it was even less than what she'd made as a secretary at an insurance company two years ago. But still, the idea of getting a job as a writer was appealing.

"Now, I know you have to think about this. Can you give me an answer by next Friday?"

"Yes, I can. Thank you so much for the offer."

"I appreciate it. And before you go, may I ask you one more thing?"

"Of course."

Flagg stood up, opened the drawer of a metal filing cabinet behind his desk and pulled out a copy of *Lady in the Desert.*

"Would you sign my book?"

Phoebe called Katie to tell her about the job offer as soon as she got home, but her friend didn't answer. So, she spent an hour doing some overdue housework, and then went downstairs to the grocery store where she still did her shopping. She thought she deserved a treat, so she bought a small steak, along with some lettuce and a of couple cans of spinach. She hadn't made her mother's famous creamed spinach for a while, and she had a sudden urge to have that with her dinner.

She ran into one of her elderly neighbors as she walked up the steps to the apartment building's door.

"Hello, Mrs. Pickering. Here, let me hold the door for you."

Phoebe shifted her bag of groceries to one arm and kept the heavy door open for the sturdy, gray-haired matron who always dressed as if she were on her way to church.

"Thank you, Mrs. McFarland...oh, dear, I keep forgetting. It's Miss Kelley, isn't it?"

"That's all right, it took me a while to get accustomed to using my maiden name again."

"Are you writing any more books, dear?"

"I'm thinking about it, thank you."

"You'll do splendidly, I'm sure."

And with that endorsement, the majestic lady marched away.

Phoebe had developed a taste for westerns after her time in Arizona, and as she ate her dinner, she dipped into a copy of Zane Grey's *Riders of the Purple Sage*, which she was rereading. Later she tried Katie again, and got her.

"Oh, Phoebe, I meant to call to find out how the job interview went, I'm sorry. But I had to drive over to Oakland to see someone about buying a used movie camera I've been wanting."

"Which one?"

"The Bell & Howell 172A. It was in perfect condition, and I didn't even ask the guy why he wanted to sell it."

"That's great!"

"So, how did it go today?"

Phoebe gave Katie the full report, concluding with Flagg's request for her to sign his copy of *Lady in the Desert.*

"I love it! Both the job offer and the autograph. Are you going to take it?"

"I don't know. I'm not that intrigued about writing advertising copy. And the pay isn't great. But it wouldn't be the worst way to make a living. At least for a while."

"You mean while you decide what to do next?"

"I suppose. I'm feeling kind of aimless again. I love going to the stores and talking to people about my book, but I only have one more signing and nothing else on the horizon."

"Then you must write another book immediately!"

"Oh, sure, I'll get on that right away."

"And I think I know just what you should write. A western."

"A western? You mean like Zane Grey?"

"No, not like Zane Grey, like Phoebe Kelley. *Lady in the Desert* is a western, even though it didn't have cowboy shootouts or battles with Indians."

"Mr. Flagg at the travel agency thought the book was a western."

"See? You already know what you're doing. You could write a story and set it on a dude ranch."

"Hey, that's not a bad idea. There were plenty of entertaining people at the H Double Bar the last two seasons. And not just the guests."

"Well, write to that publisher of yours...what's his name?"

"Arthur Mackenzie."

"I'll bet he'd love another book from you."

"Thanks, Katie. I'll send him a letter tomorrow."

"When do you have to give a yes or no to the travel agency?"

"On Friday. I could still write my own book even if I start working there, though it would take me longer. I just need to figure out if I'd be happy doing their work. I'm not desperate for money, and I don't want to get stuck in another job where I find myself frustrated all the time, like I was at Universal Insurance."

"Ugh, you do not want to feel that way again."

"Exactly."

Then Phoebe remembered that the following day was graduation at State.

"You'll have to be at the graduation ceremony tomorrow, right?"

“Yes, to repent for my sins.”

“I’m going out with the girls from Universal tomorrow night, why don’t you join us? We’re going to the Top of the Mark.”

“Oh, I’d love to, I need to see that view again. What time?”

“We’re meeting at eight.”

“I’ll be there.”

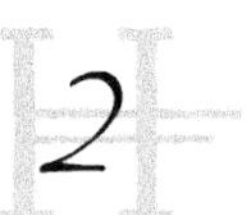

PHOEBE DID A FEW MORE housekeeping chores the following day, then spent some time in her bedroom trying to decide what to wear to the drinks get-together that night. As she rummaged through the jewelry box on her dresser, she gazed with affection at the silver-framed photo next to it. A beautiful young woman in a long, old-fashioned white dress with a ribboned waist looked with happiness into the camera lens as a little girl leaned against her, giving her a kiss on the cheek.

She went into her closet and pulled down the briefcase, taking the old leather diary out of its protective linen covering. She walked into her living room and sat down in the leather chair that had been her mother's.

Opening the volume to the first page, she ran her hand over the thick paper which held the words, *Ellender Shepherd. Her Diary.* Phoebe opened the book at random and read the words which were as familiar as if she'd written them herself.

March 23, 1915—Oh my, what a glorious evening. Virgil took me to dinner again at The Station House, and we sat on Alexandra's porch and had tea after we returned. When he got up to leave, instead of giving me his hand as usual he leaned down and kissed me, so very gently. I returned the kiss, and we looked at each other for a moment afterward. As soon as I walked in the front door I saw Alexandra grinning at me and then she said it was about time.

Phoebe closed the diary and sat for a moment, recalling again with gratitude how reading Ellender's words had changed her life.

"Thanks, Ellender," she whispered.

She moved to the old pine desk that she had refinished the previous year in a warm mahogany. Her beloved Royal typewriter dominated its surface, always within typing distance. She sat down and opened a drawer, pulling out a piece of carbon paper and two sheets of her best stationery. Rolling them into the Royal, she started to type.

June 12, 1954

Mr. Arthur Mackenzie
Mackenzie & Bedford
401 7th Street
Los Angeles, California

Dear Mr. Mackenzie,

I hope this letter finds you well.

You will be pleased to know that I have had great success with the book lectures and signings here in San Francisco. The last event, at Books, Inc., had thirty people in the audience. I think I signed about 19 copies.

I am writing to see if you would be interested in an idea I had for another novel. After spending two seasons at the H Double Bar dude ranch, I think I could come up with a good story about the kind of life and experiences which people have on dude ranches, not to mention the characters who work there. I don't have a concrete plot at present, but if you think this might be of interest to Mackenzie & Bedford, I will be glad to send you a few pages once I get started.

Yours very sincerely,
Phoebe Kelley

She signed her letter, addressed and stamped the envelope, and walked down the street to the mailbox. As she headed home to get ready for her evening out, she told herself she'd better come up with a story in case Mr. Mackenzie *is* interested.

Sitting in the breakfast nook the next morning, drinking the first of what would probably be many cups of coffee, Phoebe decided to start making some notes for the new book. She rummaged through her desk and pulled out a pad of paper. Something fell out from between its pages.

It was a snapshot of Virgil she'd taken at the ranch back in April, just before she left Arizona. He was standing next to his old Chevy truck, smiling the way he always did: open and cheerful with a touch of shyness. He was in a pair of dark jeans and white shirt, with his favorite roadrunner bola tie hanging from the collar. Behind him was the ranch's office, an expanse of clear sky, and Hunter's nose peeking around his shoulder from the bed of the truck.

Virgil had come to Tribulation before she drove back to San Francisco, and they'd had dinner at Mary and Sam's house, in the private area behind the ranch's cabins.

Phoebe propped the picture against a stack of books on her desk, and then returned to her task. She wrote down the names of everyone who worked at the H Double Bar, from Mary and Sam, to the wranglers, waitresses, cook, and maids. She wrote a few pages about the guests she had met during the two seasons she lived at the ranch, about helping Mary with everything from paperwork to serving and holiday decorating. She omitted a couple of names, wishing she could forget them.

The following week she began adding some descriptions to all these "characters," jotting down ideas and organizing the other snapshots she'd taken at the ranch. She ran a few of these past Katie when they went out for dinner on Wednesday night. She also brushed up on the talk she was giving on Saturday at the Woman's Athletic Club.

Phoebe knew she'd been avoiding making a decision about the travel agency job. So, on Thursday she made a list of the arguments both for and against it. They were evenly split. She went to bed that night hoping the next day would bring with it some clarity.

Friday morning she woke with a vague sense of unease and it wasn't until she was drinking her second cup of coffee that she realized what it was. She had forgotten to put something in the "Against" column. If she had a full-time job, she wouldn't be able to go to the H Double Bar whenever she wanted. And even if she could get away for a holiday visit, it would only be for a few days before she'd have to drive back—if they would even give her enough time off.

Her hand jerked and she spilled some of her coffee on the placemat. As she mopped it up she glanced at her kitchen clock, and knew what she had to do. She showered, dressed, and sat at her telephone table until a few minutes after nine. Then she picked up the phone, dialed the travel agency, and asked to speak to Mr. Flagg, hoping he wouldn't be too disappointed when she turned him down.

Phoebe and Katie went to Blum's for milkshakes the following Wednesday afternoon, taking a table by the window. They chatted for a few minutes about the job decision. Her friend understood, and they moved on to discuss Katie's latest film project.

Watching the tourists wander Union Square in the tepid sunshine, Phoebe said, "I got a letter from Mr. Mackenzie yesterday. He likes the dude ranch novel idea."

"Why didn't you say something earlier? That's great! Now what?"

"Well, he wants an outline of the story, which I don't really have. And he said that there has to be a romantic angle somewhere, because that will make the book sell better with women."

Katie laughed. "He's right, it's the same thing with screenplays. Certain aspects of your story have to mirror real life or audiences won't believe it."

"I guess so. It was easy to write about Ellender falling in love because I had her diary to draw from."

"If you're going to write a western, the cowboys should probably carry guns," Katie mused. "And use them," she added with a grin.

"I don't think the wranglers on dude ranches have guns. They sure don't at the H Double Bar...at least I never noticed any."

"Don't they have to be armed against rattlesnakes or coyotes or something? Anyway, remember that guy from the bookstore who thought you should have written Ellender's story as a history book instead of a novel? No one can tell you what to do. It's your story, you can write whatever you want."

"That's true...."

"You don't sound very excited," said Katie.

"I am…I guess. I love the ranch, and it would be fun to write about it, but the idea doesn't grab me like the diary did."

"That's because it affected you so personally. You mustn't doubt your ability, you've already written a successful novel. Coming up with a new idea is different, but I know you can do it. You just have to sit down and give it some serious thought."

"Yes, Miss Palmer," Phoebe said, sounding like a chastised student.

Phoebe spent the next couple of days making notes for a story, but threw all the pages away. She got more frustrated as the wastebasket filled up, so she took a break and walked a couple of blocks to I. Magnin.

Wandering the aisles, she came across a selection of patio dresses, and remembered how much she liked the one that Mary wore for special occasions at the H Double

Bar. She took a few off the rack to try on, and decided on a deep brown dress with copper-colored contrasting fabric on the heavily pleated skirt, and in a V-shape on the bodice. Rows of sparkly gold rickrack decorated the skirt and its hem, and the edges of the sleeves. It was a flattering style, and even though she couldn't think of an occasion where she would wear it, she wanted to have it in her closet. She also picked up another two pairs of white gloves, and went back to the apartment with more of a spring in her step.

Phoebe's phone rang on Sunday evening and she was tickled when she heard Mary's voice.

"Mary! I'm so glad to hear from you. Where are you, exactly?"

"We're still on vacation in Wyoming with Sam's family. Joe loves it here in Cody, and he's mad about the rodeo. He insists on going every Friday night. He's turning out to be quite the cowboy."

"What? He's only ten."

"Well, Jack and I were riding when we were younger than that. Our parents put us on horses almost as soon as we could walk."

"I keep forgetting what a horsey life you and Jack had had growing up."

"Well, Jack never really took to cowboying. He just wanted to go to college and move to the big city."

"He got that wish, at least," said Phoebe.

"True...anyway, I'm calling to ask you a big favor."

"Anything."

"Will you come back to the ranch again in the fall and help us out this season?"

When Phoebe didn't respond, Mary asked, "Are you still there?"

"Sorry...I'm just surprised that you want me. I thought everything was running smoothly, especially with your new employees."

"Well, that's the problem. The woman I hired to be the secretary/bookkeeper has left, and I don't know if I can get anyone else. You're the only one that I can count on."

"What do you mean? Aren't there enough qualified women looking for jobs? Tribulation is a small town, but they teach business skills at the high school, don't they?"

"Qualified isn't the issue. We've got competition."

"You've never worried about the other dude ranches before."

"There's never been a place like the Desert Grande before."

Phoebe heard the worry in Mary's voice.

"What's the Desert Grande?"

"It calls itself a 'guest' ranch, not a dude ranch, which means it's less authentic than a place like ours, because we also run cattle. No one is really sure who owns it, but someone bought the old Twitchell place about two miles west of town. They remodeled the main house, added a bunch of rooms to it, rebuilt and expanded the barn and stables, put in a skeet shooting and archery range, and bought a bunch of Jeeps."

"What for?"

"Taking people on backcountry desert trips. They offer horseback riding, of course, but they figure some guests might not always want to do anything that... *strenuous*." Mary's voice dropped an octave.

"It sounds more like a resort. People who want the real dude ranch experience won't go to a place like that, will they?" asked Phoebe.

"Some people won't, certainly not our regulars.

But they have also opened up their dining room to anyone who wants to eat there, like it's a regular restaurant. They have a snooty chef from a hotel in Reno or Las Vegas or one of those gambling towns. And they are snatching up wranglers from the other ranches."

"They haven't lured away Gene and Lorraine have they?"

The Bowmans were Mary's head wranglers, and the only married couple with that title in Arizona.

"No, thank goodness. They tried, and Gene told them where to get off. Carl and Bob also turned them down. But what if the Desert Grande's owner starts throwing more and more money at my people? They're only human."

"Mary, stop. I think you're getting too worked up. You have loyal employees and guests, and you get new visitors every year because people go home and tell their friends how much fun they had at the H Double Bar. I'll bet this other place charges a lot more money too, don't they?"

"Not really. Even with all of their special activities and expensive décor and food, their fees are only a little bit higher than ours. It looks like they're trying to put us and all the other smaller ranches out of business. Oh, and they are also opening a month before everyone else on the weekend after Labor Day."

"My god, won't it still be too hot?"

"Get this. They installed central air conditioning in the main building. I'll bet that cost more than remodeling the whole place."

"Where is all this money coming from?"

"Nobody knows, but I'm really worried…"

Phoebe cut her off. "Mary, I've never heard you sound like this. Now look, I'm serious. You're going to be fine. This is just a new kind of competition. You need to keep doing what you do best, and that means making sure your guests are happy, spending time with them, seeing to their needs. People come back to the H Double Bar because of you, Mary."

"Thanks. But we aren't going to take this lying down. Which is why I need you."

"Well…"

"Wait, before you say no, hear me out. I know you are looking for a job, and you've been spending time with your friends. I can't do anything about them, but I am willing to pay you to come out here to help me run the ranch like you've done the last two seasons."

"But…"

"I'll pay you a salary because you wouldn't just be helping me with the correspondence, and checking in the guests. We want to offer more things for people to do in the evenings, so we bought a bunch of new board games and Sam will put in a horseshoe pit. But the big thing is our rodeo."

"You're kidding."

"I talked to some people here in Cody and got a lot of advice on how to stage a small rodeo with events for the dudes and the cowboys. I also wrote to George Pierson out in California. He's got a big dude ranch, and they put on this kind of rodeo all the time. So, I think we can pull it off, but I'm going to need help with organization, and with the influx of tourists who will come just to see and participate in the rodeo and, well, with everything. I know it's a lot to ask, but I'll make it worth your while to give up getting a job there in San Francisco, and…"

"Mary, would you please shut up for a minute? Of course I'll come."

Mary's intake of breath sounded like a sob.

"Oh...honey, thank you. I can't tell you how much I appreciate this and wait...Sam wants to talk to you."

"Hi Phoebe. Sounds like you're going to come back to help us out?"

"Yes, I'd love to, Sam."

"I think Mary is worrying too much about those Desert Grande people, but it will be wonderful to have you here again."

Phoebe could hear the smile in Sam's voice.

"I can't wait to see you all."

"Thanks. Here's Mary."

"Phoebe, can you get here before Labor Day? We're going to open mid-September instead of mid-October, and there's a lot of stuff that needs to be organized first."

"Sure, how about the last week of August? I just started working on a new book and I'd like to get some of that under my belt, and find someone to sublet the apartment."

"You're writing again? That's wonderful!"

"I hope so. And Mary…thank you for asking me. I wanted to come back to the ranch again."

"Well, why didn't you say something?"

"I didn't want to seem presumptuous...you know, assume you actually wanted me, or if I'd just be in your way."

"You could never be in my way. We all love it when you're here. What a silly thing to say."

"Okay, you're sounding like yourself again."

"I always sound like myself."

Phoebe laughed and said, "Let me get some paper and a pen. I need to ask you a few questions."

Two days later Phoebe met Katie in her office at San Francisco State College to help organize her books and papers before shutting it up for the summer.

"What's happened? You're practically glowing."

Phoebe grinned. "Mary asked me to come back to the ranch in the fall to help out again this season."

"Wow. You really want to go, don't you?"

"I really do, and I didn't realize how much until I talked with Mary."

"You said she didn't need help this year."

"That's what I thought. But things are different."

Phoebe told her about the Desert Grande, how worried Mary was about losing business to the new place, and what she and Sam planned to do about it.

"From what you've told me, I don't think Mary has anything to be concerned about," said Katie.

"I told her the same thing. But she's putting up a fight, which is why the H Double Bar is going to start offering more activities. They aren't going to copy the other place, just give more to the folks that want that real dude ranch experience."

"So, you're going to run a rodeo for them?"

Phoebe laughed. "No, I'm just going to wrangle the crowds. And do what I've done before, help with the paperwork, check in the guests, probably find people to entertain in the evening, the usual stuff."

"I haven't seen you this excited since…well, since your book came out."

"I am excited. And even though I don't want her to, Mary said she's going to pay me a salary, so I can put a little more money in the bank."

"I'll bet you couldn't talk her out of that."

"Nope."

"When are you going to tell Richard?"

"I'll get around to telling all my friends, and that includes him. I know he'd like us to be something more, but I'm just not interested. I'm actually meeting him for drinks on Friday night, and I'll tell him then."

"That will be an interesting evening. Have you told anyone else in Tribulation yet?"

"I called Virgil after I talked to Mary. He's going to come out and visit as soon as I get settled."

"Did you call your cop friend, Steve?"

"Well, no. I thought I'd just write him a letter. I'm also going to write to Barbara, the head librarian there in town. We always have fun when we get together."

"I see."

"What?"

"The only person worthy of the cost of a phone call was Virgil?"

"Well, I know him best," Phoebe said defensively.

Katie just smiled.

"I wouldn't have Ellender's diary if it wasn't for him, and I wouldn't have my book. So, he's very important to me."

"I see."

"Will you stop saying that?"

"Okay, I just think it's interesting that the person you want to spend the most time with is a man old enough to be your father."

"Oh, it's not like that."

"Whatever you say, Phoebe," she said with an innocent smile. "So, what are you going to do about your apartment? Are you going sublet it again?"

"Yes. I'm leaving at the end of August, and I thought I'd ask the girls from Universal if they know someone who'd like to take the place for a few months."

"Well, I know someone. Me."

"What do you mean?"

"Sublet your place to me."

"Why?"

"I need a bigger apartment. I have so much filmmaking equipment, so many books, and I just need more space. You've seen my flat, it's crammed to the gills. Your place has three bedrooms, and I can use one of them just for storage."

"But it would only be from this fall to next spring. Then what will you do?"

"I'll figure that out later."

"My place is farther away from State than where you are now."

"That doesn't matter, I've got my car and the streetcar goes out there, too. Now, how much do you want for the sublet?"

Phoebe thought for a moment and named a figure that made Katie roll her eyes.

"That's less than the rent I pay now. Come on, give me a figure that's fair."

"It's very fair, I'm getting someone I can trust to take care of the place. That's my final price, take it or leave it."

Katie glared for a moment, and then extended her hand with a smile.

"Deal."

JULY WAS FLYING BY, and Phoebe spent a good part of each day packing for her trip and getting the apartment ready for Katie to move in. The only place that needed attention was the small guest room, which had been her mother's sewing room and which Phoebe had been using for storage. She knew Katie would want to have as much free space as possible, so Phoebe took linens, books, and photo albums off the bed and out of the small dresser and put them into the closet.

She then dug into her own closet for the clothes she had worn the last two years at the ranch, and which she had never worn in San Francisco. Anything she planned to take with her went into the larger guest room, and the bed was soon covered with books, records, and a collection of typing supplies.

She had multiple piles of garments: the slacks, shirts, and dresses she wanted to take with her, plus jeans, snap-front shirts, and the newly purchased patio dress. Her loafers, moccasins, and two pairs of Keds were in a neat row on the floor, along with her Acme cowboy boots. She went into the attic and brought down two suitcases, running her hand over the embossed LK initials on the largest one, which had belonged to her father, Lewis Kelley.

She decided she needed a new pair of jeans, so she spent one afternoon at the Emporium on Market Street, eventually choosing a flattering side-zip pair of denim pants with mother-of-pearl snaps on the pockets. She could get more in Tribulation if she needed them.

An enthusiastic letter from her librarian friend Barbara Burington arrived midmonth, asking Phoebe to get in touch as soon as she got settled at the ranch. She also got a chatty missive from Virgil about Hunter's antics in the new car, and a renewal of his delight that Phoebe was coming back to Arizona. Nothing came from Steve Magly, but Phoebe didn't notice.

A few days later Phoebe opened her mailbox to find a fat envelope from Mary, which included a letter and a pile of newspaper clippings. Mary's note was short and to the point, as usual. She thanked Phoebe again for coming back to help her, and said she bought a new record player for the *casa* where Phoebe stayed during her ranch visits. "So you won't have to pack yours again for the long drive," she wrote.

Phoebe sat on her couch and started going through the pile of newsprint. Mary had clipped them together with a separate piece of paper on which she had written, "Read these!!" All the articles were about the Desert Grande Guest Ranch and the new manager, a woman named Thelma Powell.

One of the articles included a photo. Powell was a tall, thin woman, who'd posed standing by the registration desk talking to a cowboy wearing clean jeans and very shiny spurs. She was in a simple black dress, pearl earrings, and had four strands of pearls around her neck, which Phoebe thought was a little strange for the manager of a dude ranch.

Most of the articles were from the local paper, the *Tribulation Mining-Register*, and the stories were either about how many jobs the new ranch would bring to town, or opinion pieces about how the place was ruining Tribulation's dude ranching reputation. Mary also sent along some stories from the *Arizona Republic*, the Phoenix paper. The reporters had dug a bit deeper into the Desert Grande's ownership, but came up empty. Thelma Powell's background was also mysterious.

Mary had scribbled comments on a few of the clippings. She wrote "See what I mean?" on most of them, with "I was right about these people," and "No one has seen this woman in town" written on two of the longer articles. Phoebe read each one, put them back in the envelope, and then set it next to her books.

She looked at her watch and remembered that Katie was coming over in a few minutes to bring along some of her things. She wanted to get her filmmaking equipment and books into the apartment as soon as possible, since it wouldn't be in Phoebe's way.

Katie arrived on time, and two hours later, after organizing the latest collection of boxes and cameras, the women sat down with glasses of lemonade.

"Don't you think you're going to feel crowded once you bring everything over here? I mean, it's like you're actually moving in, not just subletting and living with someone else's things," said Phoebe.

"Nope. Luckily, you're not big on cooking, so

there will be room for my kitchen things and my dishes. I don't have a lot of clothes, and I can put extra books in my office at State. Just having the one extra room will make the difference."

"Okay, glad to hear it, I was worried you might end up regretting your decision."

"No chance. How's your own packing going?"

"Fine. I'm putting some of my stuff in the other guest room so it'll be out of your way. Oh...did I tell you Mary bought a record player for me, so I'll leave mine behind. I know yours is better, though, so I can just stick it in the closet or something."

"Don't worry about being too organized. I'll rearrange everything once you're out of town."

Phoebe's friends knew she planned to leave for Arizona the last week of August, so they arranged many evenings together as the month progressed. Katie took her out to dinner at Ernie's in North Beach for her birthday on the thirteenth. Since it also happened to be a Friday, Katie teased her friend about the unlucky omen for her upcoming trip.

"Hey, I've had a few Friday the 13th birthdays and nothing bad happened. They were fun...well except maybe a hangover from going out and having my first legal drinks on my twenty-first."

Phoebe looked around the restaurant. "I keep forgetting about the red flocked walls in here, and always end up wearing something that clashes with the décor. I feel like I should be celebrating Christmas."

Katie smiled, taking in Phoebe's emerald green taffeta dress. She took a small wrapped box out of her purse and placed it on the table.

"Happy birthday."

Phoebe carefully removed the paper and ribbon. She opened up the white box and pulled out a brown plastic cowboy hat. Laughing, she said to Katie, "Okay, I know you, this is symbolic of something."

"Yes, it is. When you get to Tribulation, Mary will give you a new Stetson, which is my birthday gift this year."

"Oh Katie, how wonderful, thank you! I've just been using one of Mary's castoffs the last two years."

"I expect snapshots of you wearing the hat during the various dude activities."

"I promise."

"And I want some of them taken at this rodeo they are planning. Have you ever been to a rodeo?"

"No, have you?"

"Never."

"But Mary said they aren't putting on a professional rodeo with bulldoggers or events like that."

"What's a bulldogger?" Katie asked with a puzzled frown.

"Those are the guys who jump off their horses and wrestle a steer to the ground."

"Wow, that would look great on film!"

Phoebe laughed. "I'm sure it would. But since it's a dude rodeo, the events will be tamer, though I don't know yet what they are planning to do. Mary wants to advertise all over the Southwest so that people will come just for the rodeo and maybe decide to stay at the ranch.

"I didn't know this, but quite a few dude ranches run their own rodeos. Carl, one of the wranglers out there, used to actually compete in rodeos. He was one of those guys who rides on a great big bucking Brahma bull. He hurt his shoulder and had to give it up, which is why he ended up working at the H Double Bar."

"Didn't you tell me he's just in his midtwenties or something? He must have started young."

"I think he did. Anyway, I found a book at the library about the history of rodeo and what is supposed to happen in each event, and it was really helpful. Did you know that women used to compete right alongside the men? They did bronc busting, even bull riding. They don't do that anymore, though. There were some great more-recent photos of women trick riding."

"Wow, look at you with all that rodeo lingo under your belt already."

Phoebe laughed. "I didn't know anything until I read the book. I love the title, it's called *Man, Beast, Dust.* I ordered a copy from Books, Inc. so I can take it with me."

"That would be a great title for a movie. And it sounds like a very succinct description of what your life is going to be like out there."

"Dust, definitely."

Phoebe's friends from her days at the insurance company took her out for drinks at the Fairmont Hotel's Tonga Room the next night. This had become a tradition over the past two years, to give her a great send-off before Phoebe left for a season at the ranch. They gave her birthday and farewell presents, both practical and funny, including handkerchiefs, socks, liniment for sore muscles, typewriter ribbons, a plastic horse complete with saddle and reins, and a new ballpoint pen.

None of those girls had ever taken a long car trip by themselves, so it was also a tradition for them to ask Phoebe for driving details. This year, she surprised them.

"I'm not taking 66 through Kingman this time."

"Why not?" asked Bobbie.

"Because I need to get out to the ranch fast. Mary

needs all hands on deck to get ready to deal with the people at the Desert Grande."

She had told them about the new place in Tribulation, and they were all outraged for Mary.

"So how are you getting there?" asked Alison.

"I'll drive down 101 and spend a night in Santa Barbara. Then I'll pick up 60 due east toward Blythe and then into Arizona."

"So you won't see your friend in Kingman or your cousins in San Bernardino this time?" Phyllis said. "And you're doing the whole thing in three days?"

"No, and yes. I think I can manage it. If not, I'll just pull over and find a motel. I'll get to the ranch late on the third day if it works out. I'll send you all some postcards so you know I didn't get lost in the desert along the way."

The Saturday before Phoebe left, Katie came over to the apartment to pick up a set of keys.

"I say this every time, but I'm really going to miss you," Phoebe told her. "And I'm sorry you can't make it out to visit over your break. You still haven't seen the ranch."

"I know, I'm sorry, too. I've got to get that new history department chair to stop putting me on committees and assigning me more classes. I'll keep trying, we'll find a way for me to visit as long as you keep going out there."

"I'll hold you to that."

An hour later Phoebe walked Katie out to her car and hugged her friend tightly. She waved as Katie drove off, then sprinted back to the apartment, pulled out a pile of notes and maps, and took one final look at her route.

Phoebe got up at six on Monday morning, showered, and dressed in a pair of black twill slacks, a white button-down shirt, and her white Keds. At the last minute, she pulled a small purple chiffon scarf out of one of the suitcases, tied it around her neck, and slid the knot off to the side. She ate a hearty breakfast of eggs and bacon, washed the dishes, and then made a bologna sandwich, and dropped it in a paper bag along with an apple and a small jar of mixed nuts.

A little before seven she got her Nash out of the garage across the street and drove it back to her building, where she found an empty space right in front. The suitcases, records, a bag with her shoes, and the case containing her Royal went into the spacious trunk. A box of books and typing paper went onto the back seat, along with her boots. Once she was sure she had everything, Phoebe picked up her purse, her lunch, and the briefcase which held Ellender's diary, and made a final trip down the stairs.

The briefcase fit snugly in the trunk next to the typewriter. Of everything in the car, these two items were the most precious to her. She wanted them out of sight in case anyone peeked into the windows looking for something to steal when she stopped for gas or food.

As the Nash warmed up Phoebe pulled the worn and marked-up map out of her purse and put it within grabbing distance on the seat. She took a deep breath, put the car in gear, and headed toward Post Street, down to Market and then south out of the city.

She hardly noticed the passing scenery as she drove down Highway 101. She was too worried about Mary and the ranch, and just wanted to get there. Phoebe ate lunch when she stopped for gas in Salinas, enjoying the warm breezes, reflecting that she would have more than enough hot weather when she got to Arizona.

She rolled into Santa Barbara midafternoon and checked into the Ocean Palms Motor Lodge. It was right on the beach, so after taking the suitcases and the diary's briefcase into her room and changing into the dirtier pair of Keds, she took a walk on the sand to stretch her muscles. She found a large piece of driftwood where she could sit and just watch the waves as they approached and retreated.

Back in her room she changed into a cotton dress with a matching sweater and some low-heeled pumps. She thought for a moment before leaving, and put the diary's small case on the shelf of the closet behind some pillows. She then drove to the San Roque steakhouse for dinner, which her friend Lois had recommended. She chuckled at the menu, printed in the shape of a hefty bull. She ordered a champagne cocktail, and then decided on the New York steak with baked potato.

The long drive and the big dinner made her sleepy and she snuggled into the motel's twin bed with her copy of *Riders of the Purple Sage* at eight. Just fifteen minutes later she was asleep.

Orange groves greeted her as she left Santa Barbara just after dawn the next morning. As she maneuvered onto Route 60, she felt the same bubble of joy she experienced every time she made the drive. With each mile the land became flatter, the mountains sharper, and the colors earthier. Phoebe knew some people thought this desertscape was stark and ugly, but she found it beautiful and strangely soothing. She stopped for lunch at a café in Redlands, and went into a nearby grocery store to buy a few snacks to keep her going. At Blythe, Phoebe checked in to one of the many motels lining Main Street and was out the door early the next morning.

As she neared the Arizona border, the desert changed again to the landscape she loved the most. Saguaros of all sizes marched in line with the roadway, and as always, she stuck her arm out the car window to wave when she saw the first one.

After getting gas in Quartzsite and returning to the highway, Phoebe checked her speedometer and put more pressure on the gas pedal. As long as she didn't get stopped for a speeding ticket, she'd be at the ranch in time for supper.

Although Mary had invited her up to the Watts's house for breakfast on her first morning at the ranch, Phoebe decided to fix it for herself in the *casa's* cheerful kitchen. With a plate of eggs and cup of coffee in hand, she sat at the Formica table and contemplated the view out the window. She could see just a bit of Maybelle Peak, and ate contentedly as she took everything in.

She and Mary planned to meet in the ranch office up in the main lodge later that morning, so Phoebe took an hour to unpack and organize the *casa*. The Royal went onto the big mahogany desk against the wall opposite the front door. At one time it had been a rolltop, but the roll was long gone. Phoebe preferred it the way it was, where she could see the cubbies, drawers with carved knobs and, best of all, its huge surface, which nearly dwarfed her typewriter. Plenty of room to keep a pile of typed sheets as they came out of the machine.

The large living room had the comfortable furniture she'd enjoyed on previous visits: a couch covered in a deep brown textured fabric, a mesquite wood coffee table, a couple of side tables with lamps sporting rawhide shades, and a bright turquoise-and-red blanket draped casually over the back of the couch.

The stone fireplace, flanked with bookcases, had a mesquite mantelpiece, and here Phoebe placed the photo of Ellender, along with another framed image of her parents. She put her dictionary and other books into one of the bookcases, and saw that Mary had placed a few novels into the other one. The new phonograph sat on a sturdy oak table under the window next to the desk, and Phoebe stacked her records against it.

When she was ready to head up to the lodge, she pulled on a pair of jeans and a short-sleeved cotton shirt, and her grubbiest pair of loafers. She smiled at the sight of the new black Stetson hanging from a hook on the wall by the kitchen entrance.

Supper at Mary and Sam's the previous evening had been both a welcome and a belated birthday celebration. Mary had proudly presented her with Katie's gift, Joe gave her a new mechanical pencil, and Mary and Sam gave her a bracelet set with silver western charms: a horse, a barn, a horseshoe, a hat, spurs, and a tiny saddle.

She put the bracelet on just before she left the *casa*, and it made a faint tinkling sound as she closed the front door. For a moment she paused to admire the sturdy rose vines which wound their way around the porch posts. She realized she'd forgotten to put one more photo on her mantel: a shot of the *casa* and the vines covered with small pink and orange blossoms, the sight she waited for each spring. The picture was probably in the pocket of one of her suitcases.

She walked past the barbed-wire fence of vertical ocotillo branches wired together and noticed that the curved path had been refurbished with a new layer of river rock. A natural fence of prickly-pear cactus shielded the *casa* from the eyes of the ranch's guests.

4

MARY AND SAM closed the H Double Bar each summer, since only Arizona natives could handle the heat, and after arranging for their cattle and horses to be transported to cooler grazing at a friend's ranch in Wyoming, they took a family vacation. They went home at least a month before reopening to refurbish, clean, and re-supply the ranch. They also took delivery of the returning livestock and made sure all the animals were healthy. This year, with the opening date set a month early, they had come back in mid-August, and had already done a lot of work by the time Phoebe arrived.

She walked toward the main lodge, set in the center of a horseshoe-shaped collection of ten whitewashed adobe cabins. They featured barn red trim which had just been freshened-up, and so had the deep turquoise front door of the lodge, with its well-worn but still bright copper hinges and door latch in the shape of a horseshoe. Brick-colored tiled walkways led down a small hill past the parking lot to another white building which had three large doors, also painted in turquoise. One led to the reception office, another to the saloon where evening cocktails were served, and the other was a storage room.

Phoebe took in the scents from the herbs and flowers planted in the scattered strawberry pots and, pulling on the latch, walked into the spacious and welcoming lodge.

Mary was fussing with some cushions on the deep leather chairs by the unlit fireplace, and turned when she heard the door.

"Good morning, honey," she said. "Let me just finish tidying up. Would you like some coffee?"

"I would, thanks. I'll go get it."

Phoebe headed left and through an archway into the dining room, and then toward the kitchen just beyond. None of the staff had arrived yet, but Mary always kept a pot of coffee going during the weeks she, Sam, and the hands worked to get the ranch ready for guests.

Phoebe took her cup back into the main room, and then she and Mary walked through the living room.

"You got a new rug, I see," said Phoebe when she saw the turquoise and beige striped runner under the coffee table.

"Yes, I needed to get rid of the one. Remember that dude last year who wore spurs everywhere he went?"

"Oh yeah, you always knew where he was because he jingled."

"I didn't mind that he had them on in the lodge, and anyway his kids got a kick out of it. But I didn't know that he let the spurs poke holes in the rug when he sat here and watched television. I noticed it when we were cleaning up for the summer, and I could see the rug wouldn't last another season. So, I'm instituting a no-spur rule this year. Indoors, anyway."

The two women continued walking toward the small door in the far wall beyond the couch, and Phoebe opened it with the key Mary had given her. The office was spacious and well-lit, filled with windows that had spectacular and distracting views, including one of Maybelle Peak. The mountain, named for the mother of Tribulation's three founding brothers, was the highest point of a rugged range whose face changed color with shadows and seasons.

A lamp and a pen and pencil set sat on the gray metal desk, and banks of filing cabinets held the work that she would be doing that season: typing letters, typing up menus and other miscellaneous paperwork, and *Trail Notes*, the cheery newsletter Mary wrote for guests and former guests. Thanks to her two previous years at the ranch, Phoebe had organized the tasks to her liking, and she would be ready for her new duties once the dudes started to arrive.

She spent the rest of the week in the office getting her regular work together, and had supper each night with Mary and Sam. They talked about how to organize the rodeo, which would start in November, how to get people to come and watch the competition, and ways they might get the dudes from the other ranches to participate.

On the Friday before Labor Day Phoebe took a quick shower before dinner. She'd been working in the lodge moving files around, boxing some of them up for storage. It was sweaty work in the late summer heat.

Feeling refreshed and much cooler in a seersucker

dress and sandals, she walked up to the Watts's home at suppertime, knocked on the door and went in. She'd barely set foot in the foyer when Mary bounced up to her, brandishing a copy of the *Tribulation Mining-Register.* It came out on Friday afternoons, and Sam usually went into town to buy a copy unless things were busy at the ranch.

"Look at this! I do not believe the gall of these people," she said to Phoebe, sticking the paper in her face and pointing to a large ad on the open page.

"What?" she asked.

"Here, just read it," Mary said, thrusting the paper into her hand.

Phoebe straightened out the crumpled newsprint and read.

Open House

Desert Grande Guest Ranch
Monday, September 6, 1954
10:00 to 2:00

Hors d'Oeuvres
Open Bar
Tours
12007 Old Caballo Road

"Wow," said Phoebe. "That's…well, *aggressive*."

"Aggressive? It's spitting in the face of every dude ranch in the area. 'Look at us, we have enough money to serve drinks to everyone in town,'" said Mary. "Short notice, and on Labor Day, too."

Phoebe guided the fuming Mary into the kitchen, where Sam was busy putting ice into highball glasses.

"Thanks, I need a drink, too," said Phoebe, smiling at Sam and then asking him, "What do you think of this open house?"

In contrast to his wife, Sam always considered what he was going to say before he said it, and after a moment's thought he replied, "If they want to spend their money that way, that's their business. We don't have to go and watch them do it."

Phoebe and Mary gave him a look that would have shriveled a cactus.

"Are you nuts?" Mary said.

"Of course we're going," said Phoebe.

"Why?" asked Sam.

"Because you have to see what your competition is doing," said Phoebe. "*This* competition, anyway. They have thrown down the gauntlet, and we have to look them in the eye and show them we aren't worried."

"Well, I'm really not," said Sam.

"I am," said Mary. "I want to see how they've spent their money, how they decorated the place, and how generous their drinks are."

"I want to see this Thelma Powell person," said Phoebe. "She doesn't look like a dude ranch manager in the photo I saw."

"I hope they offer tours of their barn and corrals," said Mary. "I need to see what their horses look like, too."

Sam smiled at both of them. "So, what time do you want to get there?"

On the Sunday before the open house Phoebe drove into Tribulation to have lunch with her librarian friend Barbara at a new place called The Wild Burro. The sandwiches were thick, and the French fries crispy, and the women decided that this would be their new lunch spot. They talked and ate for almost two hours, and as they left the restaurant, they saw a police car parked out front. A tall, sandy-haired uniformed officer got out and walked toward them, and with a big smile on his face he said, "Howdy, Phoebe!"

Steve Magly was the youngest of Tribulation's small police force, and most people in town considered him the best of the bunch. He put out his hand to Phoebe and held hers for a moment, then turned and said, "Well, hello there Barb."

"Magly, I've been telling you for fifteen years not to call me that," she said, rolling her eyes. "I am not a sharp object."

"Oh, yes you are," he replied, laughing.

Phoebe stared at the two of them, and Barbara spoke first.

"We went to Tribulation High School together," she said. "He was a year ahead of me and played football with my brother. He was so annoying it was like having two brothers. He always called me Barb, and I've always hated that name."

"Which is why he uses it, no doubt," said Phoebe.

Steve just smiled at both of them."Fancy getting supper sometime?" he said to Phoebe.

"Sure, it's going to get pretty busy at the ranch soon, we open on September 17. Maybe one night this coming week?"

"How about Wednesday? I'm off duty that night. Pick you up about seven?"

"Perfect, see you then."

Steve got back into his squad car and drove away down Center Street.

Phoebe turned to Barbara."So, did you guys ever date in high school? I guess if he was more like a brother, you probably didn't?"

"No, and besides he isn't my type."

"What is your type?"

Barbara looked pensive for a moment, and then said, “I’ll tell you one of these days.”

That evening Phoebe called Virgil a few times but there was no answer. She felt a prickle of worry, but decided to just keep trying.

At noon the next day Phoebe walked out of the *casa* and headed toward the Watts family home. She knew Mary wanted to wear a patio dress for the event at the Desert Grande, so Phoebe decided on something different. She chose a sleeveless red poplin dress with white polka dots and a large split collar whose points reached her shoulders. The matching belt emphasized her slim waist, and she wore a pair of white espadrilles on her feet. Her accessories were pure western, though: the roadrunner earrings, her new charm bracelet, and a small turquoise and silver ring she’d found in an antique store in San Francisco. Mary had told Phoebe not to wear gloves and a hat. “You don’t want to look like a dudine,” she’d said.

When Mary and Sam came out of the front door to meet her, Phoebe wasn’t surprised to see Mary had gone all out to impress the owners of the Desert Grande. She was wearing a new patio dress, a black one with shimmering silver metallic rickrack. The crinkly skirt flowed as she walked, thanks to her last-minute addition of a stiff petticoat. She also had on her best jewelry: a stunning turquoise and silver squash blossom necklace with earrings and a wide cuff bracelet to match. Black open-toe sandals completed the look.

Sam, ever subdued, had donned black slacks, a short-sleeved black snap-front western shirt with red embroidery on the yoke, black cowboy boots, and his best cowboy hat.

Joe, who did not look happy about the excursion, was in a red-and-black striped shirt and, like his dad, black slacks and boots. Mary told Phoebe Joe had tried to get away with wearing his favorite grubby cowboy hat but she had made him wear the new straw one she'd just bought.

Phoebe beamed at the three of them.

"Mary, you look amazing," said Phoebe. "Sam and Joe, you'll make everyone else feel like a dude."

Joe chewed on a fingernail and looked longingly toward the far corral where the horses milled around under the shade of a *ramada*.

"Darling, you're the perfect blend of city girl and ranch girl," Mary said to Phoebe.

"Thanks," she replied. "I thought you two should stand out as the westerners at this shindig."

Mary laughed, and they all got into the dark green Woody station wagon, which had H Double Bar Dude Ranch painted in black and gold on both of the front doors. Phoebe noticed it had been newly washed.

Fifteen minutes later they pulled into the circular driveway in front of the enormous wooden lodge that was both the lobby and headquarters of the Desert Grande Guest Ranch. A porch with posts made of massive logs flanked the front entrance, and the ranch's name was carved into a horizontal log above the front door. The parking lot was on the south side of the building, and Sam maneuvered the Woody in next to another station wagon which also had a name on its doors: Lazy M Dude Ranch. There were at least twenty parked vehicles, and Phoebe saw more arriving as they walked toward the lodge.

Just inside the door was a large reception desk staffed by a smiling young woman in a green patio dress, whose job seemed to be directing visitors toward the bar, through an arched doorway to the left. Phoebe saw Joe gaping at the many mounted animal heads on the wall behind the desk. A stairway made of peeled logs swooped up to the right toward an open walkway set with rows of doors on the second floor that Phoebe assumed were some of the rooms.

She and Mary went into the bar first, while Sam stayed behind for a few minutes to let Joe study those game mounts.

The large barroom was built of wide logs and sparsely decorated with Indian rugs and more animal heads. Small round tables with striped linens covered nearly every inch of floor space. The bar itself was covered with plates of finger foods, and three bartenders efficiently filled drink orders from the crowd.

"There's Jim and Laura," Mary said, heading toward the couple, who'd spotted her and were smiling.

Jim and Laura Stevenson ran the Bar K Dude Ranch, farther west of the Desert Grande. It was mostly a working cattle ranch, and they took a few dudes who wanted a more rugged experience. They were both originally from farm families in the Midwest, and had come to Arizona for college, where they met, married, and decided to stay.

Jim had started working as a wrangler at dude ranches around Tucson, and Laura worked in housekeeping. A few years later they decided to get their own place, and they bought the Bar K just after the war. The couple had no children, but they had a large collection of dogs who provided extra entertainment for the kids who came to stay. Some people thought they'd named their ranch Bar K for the dogs, because the name looked like the word *Bark,* but that was its original name, and they'd kept it after they bought the property.

Laura and Mary were especially close, and gave each other a quick hug.

"Phoebe, how nice to see you," said Laura.

"You, too. How are you and Jim doing?"

"We're fine, and obviously just as curious as you are about this place," Jim replied.

Mary gave him a grim smile, and said, "Have you taken the tour yet?"

"No, they are staggering the groups so they don't have a crush of people wandering around. I think they will be back in about fifteen minutes."

At that moment Phoebe caught sight of Thelma Powell in the doorway, surveying the crowd. Mary, Laura, and Jim saw her eyes widen and turned to watch as Powell walked into the bar and started to greet visitors.

The three women immediately sized her up. She was thinner than that newspaper photograph, and taller. She was probably about forty, and had short, curly dark hair that was almost black but did not look like a dye job. She was wearing tight black western slacks with pearl snaps on the pockets and tucked into black Acme boots with silver stitching, Her shirt was silver satin with black piping and green sequined cactus embroidery above the pockets. The final touch was a wide black belt with a shiny silver buckle shaped into the letters DG. At the shirt's open neck were the four strands of pearls Phoebe remembered from the photo.

Phoebe glanced at Mary, who returned a look with an expression that said, *I don't want to be impressed, but I'm impressed.*

All eyes followed Miss Powell as she moved smoothly through the crowd, shaking a few hands and exchanging pleasantries, mostly with the men. Phoebe saw her turn toward where she stood with Mary and the

Stevensons, and Powell's eyes seemed to harden as they lighted on Mary.

She walked up to Mary, smiled, and put out her hand. Phoebe noted her eyes were an unusual light hazel color, which seemed almost yellow in the artificial light.

"Mrs. Watts, isn't it? From the H Double Bar? It's such a pleasure to meet you."

Mary smiled back and returned the handshake.

"Yes, it's also a pleasure to meet you, Miss Powell. This is my sister-in-law, Phoebe Kelley. And Jim and Laura Stevenson…"

Powell finished her sentence.

"Of the Bar K. It's lovely to meet all of you."

Sam and Joe joined them, and Mary made the introductions.

"I hope you will take the tour, and please enjoy the drinks and hors d'oeuvres. We have drinks for the kids, too," Powell said.

"Thank you," said Mary, and watched Joe take off toward the bar, followed by his father.

"Well, I must make the rounds, and I see that Hank is ready to take more people on the tour, so feel free to join the group."

With that, Powell left them, after giving them another smile and Mary one last look.

When she was out of earshot, Phoebe said, "What was that about?"

"What?" said Mary.

"The way she kept looking at you," said Laura. "She obviously knew who you were."

"She knows who everyone is," said Mary.

"But she seemed to be especially interested in you," said Phoebe.

"I don't know why."

"Oh, Mary. It's because you are a force in town and in the world of dude ranching, everybody knows that. You have done so much work to get publicity for ranchers," said Laura.

"That's just good business."

"And that's what scares her, I'll bet," said Jim, as Laura nodded.

A deep voice then penetrated the conversations in the crowded bar.

"Next tour leaves in one minute! Please meet in front of the reception desk."

All three women put their drinks down on a nearby table.

"Let's go," said Phoebe.

An hour later the friends said goodbye to each other, and Phoebe got into the car with Mary, Joe, and Sam. She could tell Mary was thinking hard about what she'd seen, and as soon as the door closed she let go.

"They sure look good on the surface," she said.

"Yes, everything was pretty shiny," said Phoebe.

Joe questioned the word "shiny."

"I mean, everything was brand-new, it wasn't used or hadn't gotten dirt all over it yet," said Phoebe.

"Their Jeeps were shiny," said Joe.

Mary laughed grimly. "They won't be for long. The horses sure looked beautiful, though they only have twelve of them, and I counted rooms enough for sixty people."

"That's because the guests will be riding around in Jeeps, or swimming, shooting skeet, and drinking," Phoebe said with a laugh.

"Then they shouldn't even call themselves a guest ranch, much less a dude ranch. They are really a resort, but they are trading on the name. As big as they are, they don't even have a chuck wagon for desert lunches. They just take people out in the Jeeps for rides. And speaking of vehicles, did you see those two new Chrysler New Yorker station wagons? I heard someone say they drive all the way out to the Phoenix airport to pick people up."

"It's just a novelty, Mary. They'll get a lot of people at first, and then only rich people who don't ride will stay there."

"Well, that Thelma Powell looks like the well-paid secretary of a millionaire business mogul. You have to like people to be a dude rancher. And I don't care how much she smiles, that woman does not like people. She's the manager, but not the owner. I wonder who she works for? Did you hear anyone mention who that might be?"

"No, but I wasn't really listening to all the chatter in the bar," said Phoebe.

"And what's with all the logs everywhere? Are they trying to look like a Wyoming dude ranch?"

"They have their Arizona touches, too," said Sam. "Those were some very expensive Navajo rugs on the wall in the bar."

"That's even worse. They're trying to be all kinds of dude ranch at once. I don't know what it is, but there's something fishy about that place."

"Her clothes were gorgeous," said Phoebe.

"That shirt did not come off the rack," said Mary. "I'll bet she commissioned it directly from Nathan Turk in Los Angeles."

"And I'll bet that it cost a bundle," Phoebe said with a shake of her head.

"It did. I wonder who paid for it?" said Mary.

"Whoever does own the ranch probably wants her to look as expensive as the décor."

"She has that new Italian haircut," Mary grumbled.

"Italian?"

"The short, curly hair. That Italian actress, what's her name...Gina Lollobrigida, that's how she wears her hair. You see it in all the magazines."

"The men sure thought Miss Powell looked good," said Sam with a laugh.

"I'll bet they did," said Mary.

"The snacks were good," said Joe.

5

THE H DOUBLE BAR was on schedule to open September 17. All but one of the seasonal staff members lived in town and came in during the day, and all of them had worked for Mary before.

The ranch's full-time wranglers and top hands Carl Royston and Bob Easley were responsible for getting the cattle and horses down from summer pasture in Wyoming. They'd arrived the day after the open house. Mary and Sam inspected each animal and gave heartfelt praise to the two men for their work.

Carl had gotten married the previous fall and now lived in town with his wife Susie, who taught at the Garcia Elementary School, but Bob was still a bachelor. He had his own separate cabin near the bunkhouse, where the seasonal wranglers stayed. Two young men who worked as hands during the season lived in a small cabin near the barn, and the one out-of-town waitress stayed in a large, multi-bedroom cabin on the opposite side of the ranch. Mary knew that young men and women would always find a way to get together, but she didn't want to make it easy for them.

Phoebe had her paperwork in order, so she helped make beds and lay out towels in the cabins, and also did a lot of grocery shopping to help stock the pantry. She ran into other dude ranchers when she was in town, and their conversation always turned to the open house and the Desert Grande. Most ranch owners were resigned to facing a new kind of competition, while others shared Mary's opinion that they needed to fight the new place by offering the most authentic activities they could. Everyone knew that the H Double Bar was going to throw a rodeo that their own guests and wranglers could participate in, and while this might pull people away from the activities at their ranches, they secretly hoped it would do the same thing to the Desert Grande.

Phoebe checked the mail every day, but there was nothing from Virgil, and her phone calls went unanswered.

On Wednesday night, Steve Magly showed up right on time in his personal car, an immaculate turquoise and white Oldsmobile. He opened the door for Phoebe and then got behind the wheel, spinning some gravel as he left the ranch parking lot.

"Do you want to go to The Red Lamp? They have a new cook, and his steaks are the best in town."

"Sounds great."

The Red Lamp was the largest restaurant and bar in town. It was popular with the dudes because of its western décor: cattle horns, branding irons, and Indian rugs filled every space on the walls, and the chairs all had cowhide seats. Locals also showed up on most Friday and Saturday nights to enjoy the generous drinks.

As they walked toward the restaurant Phoebe realized that the sight of Tribulation's buildings, old and new, its desert landscape, the varied smells from the restaurants, and the western-garbed dudes were as familiar, and as welcome, as those in her neighborhood in San Francisco. She felt a peace in the place, a comfort of being where she was welcomed and where she belonged. It was a startling but not unwelcome thought.

Steve said hello to a number of the diners and bar patrons as they made their way through the main dining room. He also chatted up their waitress, Bernice, and she made sure they got their drinks and steaks quickly.

It was past nine when they left the restaurant. Phoebe said she could tell there was someone better in the kitchen this year. Steve drove to the edge of the H Double Bar's parking lot and helped Phoebe out of the car. He walked her down the path to the cactus fence, and she told him she could make the rest of the way herself. He had never kissed her good night on any of the dates they had the previous year, but now he leaned toward her. To her surprise, he kissed her on the cheek.

Squeezing her hand, he then said, "Thanks for a great evening. I'll wait here to make sure you get safely to the door."

Phoebe pointed to the bright light on her porch just a few yards away and laughed. She thanked him and walked toward her *casa*, opening the door without looking back.

She went down to the reception office the next day to see if she had any mail. She always smiled when she saw the copies of *Lady in the Desert* that Mary put in a prominent place near the front desk. She had even made a colorful sign explaining how the book was inspired by the history of the H Double Bar and that each one was autographed by the author. *Only $2.95!* was in larger lettering at the bottom.

Phoebe went through the stack of letters and found a postcard with a photo of Philadelphia's Independence Hall on the front. It had a short note from Virgil on the back, and she read it while Mary sorted everything else.

> *Phoebe—my uncle died and I needed to jump on a train to get back here in time for the funeral, so I didn't have a chance to call you. I hope all is going well at the ranch. I'll be home on the 12th.*

"Is everything okay?" asked Mary, watching as Phoebe read.

"Oh yes, fine. I haven't been able to reach Virgil on the phone, and it turns out he had to go to Philadelphia to a funeral. He'll be back on Sunday."

"Why don't you invite him for supper on our opening evening? We only have a small complement of guests for Friday night, just three couples."

"That would be great, thanks Mary," said Phoebe. "I'll call him on Monday."

Phoebe had her own phone line and paid the bill herself. She didn't mind splurging when the occasion called for it.

She took the postcard into her own office in the lodge, and just before lunch went back to the *casa* and propped it next to the photo of Ellender on the mantel.

The final week before opening day was busy, but not frantically so, since Mary and Sam had everything planned down to the minute. Now that he was older, even Joe had special chores to do, mostly in the barn making sure the tack was in the right place and in good condition. Phoebe was ready, too. The paperwork in her office and at the reception desk down near the parking lot where guests checked in was in apple-pie order. She knew who was coming on the first weekend, and knew which cabins Mary had assigned them.

Phoebe found time on Monday evening to call Virgil, who picked up the phone almost as soon as it rang.

"Hi Virgil, it's Phoebe. How are you doing?"

"Hi, Phoebe. I'm good, I got home earlier than I expected yesterday."

"I was sorry to hear about your uncle."

"Thanks, it wasn't much of a surprise, he was in his nineties."

"Wow. Did you see any other family members?"

"Just a cousin and his wife and their grandkids. There aren't many of us left. But it was a nice trip, even if it was for a funeral."

"I'm happy for you. So listen, are you free to come up here on Friday? It's opening night and Mary and Sam would love to have you join us for the first supper of the season."

"I'd like that, and I can stay over with my buddy Frank in town."

"Oh, Mary says there are plenty of empty cabins this week and that you are welcome to stay in one of them."

"I couldn't do that. I wouldn't want her to have to clean up after me..."

"Yes, you can do that, and she will be insulted if you don't stay here."

Virgil chuckled. "Well, I don't ever want to be on Mary's bad side. Thank her for me, will you? How about if I get out there in the late morning? Will you have time to break away and get some lunch?"

"I think so, but I should be back by midafternoon to help Mary check in the guests."

"Perfect, I'll see you about eleven then."

On Thursday evening, Phoebe went up to Mary and Sam's house for supper. Sam handed her a glass of Four Roses as soon as she walked into the kitchen, and Mary was already sipping on her martini.

"Well, we're ready," said Mary with a satisfied sigh. "I'm happy with the new table staff, those girls really want to do a good job."

"A few of them look like cowgirls, not waitresses," said Phoebe.

"That's because they are," said Mary. "Shannon and Sandra asked me about riding our horses in their off hours. I said that as long as the dudes weren't using them that would be okay, as long as they check in with Bob first."

"That's nice of you," said Phoebe.

"Well, it keeps the girls happy and keeps the horses in shape."

"Joe seems to be enjoying his work in the barn. Where is he, by the way?"

"He's in his room doing homework. I hope the cats also get to work in the barn keeping the mouse population down before the guests get here and start spoiling them again."

Bea and Sabine, the ranch's resident cats, were

not only fierce mousers, they also knew how to butter up the dudes for food treats and time on laps. Bea's original name was Béla, but Mary was tired of people asking why she named her cat for Bela Lugosi. So, at Joe's suggestion, she changed it to Bea.

"I saw them following Joe in there this afternoon," said Phoebe.

Joe walked into the kitchen just then and said, "Bea got a great big mouse today."

Mary smiled, and told him to wash his hands to get ready for supper.

"Is Virgil coming tomorrow?"

"Yes, as far as I know. He'll be here late morning and we're going to get some lunch."

"Well, take as much time as you want, we have everything under control."

Phoebe spent the next morning writing postcards to the girls back in San Francisco, and putting in an hour or so on the new book. All she had so far were notes for characters and action, but nothing in terms of a plot, which continued to irritate her. She didn't want to be in a bad mood when Virgil arrived, so she put her papers away and concentrated on what she was going to wear.

She decided on the seersucker dress and white sandals, with the roadrunner earrings and silver bracelet. She walked down to the registration office a few minutes before eleven and put her postcards in the basket for the ranch's outgoing mail. A moment later she heard crunching gravel and saw a beige Buick sedan pulling into the parking lot.

Virgil got out of the car and waved at Phoebe, showing his usual shy smile. She walked down to the car and gave him a warm hug. He wore a white, short-sleeved snap-front western shirt with the roadrunner bola tie, along with jeans and probably his second-best cowboy boots.

"It's great to see you," said Phoebe. "Did Hunter get settled okay with Frank?"

"Yes, Hunter loves it out at his place, and Frank's wife gives him lots of special attention. I swear, one of these days I won't be able to drag that dog away from there."

Mary came out of the office just then.

"Hi Virgil! We're so glad you're here. Did you bring a suitcase?"

"Yes, it's in the car."

"Well, just give it to me and I'll keep it behind the desk until we decide which cabin to put you in tonight."

He handed Mary a small brown case, thanking her again for putting him up.

Virgil drove them to The Wild Burro, and he remarked on how good the food was as they they spent an enjoyable couple of hours over sandwiches and fries. She told him about the open house at the Desert Grande and how she wanted to find out more about Thelma Powell.

"I started looking in the Phoenix papers after you told me about the guest ranch," Virgil said. "Nobody's writing much about the ranch or Miss Powell. You'd think they would want a lot of publicity for the new place."

"That's what I was wondering about, too. Miss Powell is a bit too mysterious, and I want to know why."

"Well, remember what happened the last time you tried to find out about somebody's past," said Virgil with a grim smile.

"You're right. But I'm just trying to give Mary and Sam an edge over those people. If it turns out she's an ax murderer I'll keep my distance."

"Please do!"

They drove back to the ranch after lunch and Phoebe took Virgil down to the barn to say hello to Carl and Bob. The large structure with a hayloft spanning its entire length was the same warm red color as the window frames on the ranch's cabins. The paint was beginning to peel and crumble off in places, but Mary didn't want Sam to touch it up.

"The dudes expect a barn to look lived in," she said.

Phoebe loved the smell of the hay and other feeds, and didn't even mind the faint scent of manure. I really am turning into a country girl, she said to herself.

"Hey, stranger!" said Carl, shaking Virgil's hand.

"Howdy, Virgil," said Bob, the quieter of the two.

"Good to see you, boys. How are you finding married life, Carl?"

He winked. "Suits me down to the ground. Susie is at the elementary school, though school boards don't usually let women be teachers once they've got married. But it's hard to get ladies to come out here, so they bent the rules for her. She loves it, and as long as she's happy, I'm happy."

Phoebe and Virgil spent a few more minutes with the hands, and then walked up to the lodge. She introduced Virgil to the new staff members, and he said hello to the ones he'd met last year.

"It's about time for the guests to start arriving, so I need to head down to the reception office," said Phoebe. "Let's get you into your cabin before I get too busy."

"Should I just come to the saloon at five?"

Phoebe laughed. "You are a regular, aren't you?"

THE SALOON WAS in a large room next to the office, and the first guests began to trickle in just before five, where Phoebe, Mary, Sam, and Virgil were already in place.

The three couples were all in their fifties, and one had been at the ranch before, so there was much happy chatter when they checked in. Phoebe directed the new people to the carved mesquite wood bar which spanned the entire wall on the right. Its brass footrail had been newly polished, and it gleamed in the light of the large overhead light fixture set with deer antlers. Behind the bar were frosted glass sconces which provided a soft light for Sam as he made drinks. The room had circular tables and chairs decorated with bright Southwestern upholstery and linens. Two electric fans rotated slowly, and the open front and back doors let in a light cross breeze.

The guests were all in western-style clothing, and two of the women also wore patio dresses, though in brighter colors than Phoebe's copper and Mary's off-white versions.

Phoebe smiled at the sight of the old dynamite box full of coloring books, crayons, and board games against a back wall, along with a few toy pistols and bow and arrow sets, ready to be put into action when kids came to stay. Children were usually back in school this early in the season, though occasionally a family booked reservations when fall was the only time Dad could get time off for a vacation.

Sam handed Joe a drink. He made a face and walked away, sitting on a chair by the back door with the comic book he'd brought with him. Phoebe looked at Sam who smiled and said, "He wanted a Roy Rogers but I forgot to get a supply of cola, so I had to make him a Shirley Temple. I think he feels his manhood has been insulted. And he's just glad there are no other boys here to see it."

Phoebe chuckled. "What's a Shirley Temple made with?"

"Ginger ale with ice and marischino cherries and grenadine. Makes it nice and pink for the girls. Otherwise, it's the same drink but the cola hides the 'pink' color for the boys."

Some of the adults were on their second cocktail, and the noise level increased as the hour wore on. At about one minute to six a sound came from the lodge. The waitress named Sandra was running a bar through an iron triangle, and one of the women exclaimed, "Just like the movies!"

Mary laughed. "That's what we hoped you'd say. Now, if you will all head toward the lodge, our supper awaits us."

The dining room was on the left side of the lodge, through an adobe archway which separated it from the living room. A chandelier made out of a wagon wheel was the focal point of the room. The refectory-style tables were covered in red and turquoise striped cloths with matching napkins, and the chairs were upholstered in a pale turquoise. Baskets of bread, candles, and little copper bowls filled with pebbles and small succulents lined the table. Mary and Sam always sat apart from each other with the guests, and Joe usually sat with his dad. Each of the tables could seat ten people, but tonight they squeezed in an extra chair since there were eleven of them for supper. The crowding made everyone laugh, but no one minded, and strategically placed fans kept the group comfortable.

Mary always served prime rib on opening night, along with mashed potatoes and gravy, summer vegetables, and both cornbread and Irish soda bread. Whenever there were new guests, she gave a short talk about the history of the H Double Bar and the town of Tribulation. The kids who came to the ranch were especially fond of the story of the three Butler brothers who had come to the area after the Civil War and found gold. Two of them died rather gruesomely (rattlesnake bite and mine cave-in) which always brought exclamations of horror or glee from the younger crowd. Leroy, the surviving Butler brother, eventually prospered and founded the town of Tribulation, named for the troubles of his earlier days.

As everyone ate their strawberry shortcake dessert and had coffee or after-supper drinks, Gene and Lorraine Bowman came into the lodge to take down names for the next day's trail rides. They dressed in jeans, simple white cotton shirts, and their best hats when they were first introduced to the dudes. Gene made sure to let everyone know that they had horses for every level of rider, and urged the new people not to exaggerate how much experience they'd had on horseback. Mary also made a few announcements.

"Our weekly chuck wagon lunch will be held on Sunday. You can ride your horse to the picnic spot, or Sam can take you in our Jeep, and we can make multiple trips for those who don't want to ride. I'll give you more information about that on Saturday.

"We also have some board games on the bookcases out in the living room area. Feel free to take those out whenever you want. Our television is brand-new, and you are of course also welcome to play the piano. We've put in a horseshoe pit behind the building with the saloon and registration office, and have some outdoor lighting in case you are still playing when the sun goes down. And we've set up an archery range out in the open area behind the far cabins, numbers eight through ten. You'll see there's a plywood barrier there, so just walk around it and you'll see the targets set up."

She smiled at Joe and continued.

"And don't worry if your arrows go astray. We're paying Joe a nickel for each arrow he picks up at the end of the day after everyone is finished."

The adults gave Joe a round of applause that made him blush.

"For now, we just want to say welcome to the H Double Bar, and please enjoy the rest of your evening. Sam and I will be around until about eight tonight, but you all have our phone number in case you need anything after hours."

Virgil turned to Phoebe before they left the dining room and said, "It's not very late, do you want to go into town for a drink?"

"That would be fun. Let me go get my purse and I'll meet you in the parking lot."

They got one of the last free tables at The Red

Lamp. Phoebe and Virgil ordered their drinks and talked about how well the evening went.

"I'm so glad Mr. and Mrs. Ridgway are here again, they've been coming to the ranch for at least ten years. Mary needs her repeat customers."

"I'd come back, too, if I'd stayed at the H Double Bar. She and Sam have done a wonderful job with the ranch. The Desert Grande might give them a little trouble, but I don't think they'll be a problem in the long term."

"I hope not," said Phoebe.

She looked around for their waitress and then noticed Steve Magly sitting at a table in the farthest corner of the bar. A blonde woman she'd never seen before was sitting with him, their chairs pushed close together.

"Hmmm," she said.

Virgil turned to see what she was looking at.

"Isn't that Officer Magly?"

"Yes, but I don't know who that woman is. He didn't mention he was seeing anyone when we had supper last week."

Virgil looked startled. "You went out to dinner with him?"

"Yes, I'd seen him a few days earlier when I was having lunch with my friend from the library, do you remember her? Barbara? They went to high school together, which I didn't know."

Virgil fiddled with his bola tie. "So, will you be getting together again?"

"We don't have any plans, but if I run into him we might. I also thought it would be fun to go out with both him and Barbara. The way they talk to each other is hilarious."

"Oh, uh...okay."

The waitress arrived and they ordered another round. Virgil was quiet, and Phoebe rattled on about how she, Mary, and Sam were going to start planning for the first rodeo in November.

Virgil signaled their waitress again and asked for the check.

"I'm pretty bushed, do you mind if we head back?" he said.

"Of course not. Gosh, it's after ten, I should get to bed soon. I want to be up early to see how things go the first day. I have some paperwork to finish and I told Mary I would do some shopping for her. What time are you leaving tomorrow?"

"I don't have to get home by any specific time, so I thought I'd spend the day with Frank and then head back to Phoenix, probably after lunch. I guess I'll see you at breakfast?"

"Yes, I want to say goodbye before you leave."

As they left the bar Phoebe noticed that Steve and the mystery woman were still at their table. They didn't see her.

Virgil walked Phoebe to her *casa*. He waited until she was safely inside and then walked slowly toward his cabin on the far side of the lodge.

September turned to October, and though it was still hot, a change in light and desert scent told the locals that fall was coming. A steady stream of guests came and went at the H Double Bar, but even Phoebe could tell that there were fewer visitors than last year.

One afternoon in midmonth she went down to the registration office and stopped short when she saw Mary's face as she sat behind the desk.

"What's wrong?"

Mary looked up at her.

"Two sets of regular guests have not made

reservations this year, and I always hear from them by now," she said.

"I'm so sorry," said Phoebe.

"Well, at least the Hollands, the Bakers, and the Deardorffs are still coming. They'll be here at the end of the month and will stay their usual two weeks."

"That's good, don't worry about those other people. Maybe something came up and they couldn't get their usual time away from home."

"Maybe."

"I am going into town, do you need anything?"

"Yes, can you...actually, I'll go with you. I need to go to the Trading Post and get a few things. I'll drive us, meet you at the car in five minutes."

The Trading Post was the biggest and most popular souvenir shop in Tribulation. Its shelves were covered with everything from keychains, shot glasses, and books to saddle blankets and tooled leather purses. The scents of leather polish, new paper, and fresh wool created a western atmosphere that was unforced and authentic. Visiting dudes swarmed through the store like bugs clustering around a summertime porch light.

The owners were Susana Lozano and her sister-in-law Monica Baca, who managed the store and the hordes with a calm that other merchants envied. They stood out from the other shop owners because they didn't wear western-styled clothing. Both women always had on black skirts and crisp white shirts, and the only concession to color was their Bakelite bracelets and earrings. They gave Mary a discount on the bandannas, ashtrays, postcards, and other souvenir items she bought to give away to the dudes.

The store was crowded, and Phoebe and Mary exchanged quick greetings with Susana, who was behind the register helping a line of customers. They waved at

Monica, who was near the back of the store showing a collection of bandannas to a woman dressed head to toe in turquoise, from her pants and shirt to the many rings on her fingers.

Mary picked out what she needed, and they left the store, heading toward the ranch's station wagon.

As they reached the car they heard a loud noise, and a Jeep filled with cowboy-hatted dudes drove past them down Center Street. The words Desert Grande Guest Ranch was painted in bright red on its side.

"Oh, my god," said Mary.

"What?"

"That was Loretta Andrews," she said.

"Who?"

"One of the regulars who did not make a reservation this year," she said.

"Oh, I remember her. She was kind of demanding, wasn't she?"

"Yes, but she and her husband John came every season, which made her easier to bear."

"I see he's not with her."

"He's probably drinking in the bar. And flirting with the women, as usual."

"I definitely remember that about him."

Phoebe put her hand on Mary's arm for a moment.

"I wonder where they're going," she said.

"Probably out to the Maybelle Mine for a tour. I heard the Desert Grande made a deal with the new owners for a discounted rate because they will bring so many people to visit."

"You send plenty of people out there for tours and they never offered you a discount."

"That ranch has some sort of influence. And we need to find out what it is."

They got into the car and drove back to the H Double Bar in silence.

Better news came in two days later.

Mary burst into Phoebe's office up in the lodge just before lunch.

"Look at this!" she said with glee in her voice. "We just got a long-term reservation." She handed Phoebe a letter written in a flowery, feminine hand on thick, cream-colored stationery.

"They want to stay for three months?" Phoebe said, after reading it over. "Has anyone ever booked a stay that long?"

"Once, fairly soon after we opened back in 1948. An older couple, they were so lovely, but they kept changing their departure date. I was afraid they were going to move in. Turns out they were just trying to avoid spending time with their children."

"Wow. So, who are these people?"

"I don't know, they're Glenn and Jayne Carter from Carson City, Nevada. They want to stay somewhere warm from the end of October until January, with the possibility of extending their reservation. Isn't this great? They will get here in time for the rodeo."

She bounced back out the door and Phoebe smiled, happy that Mary's spirits had improved.

7

Monday, October 18, 1954

Dear Katie,

I'm glad to hear you asserted yourself with the department chair, and I'm sure it will take a while for him to recover!

Thanks for asking about the ranch. Mary and Sam have been worried because the guest numbers are lower than they have been the last few years. The Desert Grande has been siphoning off the dudes in a steady stream, but we got a reservation for a long-term stay a couple of weeks ago, so that's given them some breathing room.

We've been working together nearly every evening to plan the rodeo. I go up to their place once supper is over and after Mary makes sure the guests have everything they need for the night. Their dining room table is covered with papers and letters and newspaper clippings about other rodeos.

Mary put ads in a couple of industry magazines about getting some professional people to come and put on an exhibition, but we haven't heard from anyone yet. So she put some small ads in local papers in cities that have big rodeos, like Cheyenne, Prescott, and Salinas. Maybe that will get someone's attention. In the meantime, we've just been talking about what rodeo-type events the dudes can do safely.

You wouldn't believe it, but some ranches let their dudes try bronc riding, even bull riding. Mary says she has had guests in the past who would happily try any of these, but it's too dangerous and she doesn't want anyone to get hurt. And we also want to have something for the kids to do. The first rodeo will be the Saturday after Thanksgiving, when we usually have more families. We hope we will, anyway.

Mary is going to open up the rodeo to dudes from other ranches too, so she and Sam have been visiting a few of their friends at other spreads (how about that for local lingo?) to talk about it. So far, they love the idea. And to keep things interesting the H Double Bar wranglers, and the ones from other places, will also compete. They get to do the real rodeo stuff, like bronc riding (well, the men will), and the women wranglers will do what's called barrel racing. The dudes will do the kiddie version of rodeo events, and we're still working on that.

Mary sent out a special newsletter to all of her former guests, letting them know about the rodeo. And she had some signs made which most of the businesses in Tribulation are putting into their front windows. Anyone who wants to see the rodeo can come, and the local Lions Club is going to sell food and keep the proceeds for one of their charities. Mary is also having fun thinking up ideas for prizes. The one thing that makes me roll my eyes is what she's calling this event: a "dudeo." I told her if she used that word I would pack up and go back to San Francisco, but she knew I was kidding. Sort of.

Carl is a huge help with all of the planning, since he was in the rodeo himself. He is trying to talk Mary into letting him do his bull riding again, but she's worried about his old injury, and so is his wife, Susie. And they don't know where to find the right kind of bull, I guess. Oh, and Mary put an ad in Western Horseman *back in August, too.*

I haven't done much work on the new book. I could tell you it's because I've been busy but it's really because I'm just not inspired. Even being here at the ranch hasn't given me any plot ideas. I'm feeling pretty frustrated, but I'm not going to worry about it. I really do have a lot to do, and Mary needs me more this year. I'm just taking notes about the people I meet, and I'm sure I'll have a lot to scribble about once we have the rodeo.

Has Mrs. Pickering asked you a lot of personal questions yet? She's inquisitive, but harmless, and will probably be thrilled to know that a female professor is in the building. Speaking of which, good luck with midterms. Try not to be too hard on the kids this year.

Love,
Phoebe

Phoebe pulled the paper out of her typewriter and addressed an envelope. She then took a postcard off a stack she kept in the corner of the desk in her *casa*. It had a historic image of Tribulation on the front, which Barton's general store carried in a rack by the cash register. She wrote a short note to Virgil, giving him a few details about the rodeo, saying she hoped he would come to town to see it. She hadn't heard from him in the last month and was a little disappointed, but she kept up her end of the correspondence anyway.

She took her letters and walked down to the reception office. It was just after lunch and Mary was saying goodbye to a few outgoing guests. Phoebe smiled when she saw that one of the women had a copy of *Lady in the Desert* under her arm.

She was up-to-date with everything in her office, and it would be a couple of hours before the guests arrived. It gave her time to work on her writing, but the thought of it irritated her since she was still lacking inspiration. So she picked up the book about rodeo she'd brought with her and kept on top of the shortest filing cabinet and took it into the dining room, where the afternoon crock of lemonade and plate of cookies were in their places on the sideboard. She filled a glass, took two cookies, and sat at the table closest to the open window overlooking the back patio and swimming pool.

Three people were lazing in the water on air mattresses. The splashing was a cheerful and not obtrusive noise, and Phoebe settled in to eat as she slowly turned the pages of the heavy volume.

It had been published seven years earlier, so some of the famous names in the book might not even be around anymore, but it was still thrilling to read about them. She flipped through the chapters, looking at the photographs. She smiled at one captioned “Cowgirls’ Attire (1910),” which showed three young women smiling at the camera, wearing leather chaps, plain shirts, various sizes of cowboy hats, and bandannas, standing by a ladder that looked like it led to the announcer’s booth in a grandstand. A couple of cowboys sitting on a nearby fence had managed to get into the shot, too.

She got lost in the collection of photos, and then read the section about cowgirls. The author thought highly of them, writing, “When it is a question of sheer courage and grit among the athletes in various branches of sports, great tribute must be paid to the cowgirl who competes in rodeo.” She reflected on the sports she’d attempted when she was in school. No one would ever have used the word grit to describe her.

Mary waylaid Phoebe as she walked toward her office in the lodge the following Friday morning.

“Would you come with me to check the cabin I’m giving to the Carters? They arrive later this afternoon.”

“Sure, what are you looking for?”

“Just to make sure everything is perfect. They are our first long-term guests, and I want the cabin to be very welcoming.”

The women walked to the next-to-last cabin on the left side of the lodge. It was the second largest, and could accommodate a big family if needed. Mary took a key from the pocket of her Capri pants and opened the door.

"Oh, it's lovely," said Phoebe.

The cabin had a short entryway that led to a sitting area with a couch upholstered in a deep brown fabric with understated red accents. It also could fold out into an extra bed. A small mesquite wood coffee table sat in front of the couch, and Mary had placed a pottery vase of bronze chrysanthemums in its center. As with all of the cabins, there was a floor lamp with a rawhide shade, a copper ashtray stand, and mesquite end tables with matching table lamps. Beyond was a spacious main bedroom with two double beds covered with bedspreads in bright stripes of red, beige, and turquoise. The wooden floor gleamed and each bed also had a small rag rug next to it as well as two mesquite nightstands with rawhide-shaded lamps. Behind a turquoise painted door was the bathroom with a large shower and two sinks.

"This is perfect! There's no way they won't love this. And it certainly is big enough for a comfortable long stay."

"Thanks, I'm glad we had already put in new floor coverings and linens," said Mary.

"Isn't it kind of large for two people though?"

"They asked for a room with two beds, and I did not ask them why. Besides, they will be here for three months at least, and they can't be cramped into one of the smaller cabins. I decided not to give them the big cabin with the suite, because I'm still hopeful we'll get some families or groups of friends who want to room together, especially when we get closer to the holidays."

"Smart."

"Don't let me forget, I want to put a plate of

cookies in here just before they check in. They are driving from Carson City so it could be anytime between three and five this afternoon. I hope they arrive in time for cocktails. That's always our best first impression."

Phoebe laughed. "Oh yes, you have to make sure the guests know how good your booze is."

At precisely three a black Buick Skylark rumbled into the ranch's parking lot. Phoebe had just walked into the reception office to check the mail, and Mary was at the desk as usual, waiting for her afternoon arrivals. They looked out the window and then looked at each other.

"Here they are," said Mary.

As they watched, the driver's side door opened and a tall, well-dressed man emerged. He was probably six feet two with broad shoulders and a muscular neck. He wore a salt-and-pepper tweed jacket with a white shirt, a red-and-black striped tie, and gray slacks. The jacket was tight enough to show how muscular the rest of him was, and Phoebe could see the shine on his shoes. He was not yet middle-aged, but his hair was completely silver. Thick and slicked back, it complemented his face rather than aging it. He looked around, smiling, revealing very white teeth, and there was an air of mastery about him. He then went to the passenger side of the car and swung the door open.

The woman who stepped out was petite, and Phoebe thought she must be only a couple of inches over five feet tall. Dressed in a powder blue sweater twinset, black skirt, and low-heeled black pumps, she looked like a faded photograph next to her husband. Except for her hair, which was a deep, natural red, cut short but not stylishly. Watching them walk together toward the office, Phoebe thought how mismatched they appeared. He looked like a big-city plainclothes detective. She looked like a worn-out schoolteacher ready for the term to end.

Glenn and Jayne Carter walked into the office, and Glenn introduced himself and his wife to Mary and Phoebe. His voice suited his size.

"Well, it's so great to be here!" he boomed.

"We're happy to see the both of you," said Mary. She then smiled broadly at Mrs. Carter, who took a final drag on her cigarette and put it out in the copper ashtray on the reception desk counter.

When Mrs. Carter said, "Thank you," her voice wasn't as understated as her appearance, and was as strong as her husband's, though not as loud.

Mary walked them through the check-in process, and then reached for the phone to summon one of the staff to carry the Carters' luggage to their cabin.

"I'll take them over there," said Phoebe. "We'll get you your bags right away," she told them.

Glenn thanked her and took his wife's elbow. She had a large black alligator skin purse on her left arm, and they followed Phoebe out the door.

It was just a short walk to the cabin along the tiled pathway.

Glenn took a deep breath."Ah, just smell that fresh air," he said.

"It's not as pleasant in Carson City?" asked Phoebe.

He laughed. "Oh, it's fine, I'm just used to the smell of gasoline fumes."

They reached the cabin, and Phoebe used the key Mary had given her, opening the door and gesturing for them to go in. She saw the cookies in place on the coffee table next to the flowers.

"Say, this is nice, a good size. What do you think, honey?" he asked his wife.

Jayne Carter put down her purse and took out a pack of cigarettes and a chrome lighter.

"It's fine, dear. We'll be very comfortable."

"Well, I'll leave you to settle in," said Phoebe. "Cocktails are at five o'clock in the saloon, which is the door next to the reception area where you checked in. And we serve supper at six."

Glenn thanked her as Jayne sat on the couch, smoking and not looking particularly happy.

Phoebe went back to the reception area. Mary was just getting off the phone, and said, "Well, that's an interesting couple, what did you think?"

"I can't decide if Mrs. Carter is shy, unfriendly, or just unhappy that she had to come to a dude ranch."

"We have plenty of time to find out what she's really like," said Mary. "Oh, I forgot to tell you. I met with Helen a couple of days ago and we made some changes to the menus for next month. I have to make sure we don't repeat meals too often now that the Carters are here for the long haul. We don't want them to get bored with our food."

"Just give me the new information and I'll type up the menu cards. But I can't imagine anyone being bored with Helen's meals," said Phoebe.

Helen was the ranch's cook, the highest-paid and most valuable member of the staff. Everyone expected to eat well at a dude ranch, and if they didn't, word got around and that was very bad for business. Helen lived full-time in an apartment in town which Mary and Sam partially paid for each season—a nod to her status and skills.

"She told me that Powell woman has called her three times to offer her a job at the Desert Grande. Thank god she's loyal to us," said Mary.

"You treat her well, and the guests love her food," said Phoebe. "She would never do that to you. Besides, she's what, fifty years old now? She knows her own mind and she also knows people. If she wasn't cooking here she could run a business."

"I asked her once if she ever wanted to open her own restaurant and she just rolled her eyes and said, 'I don't need that kind of aggravation.'"

"Then count your blessings and don't worry about it," said Phoebe.

The Carters were a bit late for cocktails that evening, so they didn't so much arrive as make an entrance. Phoebe thought that was probably how Glenn Carter always showed up. He was in full dude regalia: dark blue satin shirt with white piping and buttons, new jeans, and new tooled brown cowboy boots. Jayne, on the other hand, was in the same clothing she had arrived in, but had just added a three-strand necklace of pearls and large pearl stud earrings.

Mary greeted them and introduced them to the four other couples in residence. Glenn shook hands with the men and winked at the women, while Jayne smiled grimly. She then made her way to the bar and asked Sam for a highball. Glenn heard her and said over his shoulder, "Hey honey, order me one too, will you?" He was talking with one of the men, the only one who came close to him in size and taste in clothing. Once Glenn had his drink, the two men went off into a corner, talking all the while.

Jayne was standing by the bar alone with her drink and a cigarette. Phoebe went up to her, said hello, and gestured toward Glenn.

"They seem to have found something in common pretty quickly," she said with a nod toward the corner.

Jayne actually smiled and replied, "My husband is in real estate. He can smell a prospect across a crowded room no matter where we are."

Phoebe wanted to ask how staying for three months at the H Double Bar would help his business, but Jayne volunteered the information.

"We're here scouting property for a big client," she said. "Glenn is so excited, he's like a kid when it comes to the Old West stuff. He took a few horseback riding lessons before we drove out here."

"What about you? Are you interested in riding?"

Jayne gave her a strange look.

"Not really, I'm just looking forward to a rest. We've been very busy the last few months. I'm the bookkeeper and secretary for our business and I've had a lot to do."

She peered out the nearby window and said, "I think I will like it here after all."

"I hope you will," Phoebe said. She wondered what "after all" meant, but didn't ask, and then excused herself, wandering over to talk to one of the other women guests, a nurse from San Francisco. They were soon exchanging stories of their favorite restaurants. Mary joined them, hoping to hear some food ideas.

A few minutes later a couple from Montana, Russell and Laura White, touched Mary on the elbow, and Russell asked her a question.

"We've been to some dude ranches in our own state, and in Wyoming, but they don't serve alcohol. They told us it's a rule or something. How are you able to open a bar?"

"Thank you for asking, Mr. White. It's generally a rule at dude ranches not to offer alcohol, and ranches often can't get a license. But we have a good relationship with the authorities here and were able to do the paperwork to offer the choice to our guests."

"What do you do if someone has too much and gets drunk and rowdy?"

"Well, we have never had that problem, we have wonderful guests. But if it does happen, we have some big, strong cowboys who can deal with them."

With that, Mary winked and walked away.

AT TEN THE NEXT morning, Glenn Carter joined five of the other guests and walked the pebbled path down to the corral, where the wranglers had gathered the ranch's horses. Phoebe joined them, as she liked to watch Gene choose the horse for each guest whenever she could, always hoping she would learn something. She especially enjoyed eavesdropping when Lorraine took charge of the trail ride.

Glenn was in his new jeans again, paired this time with a cotton, snap-front shirt in stripes of bright orange and blue. His boots and new Stetson were black. Gene greeted everyone and asked each of them about their riding experience.

"I've had a few lessons, but I'm no cowboy," Glenn said. "Better pick me out a tame steed."

Gene thanked him and brought Glenn over to a light brown, stocky horse with black mane and tail.

"This is Huck," he said. "He is good on the trails with new riders. He just likes to contemplate the scenery as he walks."

Glenn laughed and said Huck sounded perfect. Gene picked out a blanket and saddle and soon had him ready. He did the same thing with the others, made sure everyone was safely mounted, and then got on his own horse, High Stepper.

He turned Stepper toward the well-marked trail which led from the corral into the desert, and said, "Wagons ho!" On cue, all the other horses followed him.

Phoebe walked back to her office in the lodge and two hours later, as she went out to get a glass of lemonade from the sideboard, Glenn Carter and Elizabeth, the nurse from San Francisco, walked in to do the same thing. They looked exhausted but happy.

"How was your ride?" Phoebe asked them.

"Great," said Elizabeth. "Though I thought I was in better shape. I'll be creaky tomorrow."

Glenn laughed. "Well, I survived. But it was a ton of fun, I'll definitely be taking more of those rides."

"Did Gene tell you that Huck will be your horse while you're here?"

"Yes, and he said that since Jayne and I will be around for quite a while, I might get a different horse if I improve. That remains to be seen."

Phoebe said, "Your wife told me she doesn't plan on taking a trail ride."

Glenn's smile wobbled a bit, and he said, "Probably not. She's not the outdoorsy type, but I'll keep working on her. Oh, there she is."

He'd been looking out the front window, and saw Jayne pull into the parking lot in their Skylark.

“Ah, she’s been doing some shopping,” said Glenn. “Guess I’d better go see what the damage is.”

He strode out the front door, and Phoebe asked Elizabeth for details about her morning.

At supper that night Mary reminded everyone that the weekly chuck wagon lunch would take place the following day.

“Those of you who want to ride to the picnic area should head to the corral around eleven thirty, and Carl will get you onto your horses and lead you out there. It takes about twenty minutes. If you want to go in our station wagon, please gather in the parking lot about ten minutes to noon. Sam will do the driving.”

The guests were spread out over two of the tables in the dining room, and the Carters sat together with one other couple, though Phoebe didn’t see them make any conversation during the meal. After Mary made her announcement, Phoebe saw Glenn bend over and say something to his wife, who shook her head and reached for a piece of bread in the basket in front of her. Glenn’s face didn’t register any emotion, though the man sitting across from Jayne raised his eyebrows as he looked at his wife.

Sunday was glorious. The air was still warm, but gentler, with the softness of a summer left behind. A few clouds skittered in the sky, concentrating themselves around Maybelle Peak. The horses also liked the change in the weather, and were sprightlier this morning, though not enough to alarm the novice riders.

Only two women opted to ride out to the chuck wagon lunch in the Woody station wagon with Sam. Jayne Carter was one of them. She had changed out of her usual skirt and wore a pair of black slacks and a light blue chambray shirt, accented by the pearl necklace and earrings. Her boots looked stiff and new, and Phoebe wondered if she'd bought them in town the previous morning.

One of the waitresses stayed behind at the ranch so that Mary, Sam, Joe, and Phoebe could manage the outdoor lunch. Phoebe always helped out with setup, and they used the Jeep to drive out to the site. Gene Bowman was now in charge of hitching up two of the ranch's biggest animals, named Henry and Jesse. He also drove them out to the picnic area. The previous driver, hilariously named Chuck, had retired and moved to Phoenix to live with his granddaughter.

Mary, Joe, and Phoebe took off at eleven, and pulled into the cleared spot just as Gene was leading Henry and Jesse into a small corral. He then started to unpack the food and utensils from the wagon, and Phoebe got out of the Jeep holding a red-and-white checked oilcloth and a handful of linen napkins in the same design.

She started laying everything out on the picnic tables underneath the *ramada* that was built from four tall posts of mesquite wood which supported a lattice roof covered with ocotillo branches. Utensils, paper plates, mustard, ketchup, and pickle relish came next, followed by platters of cold cuts, bread and rolls, gelatin and macaroni salads, and dishes of black olives and peppers. A cask of lemonade sat on a small folding table nearby with cups ready to be filled.

Everything was in place by the time the riders arrived just before noon, both on horseback and in the car with Sam. Mary invited everyone to find a place at the tables. The new guests, as well as some of the regulars, inspected the chuck wagon first, exclaiming at how ingenious it was. Mary then announced that dessert, cherry pie and chocolate chip cookies, would be brought out after they finished, and coffee and tea would be waiting for them in the lodge when they returned to the ranch.

The noise level increased as everyone ate and talked with each other. The guests had started to form friendships and spent a lot of their time together, which Mary was always happy to see. Glenn Carter chatted with Ted Holloway, who was also in real estate in his native Pennsylvania. His wife Mamie, who had come out in the Woody, tried to start up a conversation with Jayne Carter but didn't get very far. Jayne sat and smoked, staring off into the distance, though she did respond when someone asked her a question. Joe had both pie and cookies, and ignored his mother's frown.

When lunch was finished, the riders got back onto their horses, and Sam took Jayne and Mamie back to the H Double Bar. Joe went with them. He decided not to get into his mother's vehicle and therefore avoid a lecture about eating too much dessert.

Phoebe went to the Watts house after supper for drinks that evening, and asked Sam what Jayne Carter was like.

"What do you mean?"

"Well, what did Jayne do? Did she seem happy or bored or what?"

"She didn't say anything," said Sam. "That Mamie woman chattered the whole way."

Phoebe looked at Mary, who said, "I already asked him, and it would have been hard to keep an eye on her while he was driving on that road."

"But she never said a word?"

"Nope."

Mary asked Phoebe, "Why do you want to know?"

"I just think she's interesting. She doesn't act like she wants to be here at all, and is only taking this trip because her husband wanted to."

"I've seen that before," said Mary. "Most of the women end up having fun, they just have to find something they want to do. Though it doesn't happen for everyone."

"I guess. She just seems bored, and on the edge of being irritated with her husband."

"I've seen that plenty of times, too."

With the dudeo planned for the following month, Mary, Sam, and Phoebe spent the final week of October nailing down all the details.

Many of the ranch's former guests wrote in to make their usual reservations early just so they could come to the rodeo. Mary was discouraged by the response to her ads, though. A few men had written to ask how much she would pay to have them come to do bronc riding or roping, despite the fact that the advertisements had been clear that she would only pay for lodging and food.

"I guess I was naïve," she said one night. "I thought these guys loved their sport and would be happy to show off their skills."

"I think most of them only go to the sanctioned events," said Sam. "That way they earn money and a place in the bigger rodeos."

"I'm sorry, Mary," said Phoebe. "But you have a good list of wranglers from the other ranches who are coming and want to compete. Between the bronc riding and barrel racing we will still put on a good show.

"And the dudes will love the fun stuff you have planned for them. I'll bet lots of people will want to come and watch the events, and you've done enough advertising so they know about it. We still have Carl, too, though Susie will shoot you if you let him ride on a bull. Maybe he could do something else?"

Mary looked more cheerful. “Yes, that’s true, we’ll find something for Carl that won’t kill him.”

All the guests were still in residence for Halloween, and they had been encouraged to wear costumes. Nearly everyone brought along something fun, and Phoebe had put on the outfit Mary had put together for her two years earlier: scruffy denim overalls, plaid flannel shirt, boots that were too big for her, and a smashed, dirty Stetson. Carrying a pickax and a stuffed burro, she walked into the saloon to hoots of laughter, and explained to everyone that she was supposed to be one of the Butler brothers working the Maybelle Mine.

Glenn and Jayne Carter did not dress up, though Glenn’s shirt was more flamboyant in color and design than some of his others. Phoebe wondered if he considered his dude clothing costume enough.

Guests snacked on popcorn balls during cocktails, and as they entered the dining room for supper, they saw the tables illuminated with small carved pumpkins with votive candles inside. The supper wasn’t exactly Halloween-themed, but it was hearty: fried chicken, mashed potatoes, green beans with cheddar cheese sauce, and a carrot and raisin salad. Dessert was a devil’s food cake with what Helen called White Mountain frosting, a marshmallow-like concoction which she had decorated with thin streams of chocolate sauce to make a spiderweb design. The happy guests went back to their cabins or sat in the living room in front of the television after drinks and coffee.

Phoebe walked back to her *casa*, enjoying the sharpish night air faintly scented with the sweet woodsy aroma of the creosote bush, which grew in the open desert around the ranch. Phoebe loved how the smell deepened and filled the air after the winter rains. She sat on her couch for a moment, and glanced up at the mantel. She’d found a frame for the photo of Virgil standing next to his truck with Hunter looking over his shoulder and had placed it next to the picture of Ellender and her daughter.

Wondering why she hadn't heard from Virgil, she got up and headed to the little telephone table, but then looked at her watch. It was nearly nine, probably too late to call him.

She sat at her desk instead, and took a Tribulation post card from the stack she kept in one of the cubbyholes. This one had an old photo of a store on the front, with a sign reading "Campbell's Mercantile." She took out her pen and began to write.

Dear Virgil,

How are you? Things have been very busy here, and we have a couple of guests who are sticking around for a few months. Mary is ecstatic, though I have to say they are kind of strange. I haven't done much with my writing, as we have also been busy planning the rodeo which we'll have on the first Saturday after Thanksgiving. Can you come down? We would all love to see you. What are you doing for Thanksgiving? Just drop me a line or call me some evening.

Say hi to Hunter for me.

Yours,
Phoebe

She was in the registration office when the mail arrived the next afternoon, and she gave her postcard to the mailman to take with him. Among the letters he dropped off was a large envelope with a California postmark. Mary opened it first.

"Phoebe, look at this. A woman wants to come to our dudeo and demonstrate trick riding for the audience. This is amazing."

She had a letter in one hand and a folded handbill in the other. Mary opened it up and she and Phoebe looked at it together.

Eden Williams
The Celebrated Trick Rider
And her Famous Horse
Berry-Wise

Underneath the headline was a black-and-white photo of a young woman on a stocky, light-colored horse. The bottom of the poster had a list of appearances in California and Nevada cities the previous spring.

"Is she actually standing up on that horse?" Phoebe said.

"Yup, that's a classic trick," said Mary. "She looks like she knows what she's doing, too. Here's her letter."

Mary gazed at the poster as Phoebe read the letter out loud.

Dear Mrs. Watts:

My name is Eden Williams, and I saw your advertisement in Western Horseman *magazine. As you can see from the enclosed, I am a trick rider with longstanding experience and I would like to come to your rodeo and give a demonstration. Please write to the address below and confirm that you have a place for me. I understand that you offer board and food only, as well as stabling and feed for my horse.*

Thank you in advance and I look forward to hearing from you.

Yours sincerely,
Eden Williams

Mary looked at the return address.

"Where is Sebastopol? Do you know?"

"Yes, it's north of San Francisco in Sonoma County. It's very agricultural, they grow apples and berries and lots of other produce."

"Huh." Mary was still looking at the handbill. "I wonder how she got involved with trick riding."

"I guess we'll find out. Will you write and tell her to come?"

"Absolutely, I'll do that today."

"I wonder how her horse got that name."

Carl came into the office before Mary could answer the question.

"Howdy, cowboy," said Mary. "What's up?"

Carl looked around nervously.

"Something happened before the trail ride this afternoon," he said.

"What?"

"I was saddling Mr. Carter's horse, Huck, and the cinch broke when I was tightening it. Someone cut that cinch almost all the way through, Mrs. Watts. It could have broken during the ride if I hadn't noticed it."

"Oh my gosh, that's awful," said Phoebe.

Mary frowned. "Are you sure it wasn't just worn out?" she asked.

"Nope. I know a knife cut when I see one."

"I don't like the sound of this. What did you do?"

"I pulled a different saddle for Carter, and put the other one in that big cupboard in the tack room. I don't think anyone noticed."

"Thank you for being so careful, Carl. Will you please go ahead and check all the other saddles to make sure they're okay?"

"I already did, and the rest of 'em are fine."

"Tell Gene, Lorraine, and Bob, and make sure they inspect the saddles more carefully than usual when they are getting everyone on their horses."

"Yes, ma'am," said Carl. He touched his hat and left the office.

Mary blew out a breath."That could have been a disaster."

"Have you ever had something like this before?" asked Phoebe.

"Not anything that looked like sabotage."

"What?"

"I trust Carl's instincts. If he says the cinch was deliberately damaged, then I believe him. I'll have Sam get the saddle so we can look at it."

The following Sunday Phoebe and Mary were loading supplies into the Jeep to take out to the chuck wagon lunch site when Mary noticed one of the back tires was flat.

"Oh, damn," she said. Looking around she saw Sam and waved him over.

"Honey, can you change this tire for us? Luckily, we're not running late, but we do need to get to the picnic area."

"Sure, hon," said Sam. He went out to the barn and came back with a tire, pulling a jack from the floor of the Jeep. He expertly removed the flat, and then made a face.

"This tire isn't just flat, it's been punctured," he said, puzzled.

Mary took one look at the tire and said, "That must have been deliberate."

"You don't know that. I don't see a nail or anything, but this Jeep could have run over a dozen sharp things on any of its trips," said Sam as he finished his task.

"Let's go," said Phoebe. "You can worry about this later, okay?"

"All right, but I don't like it," said Mary.

9

"DAMN."

Phoebe pulled the sheet of paper out of her typewriter, ripped it in half, tossed the pieces into her wastebasket, and went into the kitchen to get something to drink. She often got a second writing wind in the early evening and she'd come back to the *casa* right after supper to put in some work on her new novel. But not tonight.

She stood at the kitchen window with a glass of water and gazed at the star-sprinkled sky. She let her eyes wander, looking for the stars that stood out as the brightest. She took a deep breath, downed her drink, and then went back to her desk. But instead of scrolling another piece of paper into the Royal, she picked up the letter which sat beside it, reading the words over for a third time.

Dear Phoebe,

Thanks for your postcard. It's always fun to see a picture of the old Campbell's store.

I want to also thank you for the invitation to Thanksgiving and the rodeo. I have plans to eat with friends here in Phoenix and will also be busy during the weekend. But I hope it is a huge success.

Have a wonderful time with all of your friends. Say hi to Mary, Sam, and Joe for me.

Virgil

"Huh." Phoebe made an inarticulate noise and tossed the paper back onto the desk. *All of my friends? What's that supposed to mean?*

She shook her head and went back to the typewriter, but it was no use. She turned on the radio, found some light music, plopped onto the couch with the novel her librarian friend Barbara had recommended, and started to read.

She felt better the next morning and got her paperwork done in record time. She carried a new collection of menus down to Mary at the registration office to proofread.

"I see you got a letter from Virgil yesterday. Is he coming to Thanksgiving?" Mary asked.

Phoebe's good mood evaporated."No, he already has plans."

"What about the dudeo?"

"Nope."

"Why not?"

"How would I know? He just said he was busy and told me to have fun with my friends."

Mary had been sorting papers as they were talking, but she stopped, put everything on the desk, and looked closely at Phoebe.

"What's wrong?"

"Nothing. Except that I can't make any headway with my writing."

"That's not it. You're upset because Virgil told you he isn't coming."

"Well of course I am. He's my friend, too, and it seems like he just doesn't want to come here anymore."

Mary tried not to smile.

"Well, he is very fond of you, that's obvious. So, something else must be going on."

"Well, it's not my concern."

"Whatever you say."

"I hate it when you do that."

Mary did smile then, went back to her task, and Phoebe left the office.

She looked at her watch and saw that she had about forty-five minutes until lunch was served. She decided to head out to the corrals to see how the construction was going.

Mary and Sam had hired local carpenter Paul Hewson to bring a crew to the ranch to build a rodeo arena. They had added some fence to the largest corral, more than doubling its size so that there was plenty of room for events or demonstrations. Paul also knew how to construct what Mary called a "bucking chute," a place where the bronc riders would mount their horses before jumping into the arena.

He had finished that yesterday, and the men were

now building wooden bleachers on one side of the corral for the spectators. Mary told Paul she wanted enough seats for fifty people, and then asked him to also make some plain benches. Phoebe knew that Paul had managed to get some old cement blocks from a construction site, and was planning to stack them with some boards he also had on hand from another job, creating makeshift but still serviceable benches.

The rhythmic sound of hammering, the smell of new wood, and the familiar scents of the desert soothed Phoebe's rattled feelings. The morning trail riders came in a few moments later, led by Lorraine, who waved at Phoebe as everyone headed toward the barn.

Phoebe made her way back toward the lodge around four-thirty and saw the Carters' car pull into the parking lot. They had gone to Phoenix the previous morning, telling Mary they had to attend a business meeting, but would be back in time for cocktails that evening. This was the second time they had spent a night away from the ranch. Phoebe realized that things were a little less tense at meals without Jayne at the table, even though she never did anything overtly to make anyone uncomfortable. There just seemed to be a simmering undercurrent between the Carters that Phoebe couldn't put her finger on, and other guests felt it too.

She watched as they walked toward their cabin. Glenn wore a black suit and Jayne was in a navy blue dress with her usual pearls. The couple looked like they'd been to a funeral, but Phoebe thought that might be how people dressed when they did big real estate deals.

Glenn was a dude again that night in the saloon, though Jayne still only gave a nod to cowboy clothing. Tonight, she had accented her chambray shirt with a silver brooch in the shape of a longhorn bull, pinned near her left shoulder.

Phoebe went up to her and said, "What a beautiful pin." It was exquisitely crafted and Phoebe could see every hair on the animal's face.

After Sam handed Jayne her usual highball, Jayne sipped her drink and reached into her purse for cigarettes and lighter before responding.

"Thank you. Glenn bought it for me in Phoenix. I have to say I'm not much of a western jewelry enthusiast, but I do love engraved silver. And I like the sharp horns on the bull."

Phoebe thought this was an odd thing to like in a piece of jewelry but just said that it looked very lifelike. Jayne smiled, sipped her drink, and made a remark about the fall weather.

The following evening Bob came into the lodge as the guests were dispersing. Mary and Phoebe were talking to one of the waitresses, and Bob walked up to them and said, "Mrs. Watts, ma'am? May I have a word?"

"Of course," Mary said. Phoebe watched the two of them walk over to the fireplace and have a short, but obviously tense conversation. Mary then touched Bob on the arm and he left.

"What's happened now?" Phoebe asked

"Some tack is missing," said Mary.

"Well, that doesn't sound too bad. Maybe it's just been misplaced."

"Bob and Carl keep that room in perfect order. The only reason they can't find something is because someone took it."

"What's missing?"

"Two of our newest saddle blankets, and the

saddle that Carl gave to Mr. Carter after the cinch incident. Sam hadn't inspected it yet."

"Oh, that's not good. I'm sorry, Mary. This does look deliberate, doesn't it?"

"Yes, and I know who's behind all of this stuff."

"Who?"

"Who do you think?"

Phoebe hesitated a moment and then said, "Oh, not the Desert Grande."

"Well, who else has a reason to make things difficult for us?"

"But why would they do all these things?"

"I don't know, I'm not a criminal."

"Well, don't go accusing them of anything, that would just give the place ammunition against you."

"I know, you're right. It just makes me so mad. We'll just have to be vigilant. I'll ask Sam to keep an eye on the cars, and Carl and Bob are already checking the tack regularly. We've never locked the tack room, but I guess we'll have to now."

"I'm sorry, Mary. We'll get to the bottom of it."

"I hope so."

Mary came into Phoebe's office with a large box just before lunch the next day.

"Can you keep this in here? I don't have room down in the registration area, and I don't want to spoil the surprise."

"What is it?"

"The ribbons and prizes I ordered for the dudeo."

She put the box on the table next to Phoebe's desk and opened it up. Inside were three large envelopes and four smaller boxes.

"Here are the ribbons," Mary said, pulling the

colorful satin items from each envelope. "Blue for first place, red for second, and white for third."

"How many did you buy?" asked Phoebe.

"I bought thirty of each color. And take a look, aren't these cute?"

Mary opened one of the boxes and pulled out a small brass-colored trophy on a black base.

"We can't engrave them or anything, but this is something we can give to the kids who win the events."

"What a great idea. What are you giving to the wranglers who compete?" She took the trophy from Mary to admire it.

"The men will get tooled leather stirrup straps. My friend Walter in town made them, he has that shop next to The Red Lamp. And women will get a little chiffon scarf like the one you have. I asked Helen to pick up a few at Goldwaters when she went into Phoenix last week."

"Oh, perfect."

"I also need to go to the Trading Post to see if they have anything we can give away that we don't already keep around. I thought I'd do that this afternoon. Do you want to come? Sam can manage the registration desk, though we're not expecting any new arrivals today."

Phoebe said yes, and they made a plan to meet right after lunch.

After parking the station wagon on Center Street, they walked toward the store entrance and Mary suddenly waved at someone. Phoebe saw Laura Stevenson walking toward them. She and Mary embraced briefly, and Laura said howdy to Phoebe.

"I haven't seen you since that woman's open house," said Mary. "How is your season going?"

"Not bad, we have a full complement of dudes," said Laura.

"That's great, I'm so glad," said Mary. "So, the Desert Grande hasn't ruined your year."

"Not yet, anyway. How about you?"

The two women talked shop for a few minutes.

"Three of our dudes want to participate in the rodeo. Oh, excuse me. *Dudeo*," said Laura.

Mary laughed. "That word takes some getting used to, but it's unique. Glad to hear it. Just call or send me a note with their names."

"I will. Billy and Frank will try the bronc riding."

"Oh good, those boys will definitely put on a good show."

"Yes, they will. All right, guess I should finish my shopping. See you soon!"

Laura gave each of the women a squeeze on the arm and strode off toward the feed store.

After spending more than a half hour in the Trading Post, Mary and Phoebe gathered up their two bags of souvenirs: burro-shaped pins with the word *Tribulation* etched on the side, small stuffed burros, and two Tribulation-themed belt buckles. As she made her choices, Mary told Phoebe she wanted a really great prize for the stationary steer head roping, one for adults, and one for kids.

"People like to feel they've won something special," she said. "The dude events are just for fun, but roping takes skill. I think we'll have some fierce competition there for the top prize. Everybody loves a belt buckle."

As they left the store Phoebe felt Mary stiffen, and she saw Thelma Powell leaning over to read the flyer for the H Double Bar dudeo in the Trading Post's window. From her black loafers to the squash blossom necklace which set off her blindingly white Oxford shirt, she looked like an advertisement for Vassar, if Vassar had a campus in Arizona.

Thelma looked up, saw the women, and smiled.

"Mrs. Watts, Miss Kelley, how nice to see you," she said.

Phoebe replied, "Hello Miss Powell, nice to see you too. Are you doing some shopping?"

She poked Mary with her elbow, and she also said hello, in a tone that sounded friendly but which Phoebe knew was her "I really don't want to talk to you" voice.

"I've been seeing the ads for your rodeo all over town," Thelma said. "It looks to be an exciting event."

"Everyone is invited," said Mary. "I do hope you can drop by. And be sure to let your guests and wranglers know they can participate, too. They just need to call me to sign up. The dude events will be simple, of course, but we have a bucking chute for the wranglers who want to try bronc riding. And we'll have barrel racing for your female wranglers, if you have any. We plan to hold at least one dudeo each season."

"Really."

"Yes indeed," said Mary. "We will also be demonstrating trick riding. Please try to come."

"Thank you. Well, I must be off, it was nice to see you both."

She walked stiffly away, her shiny loafers kicking up dust on the sidewalk.

Phoebe turned to Mary.

"I didn't know you were planning to hold a dudeo every year."

"We are now."

Phoebe and Mary returned to the ranch and put the bags with the other prizes in Phoebe's office in the lodge. Then they both went to the registration desk to check the mail, which had just arrived. Phoebe looked casually but in vain for a letter from Virgil, though there was one from Katie.

"Oh look, Phoebe, here's the reply from that girl trick rider, Eden Williams. She accepts all of our terms, and will get here the Wednesday before Thanksgiving."

"Good thing, since you told Thelma Powell we'll have trick riding demonstrations. It will be nice to have her here for the holiday."

"Yes, she can get to know the dudes, so she'll have a sense of who she is performing for. Although I hope we get a lot of people from town and the other ranches, of course. I'm going to make some new flyers with the information about Miss Williams. I'll send Carrie to pass them around town and pick up the old ones."

They heard a rumbling of wheels on gravel and saw Jayne Carter pulling the Skylark into the parking lot.

"That woman sure gets around," said Mary. "I wonder what she does on all her trips to town? I didn't see her when we were there, did you?"

"No, but she could have parked her car off one of the side streets and gone shopping somewhere."

"How many more shopping trips does she need to take before she runs out of things to buy? Anyway, I'm going to put Miss Williams in the girls' bunkhouse with Carrie. She spends all her free time studying so she won't mind having a roommate. Well, she doesn't have any choice."

"Why isn't she at college? I can't remember."

"She's studying natural history, she's interested in desert plants and wildlife. She got into Arizona State but needed to make some money so she's taken a year off and will work here until we close for the season next spring. Luckily all the other girls live locally so there's an extra bed in the staff cabin."

Phoebe took her letter from Katie and walked out to the rodeo grounds, sitting on the now-completed bleachers. The weather had cooled but Phoebe was comfortable in her jeans and cable-knit sweater. She chuckled as she read about Katie's efforts to avoid Mrs. Pickering's pointed questions about being an unmarried college professor with ambitions to make movies. She heard a creaking sound and looked up to see Carl pushing a large wheelbarrow into the enlarged corral. He stopped in the center and tipped the wheelbarrow over, gently dislodging a bulky item wrapped in burlap. Phoebe got up from her seat and went through the arena's gate to see what he was doing.

"Hi Carl, what have you got there?"

"Oh, hi Phoebe. Take a look at this. It's the dummy head for the roping contests."

He pulled the fabric off, revealing the wooden face of a longhorn steer.

"Wow, it looks great!" said Phoebe. "Who made it?"

"Paul's wife, Vivian, she's an artist, and works with wood a lot."

"It looks so real, it's got personality. And those horns! The kids will love throwing a rope at it."

Carl picked up two metal stakes.

"Viv left openings in the back of the head. These slide into the holes, and then we put the stakes into a bale of hay to hold everything up. We'll keep this in the middle of the ring for the roping, and we can toss everything into a wheelbarrow to get it out of the way when we have events. I'm going to get the hay bale now."

Carl wheeled away and came back a few minutes later with a bale of hay wrapped with twine. Placing it on the ground he attached the stakes to the back of the dummy and pushed them into the bale.

"There, how does that look?"

"Like a steer with a body made of hay," said Phoebe, stating the obvious.

"Great, that's what it's supposed to be."

He stepped back and walked all the way around to make sure everything looked right. Then he lifted the bale with its black head into the wheelbarrow, covering it with the burlap.

"Where are you storing this?" Phoebe asked.

"In the tack room. Which we now keep locked, as you probably know."

"I heard."

"I thought I saw someone hanging around the tack room the day that stuff went missing."

"Who was it?"

"Not one of our guests, I can tell you that. Just when I was going to see what he was doing, the guy just disappeared. He must have sneaked out the back of the barn. Maybe he had a horse there or something, and I didn't have a chance to investigate."

"That's so strange. Did you tell Mary?"

"Of course. And if I see him again, I'll be sure to bulldog him."

"I'm sure you will. Which reminds me, what will you be doing at the dudeo?"

Carl gave her a goofy smile.

"It's a surprise."

"I hope it won't be a bad surprise for Susie."

"Not at all. Mrs. Watts approves, too."

"She hasn't told me what you're planning."

"She wants to surprise everybody."

Phoebe followed Carl and his awkward burden out of the corral and then veered off to walk back to her place to get ready for cocktails.

She was a little late, and Jayne Carter was the only one at the bar when she asked Sam for a bourbon and water. Phoebe sat down next to her, waiting for her Four Roses, and fished around for something to say, even though Jayne rarely invited conversation.

"May I ask you something?" said Phoebe.

"Of course," Jayne replied, finishing her cigarette.

"I've never met anyone who spells the name Jayne like you do. Well, except for that actress, Jayne Meadows. Is it a family name?"

She looked at Phoebe and her face grew soft.

"Actually, my parents gave me the usual spelling. But I had an Uncle Wayne, who was very important to me, a big part of my life when I was growing up. We lived in a very small town in Nevada, and he used to come to town to see us once or twice a year, driving a rickety Model A Ford. I remember it was usually winter, or at least it was cold, and he wore a thick, black wool overcoat with a fur collar. He always had candy in the pockets for me and my brother.

"Then, during one of his visits when I was a senior in high school, he gave each of us a $100 bill. He didn't really care what my brother used it for, but he was very serious when he gave me the bill. He said I should take the money and go to secretarial school after graduation, instead of sticking around and just taking any old job. Then I could get out of town and have a better life.

"I was startled, but I loved him and decided to take his advice, though my mother wasn't thrilled with the idea. A few weeks after this visit he died in a car accident, and I left home to take my courses. I graduated at the top of my class, and went to Reno to get a job. But before I did, I changed the spelling of my name to honor my uncle. Jayne for Wayne, you see?"

"What a wonderful story," said Phoebe.

"I met Glenn in Reno, I was a secretary in the

office where he was working. I owe…him so much. My uncle, I mean."

The supper bell rang just then, and Jayne's face settled back into its usual unrevealing expression. She got up from her barstool, sought out her husband, and they walked up to the lodge together.

10

TWO DAYS LATER Phoebe went into the kitchen right after breakfast to get another cup of coffee and ran into Lorraine Bowman, who had come into the lodge on the same mission.

"Hi Phoebe."

Phoebe smiled at the wrangler, always amazed at how a woman who had spent her life outdoors on a horse could still look so youthful. She knew Lorraine was in her late forties, older than Mary by almost a decade, but they looked like contemporaries. Maybe it was her sunny outlook on life.

She never met anyone she couldn't turn into a horse lover. The dudes adored her because she was gentle with the ones who were nervous around horses, and she gave the experienced riders the more challenging animals.

"Did you hear?" Lorraine asked her as they poured coffee into their mugs.

"Hear what?"

"That Carter woman is going to take this morning's trail ride."

"You're kidding."

"Nope. I guess her husband talked her into it. I'm heading out to the barn in a couple of minutes to get everything ready. I don't think she has any experience, and if so, I'll probably put her on Daisy. The only other novice has been riding Holiday."

"Well, good luck. I know she'll enjoy herself with you in charge."

The women parted, and Phoebe headed back to her office.

About an hour before lunchtime, Mary walked in, looking grim.

"What's wrong?"

"Glenn Carter had an accident."

"Oh, my god, is he okay?"

"Yes, luckily. Something spooked Huck on their way back, and he reared. I'll say this for him, Carter held on, though he started to slide off just before Lorraine got there and calmed Huck down. Carter wrenched his shoulder but he says it's not that bad. Dr. Calhoun is here and looking at him now. He gave him some liniment and told him not to ride for a couple of days. He isn't even mad, he kind of laughed about the whole thing, and asked if I thought he was ready for a more spirited horse now."

"Well, that's big of him. What did Jayne do?"

"She was riding behind her husband, and managed to keep her horse from panicking while Lorraine dealt with Huck. By the way, she thinks Jayne has more experience than she's letting on. She kept her horse calm, no beginner could do that."

"Why would Jayne lie about how well she rides?"

"I don't know, I'm just happy they aren't planning to pack up and leave."

Glenn was the star at cocktails that night, and he gave an account of the morning's adventures to a rapt audience. His right arm was in a sling, though his injury didn't keep him from wearing another brightly-colored cowboy shirt. This one sported a rodeo print, including images of bucking broncos, which was probably a deliberate choice.

"How are you feeling?" Phoebe asked him, as they both stood at the bar.

"Oh, I'm fine. What's a ride without a little bit of excitement?"

"That would be too much excitement for me."

Jayne walked up to them just then.

"You had a frightening experience, too," Phoebe said to her.

"Yes, it was unnerving, but Lorraine kept things from going badly."

"Did you have any trouble with your horse while all this was going on?" Phoebe asked, very aware of why she wanted to know.

"No, the horses seem to be well trained."

"Were you riding Daisy?"

"Yes, she's a lovely animal." Jayne seemed startled at her own words, and then reached into her purse for cigarettes and lighter.

Glenn took her by the elbow and excused the both of them, and they walked away to talk with the Philadelphia real estate man.

Phoebe noticed that Mary, standing by the saloon's door, had been watching Glenn as he told his story. She went up to her and asked what she was doing.

"I just want to hear how he describes what

happened today. I hoped he wouldn't make Lorraine or the ranch look bad," whispered Mary.

"He isn't doing that at all." Phoebe also kept her voice low.

"I know, I'm so relieved. He seems to be enjoying the attention, so we're just going to let him have his moment. I guess he just feels he had a real Wild West experience."

"That's why he's here."

Mary smiled, and then she escorted everyone to supper.

Mary and Phoebe devoted the next few days to redecorating the lodge for Thanksgiving. They put away the summery-colored Indian rugs and brought out others of deep orange and warm brown. They also put piles of pumpkins and scarecrows made of synthetic straw around the fireplace hearth, and piled logs on the grate for the first fire of the season, which would be lit on Thanksgiving night. The mantel also sported pilgrim and Indian figurines, along with a few smaller pumpkins interspersed with white candles in tangerine-colored pottery holders.

Mary spent many afternoons in the kitchen conferring with Helen about the holiday menu. Phoebe used specially themed paper to type up the menus, and also made place cards for everyone. Mary believed that if people spent their holidays away from home, they should enjoy a few special touches.

Phoebe managed to get away on the Monday before Thanksgiving to have a quick lunch with Barbara. She left the assistant librarian in charge of the desk, and the two women went to The Wild Burro. As they chatted in their booth, waiting for their drinks, they heard the tinkle of the restaurant's main door and Steve Magly walked in with the blonde woman Phoebe had seen during her lunch with Virgil. The hostess seated them on the far side of the room.

"Who is that?" Phoebe asked Barbara, gesturing toward the couple.

"Nora Collins," said Barbara. "She was Steve's girlfriend all through high school. But then she went away to college in California and they drifted apart. She's a secretary somewhere in Los Angeles."

"I saw them together back in September."

"I heard she was in town then because her mother was sick, though it turned out not to be anything serious."

"Is Steve still holding a torch for her?"

"Very possibly. He had a girlfriend when he was at the police academy in Phoenix but he didn't bring her back here with him. He's dated a couple of girls in town, but you see he's never married. I've often wondered if he kept in touch with Nora."

The women continued to discuss the officer's love life as they ate their salads. After splitting the check Barbara said, "Come on, I'll introduce you."

She led Phoebe across the room and when Nora saw her, she leaped out of the booth to give her a hug.

"Barbara Burington! Oh, it's so good to see you."

Nora was a petite blonde with dark eyes and eyebrows, and had an open and infectious smile. She grabbed Phoebe's hand with enthusiasm when Barbara introduced her.

"I am so happy to finally meet you. Steve told me about your adventures here in town, and I want to hear your version one of these days."

Phoebe couldn't help smiling back, and said she would love to tell her the *real* story someday, which made Steve laugh.

"I have to get back to the library," said Barbara.

"And I have to get back to my office chores," said Phoebe, and then she had a thought.

"Will you be in town during the weekend after Thanksgiving?" she asked Nora.

"Yes, I don't go back to California until the following Wednesday."

"Well, you should both come out to the H Double Bar on Saturday at eleven. We're having a rodeo…excuse me…*dudeo*…for both dudes and wranglers, and there will be some trick riding demonstrations."

"Steve told me. It sounds like a lot of fun. I'd love to come."

"We'll be there," said Steve.

Everyone said their goodbyes and Phoebe walked her friend back to work.

"She's lovely, no wonder Steve never got over her," said Phoebe.

"I don't think he'll let her get away this time," said Barbara.

On Wednesday morning Phoebe drove into Tribulation to do some emergency food shopping; Helen had forgotten to put evaporated milk on her Thanksgiving grocery list. All the parking spaces in front of Barton's general store were taken, so she had to leave the Nash a few doors down the street.

She wandered the aisles and put five cans of milk in her basket, also picking out a loaf of bread, a package of Waffle Cream cookies, and a can of Arbuckle's coffee for herself. As she waited in line by the register, she remembered that her stock of postcards was low, so she chose a few more from the rack that was just within reach.

As she drove down the long driveway into

the ranch, she saw something big in the parking area, surrounded by a few colorfully dressed dudes. She pulled in and parked her car in the spot closest to the lodge. She steadied the bag of canned milk in her arms and walked over to see what the excitement was about.

A cream-colored Oldsmobile sat idling near the pathway by the registration office, and attached to the bumper was a white horse trailer. It had an oval window on the front, a rack on top with a ladder on the side, and a tailgate with a hefty chained latch. Phoebe could see the back of a horse in the trailer's dim interior, which some of the dudes were gazing at from a safe distance.

Both sides of the trailer featured a sign painted in red letters:

Eden Williams
&
Berry-Wise

Western Pride Berry Farm
Sebastopol, Cal.

The trick rider had arrived.

Phoebe took her shopping bag up to the lodge and left it in the kitchen for Helen, then went back down to the registration office, pausing to take in the trailer and its silent passenger. She walked in just as Mary was handing a key across the counter to a young woman.

"Oh Phoebe, there you are. This is Miss Eden Williams, who will be demonstrating the trick riding at the dudeo. This is my sister-in-law, Miss Phoebe Kelley."

The woman turned to look at Phoebe, holding out her hand.

Eden was at least an inch shorter than Phoebe, and nearly a decade younger, but she had a presence that ruled the room. It might have been the confident look in her wide eyes, which were a clear, greenish hazel and made Phoebe think of pebbles seen through a rushing stream. Eden's dark hair was cut in a bob at her shoulders, and she wore simple gold hoops in her ears. A hint of cheekbone accentuated a genuine, warm smile.

"Miss Kelley, it's a pleasure to meet you."

"You too, Miss Williams. We've been looking forward to having you join the dudeo, and as you can tell from the crowd outside, so are our guests."

Eden held on to Phoebe's hand and her eyes seemed to ask a question, but it was only for a moment and Phoebe wasn't really sure she'd seen it. Eden let her go and turned back to Mary.

"I'd like to take my horse to the barn and get him settled. Can we do that now?"

"Of course," she said.

"Can I drive my trailer over there?"

"Yes, that's fine. I'd like to invite the guests to watch you unload your horse, would that be all right?"

"Oh, yes. I'd like that."

Eden put her room key in the back pocket of her jeans, and the three women walked out of the office. The morning trail riders had returned to the ranch, enlarging the crowd around the trailer. Glenn Carter was among them, but not Jayne. Two families had arrived the day before, and a collection of boys and small girls hovered near their parents, occasionally jumping in the air to try to see into the trailer's dark interior.

Mary surveyed the crowd and smiled.

"Hello everyone. I'm sure you join me in welcoming Miss Williams to the ranch. She is taking our other new guest down to the barn. Feel free to join us."

Eden got into her car and drove slowly behind Mary as she walked the wide back pathway to the barn, and Phoebe joined the crowd of dudes who followed in their wake. The car and trailer stopped in the large open area by the barn door. After she got out of the car, Eden asked everyone to step back as she approached the rig.

Unlatching the half door, she walked into the trailer and the sound of a low murmur came from inside. A few moments later a horse began backing up carefully with Eden at its side, still talking, holding on to the rope attached to its halter. He placed his back left leg on the ground, the right leg followed, and with one smooth movement the horse seemed to float out of the trailer. Eden patted the animal, and then turned him around to face the crowd.

He wasn't especially tall, and even with her limited knowledge Phoebe knew he was probably about fifteen hands high. He was sturdily built, but he looked powerful, not chunky. His body, mane, and tail were a warm, chestnut color, and a wide, white blaze ran all the way down his face, covering his nose. Phoebe gazed with wonder at the white markings all over the horse's body; he looked like he had been sprinkled with powdered sugar. He drew all eyes to him, just like Eden did.

With her hand on the horse's broad neck, Eden smiled at the gathered dudes and said, "Ladies and gentlemen, meet Berry-Wise."

Recognizing the drama of the moment, the group applauded, while the kids mostly stared. Phoebe noticed that Glenn, in the back of the crowd, was looking at Eden instead.

Lorraine had joined the group by this time and was gazing at the horse with admiration. Eden gestured to the older woman, seeming to recognize her status, and Lorraine stood with her beside Berry-Wise, stroking his large head. He looked calmly around, and as his gaze fell on the assembled children, they all started to smile.

Berry-Wise got the same warm reception from

the wranglers and part-time hands, who all gathered around, asked permission to approach the horse, and posed questions that Phoebe didn't fully understand. Bob seemed especially taken with him, and showed Eden the stall they had prepared for the horse, taking extra time to make sure he was settled. He also asked about her saddle and tack. She told him there were two saddles in her trailer, along with the rest of her gear, and he said he would unload it all for her. She thanked him, holding out her hand, shaking Bob's massive, calloused palm.

Eden chatted with everyone for a few more minutes, and Phoebe saw Mary gesture to Bob. She wasn't surprised when Mary told him to lock Eden's saddles in the tack room. She also asked him to put Eden's car and trailer in the large open area next to the barn.

Eden got her suitcase out of the trunk of her car, and then she, Mary, and Phoebe walked back to the registration office where Sam was waiting. He took Eden's luggage and escorted her to the cabin she would be sharing with Carrie.

Phoebe said to Mary, "She's certainly a beautiful girl, isn't she?"

"Yes, and I wonder if she might be part Indian."

"Really? Why?"

"Something about her eyes, and that almost-black hair."

"That might not be something she talks about."

"True. There's still a lot of prejudice around here about Indians. And it's none of our business."

11

EDEN ARRIVED at cocktails before most of the guests that night, and Phoebe took her to the bar to place her drink order with Sam. Joe was hovering around, waiting for the other kids to show up. When he heard her ask for a Roy Rogers he said, “That’s a boy drink.”

Eden looked at him and said, “Well, girls can be just like Roy Rogers, if they want to. Here, I’ll make you a deal. Watch me at your dudeo, and afterward tell me if you think it’s okay for me to have a boy drink. Deal?”

Joe smiled shyly, and said, “Deal.” Eden held out her hand, and they shook on it.

Phoebe thought Joe was probably confused by the contrast between Eden’s professed skills and her obvious femininity. She wore a simple black-and-white gingham dress with a wide black belt, and carried a white sweater, ready for the rapidly chilling evening. She had pinned up her hair and exchanged the gold hoops for clip-on copper discs, which matched the wide copper bracelet on her right wrist. Her makeup was expert and her red lipstick the perfect shade.

The rest of the dudes arrived a few minutes later, including Glenn and Jayne Carter. Mary made a point of introducing Eden to everyone, as she was more than just a regular guest, and she wanted the young woman to feel welcome. Mary took her up to the Carters and said, "I don't think you've met Miss Eden Williams yet. She's here to demonstrate trick riding at our dudeo."

Jayne put on the bland smile she showed nearly all the time as the women acknowledged each other. Glenn's face, however, seemed to freeze, and though he said, "Nice to meet you," his hand barely grazed Eden's own. When the women walked away Phoebe saw him wipe his palm on his jeans.

As everyone was enjoying their apple pie and ice cream after supper, Mary stood up and said that Miss Williams was going to talk a little bit about herself. Eden then rose and acknowledged the enthusiastic applause.

"Thank you, Mrs. Watts. I am very happy to be here, and I can tell you that Berry-Wise is, too. I live in Sebastopol, which is in northern California, and where my family were farmers. For many years I've been working for the owner of the largest berry farm in the area, called Western Pride.

"The owner, Mr. Ivar Danielson, saw that I loved horses and let me exercise some of his animals after I finished mucking out the stables and doing other chores. He raised quarter horses and one day he bought a young roan he named Berry-Wise."

One of the boys interrupted just then and got his question out before his mother shushed him.

"Why is he called that?"

Eden smiled and asked the boy his name. "Jason McIntyre," he said as his brothers, Christopher and Matthew, rolled their eyes and their mother, Gladys, tried not to. Fred, the boys' father, was a script reader for a TV series in Los Angeles, and he was as interested in Eden's story as his son was.

"Well, Jason, he's a strawberry roan, he lives on a strawberry farm, and he's a very wise horse. So, that's why he's called Berry-Wise. Anyway, Mr. Danielson hired me to start exercising his horses, too, and Berry-Wise was my favorite. About the same time, I went to some local rodeos and saw young people doing trick riding stunts, which looked like a lot of fun, so I decided to learn some of them for myself when I was taking Berry out for his run. One day, Mr. Danielson saw what I was doing."

She paused and, as expected, she had everyone's full attention. She then turned back to Jason and said, "What do you think happened next?"

"You got in trouble!" he said without the slightest hesitation, and everyone laughed.

Eden joined in and said, "Well, guess what? I didn't get in trouble. In fact, Mr. Danielson was so impressed he gave me time to practice the tricks I was learning with Berry-Wise. I entered the rodeos around where I lived, and started winning prizes. Berry's owner then made me a bargain: if I would help advertise the berry farm, he would sponsor me to travel even farther to show what a great trick riding horse Berry-Wise is."

Phoebe was impressed. Eden not only knew how to tell a good story, she made it all about the horse, and not her own skill. And she wondered if this Danielson guy knew how lucky he was.

Mary stood up and said, "Miss Williams will be happy to answer your other questions after we get our coffee. Then I'll tell you a bit more about the dudeo."

There was a clanking of mugs as people poured coffee from the urn on the sideboard. Phoebe, who had been sitting with the Graham family and their two girls, Bonnie and Sarah, got up to ask Eden if she wanted any coffee. She said no, but smiled her thanks. After everyone got settled, Mary took over again.

"Well, first of all, I am so happy you are here, not only for our Thanksgiving supper tomorrow night, but for our very first rodeo or 'dudeo,' which begins at 1eleven on Saturday. We won't have any trail rides that day, but we will still have our chuck wagon lunch on Sunday.

"We have events which both you and your kids can do, and guests from other ranches will also be participating. Our male wranglers will compete in bronc riding, and our ladies will have a barrel racing contest. Wranglers from other ranches will also join in, which will make it quite the competition. And everything will take place in our new, enlarged corral.

"Of course, the highlight of our dudeo is Miss Williams and Berry-Wise. They will perform when the events are over and prizes have been awarded."

Phoebe noted that Mary also included the horse when she described the trick riding part of the program. And she saw Eden give a faint nod of thanks.

"We have three events for our guests: pole bending, an egg and spoon race, and steer head roping."

The three McIntyre boys, along with Jacob Randolph, who was visiting with his grandparents, made sounds of masculine glee. Mary was ready for it.

"Sorry, boys, it's not a real steer. We have a head made of wood for everyone to try to rope instead."

There was a collective rumble of disappointment, and a few laughs from the parents.

"In pole bending, you ride a horse around a series of poles, like an obstacle course. The winner makes it around the poles in the shortest time. The egg and spoon race is a lot of fun. You get on a horse on one side of the corral, and you'll be given a spoon with a raw egg in it. Everyone takes off at once, and you then have to get to the other side without dropping the egg. If you do lose your egg, you have to go back to the starting point, get another one, and start over. The first rider to get across the corral with the egg still in the spoon is the winner. And in the steer roping, the winner is the person who gets the lariat around the head, and not just on the horns."

The guests had a lot of questions, and the next fifteen minutes were devoted to clarifying the rules and making sure the two Graham girls, and Jacob Randolph's little sister Ava Grace, knew that steer roping wasn't just for boys.

As people finished dessert and got up from their tables, Phoebe realized that the Carters were the only ones who didn't seem interested in Eden or her upcoming demonstration. Although Glenn paid attention when she was speaking, Phoebe thought his gaze was hostile rather than intrigued. They were also the only guests who didn't stick around to talk with Eden, or watch TV as usual.

Phoebe and Mary stayed until the last guest had wandered off for the evening.

"Well, I think you've made a few fans tonight," Mary told Eden.

"Just wait until Saturday. Berry-Wise always steals the show."

"I think you're underestimating your own appeal, dear. He's a magnificent horse, but all eyes will be on you, I guarantee it. I'm very impressed that you taught yourself how to trick ride."

"I made a few friends on the rodeo circuit, and the girls showed me the ropes. Then Mr. Danielson gave me time to practice."

"I'm surprised the other riders shared their secrets with you. Weren't they worried about competition?" asked Phoebe.

Mary jumped in before Eden could speak.

"Honey, that's how it is in the rodeo world. It's just like dude ranching. What's the phrase, 'a rising tide lifts all boats?'"

"That's true," said Eden. "When we help each other, we all get better at what we do. Which doesn't mean we don't try to win. We compete hard, and when one of us comes out on top, the rest of us try to figure out how to beat that girl the next time. But we're still good friends."

"Exactly. Dude ranchers keep an eye on what the others are doing, and we try to copy what works in our own way. But it's only to make our ranches better, not take away from the others. Well, almost all of us."

Eden gave her a questioning look.

"There's a new place in town called the Desert Grande Guest Ranch, and they have been siphoning off guests and staff from everyone else in town."

"That doesn't sound good. What are you doing about it?"

Phoebe was startled by the question, but Mary wasn't fazed.

"Our dudeo is the only one in town, and we hope it will give us an edge over those people. They offer all kinds of activities that you could do anywhere. We give guests a real dude ranch experience. So that's why I'm so grateful that you answered my ad."

"Do you think they'll send anyone from their place to compete?"

"They haven't told us if they will. All the other ranches gave me a list of which dudes and wranglers want to participate, but we are ready if someone else just shows up. We haven't opened up the competition to people in town, because we want the events to be a draw for people to come to the ranch as guests."

"Do you plan on having more dudeos in the future?" asked Eden.

"We hope so," said Mary. "We'll see what happens after Saturday."

Mary and Eden then talked about how she and Berry-Wise could manage to get some practice time in the corral on Friday.

"I'd also like to take him on a good walk tomorrow, but I don't want to interfere with your trail rides. What's a good time for me to go?"

"Early in the morning before ten would be good, as the ride takes off then. Or just after lunch and before the two o'clock ride. Talk to Bob or Gene about the best trails and when you'd like to go."

With that settled, Mary excused herself and took one final look in the kitchen before returning to her own home. Phoebe was about to do the same, when Eden spoke.

"You're the Phoebe Kelley who wrote *Lady in the Desert,* aren't you?"

"Well, yes I am. How nice of you to ask."

"I read your book. Many times, in fact. I enjoyed it a lot. Could I talk with you about it sometime, maybe on Sunday after lunch? I'm not leaving until Monday."

"That sounds lovely. Once we get back from the chuck wagon lunch, I'm off the clock."

"Great. Would you like to ride with Berry and me tomorrow?" Eden asked.

"Oh. Well, actually, I don't ride that much. But thank you." Phoebe could feel her cheeks flush.

"Really? Why not?"

Other people had asked Phoebe this question in the past and it usually irritated her, but Eden looked sympathetic, even concerned, unlike the astonished curiosity Phoebe was used to. So, it seemed easy to give an honest reply.

"Well, I grew up in San Francisco, and never had the chance to learn. I visited the ranch often when my husband was alive, and I've worked here the last two seasons, but there just didn't seem to be enough time for the people here to teach me properly. It's not their fault, it's a busy place."

She took a breath and gave Eden the reason she'd rarely told anyone else.

"And frankly, I'm a little afraid of horses."

Eden smiled. "I understand that. If you haven't been brought up around them, they can be a little scary.

"Would you like me to give you a couple of lessons while I'm here? I hate the thought of you not being able to ride, especially here. If that's something you'd like to do, of course."

Phoebe started to say no, but then hesitated. Her lack of horsiness was getting a little embarrassing. Especially if she was going to keep coming out to the H Double Bar each season. She had been on a few trail rides after getting some pointers from Sam, but she still wasn't confident enough to get on a horse as if she knew what she was doing. Bob and Carl had said they would be glad to give her some real lessons, but she kept turning them down. She was fond of both of them, but wasn't sure their approach was what she needed, especially after they'd used the phrase "throw you onto a saddle."

It only took a moment, but Phoebe realized that Eden was someone she could trust to teach her without judgment, though she couldn't have explained why.

"You know, I would like that," she said.

"Wonderful! How about Sunday, as we'd planned?

We can ride and talk about your book. Your wranglers can pick one of the gentlest trail horses for you."

"We have an afternoon ride that day, but not everyone participates, so there are always a few horses hanging around. I'll talk to Gene, Lorraine's husband, he's the head wrangler. I'll let you know what he says. We can go on one of the trails that the guests don't use, so we don't run into anyone."

"That sounds good."

"Thank you, Miss Williams, I really appreciate it."

"I want everyone to love horses, I think that's my mission in life. And please call me Eden."

"And you must call me Phoebe. Are you going back to your cabin?"

"Yes, it's been a long day."

"I'll walk you there."

Eden put on her sweater as the women walked along the tiled pathway in the sparkling, clear night air.

"Have you met Carrie yet?" Phoebe asked her.

"Yes, for a couple of minutes when I first got into the room. She's very nice, and said she's going to ask me some questions about the plant life in northern California when she has some time."

Phoebe laughed. "She's quite the naturalist. I hope you don't mind sharing the room with her."

"Not at all. The cabin is great, and I like talking to new people. Believe me, it's a lot nicer than some of the places I've stayed."

Phoebe watched Eden smile as she looked around. The windows of the occupied cabins glowed, and the sound of children's laughter joined a coyote chorus performing in the desert darkness. Phoebe said good night at the door, and then walked slowly back to her *casa.* She'd left the living room lamp on, and its warmth echoed the shimmering porch light, welcoming her home.

Thanksgiving was, as usual, a triumph. Mary served the traditional foods, like turkey, yams, mashed potatoes, stuffing, and string bean casserole, and the lodge smelled like everyone's holiday memory. Helen was a master gravy maker, and more than one guest asked for her secret every year, which turned out to be the milk and butter she bought from a dairy farm a few miles from Tribulation. Mary wanted the meal to be memorable, so she and Helen always put a few different flavors into the food.

Cumin and a dash of hot pepper surprised the guests as they dug into the stuffing, and there was an additional side dish of refried beans smothered in cheese, along with platters of cheese enchiladas. There was also a pile of what looked like puffy tortillas, and Mary announced that it was Indian fry bread.

Every year someone (usually one of the children) asked about the unusual menu, and her response was always the same.

"Indians and Mexican people were in Arizona before the Americans. I like to give my guests a taste of all of Arizona's history when they visit the H Double Bar."

Eden's face lit up as Mary spoke, and Phoebe wondered if she might be a history buff. That would also explain her interest in *Lady in the Desert*. As she ate, Phoebe also listened to Ava Grace, the Randolphs' granddaughter, who was enchanted with the lady and her "strawberry horse."

Phoebe'd intended to watch Eden take Berry-Wise out for his afternoon exercise on Thanksgiving afternoon, and so did everyone else. When asked, Eden said she would leave around one. Phoebe went down to the small corral near the barn doors a few minutes before the hour, accompanied by all of the children and most of the parents.

Eden came out a few minutes later, leading her saddled horse. She wore the jeans she'd had on the day before, along with a denim shirt. Her battered boots fit perfectly in the stirrups as she got on Berry's back in one quick movement and walked him out of the corral and toward the trail that Gene had told her about that morning. They ambled slowly at first, and then the horse began to trot, breaking into a lope. Just before they reached a large rock formation, Eden stood up in the stirrups, leaned backward, waved a bandanna at her audience, and then horse and rider disappeared from sight.

Mary had arranged for Eden to have the new corral to herself on Friday morning, so she and Berry-Wise could practice. A few of the guests asked if they could watch, and Eden said they would enjoy her performance more if they waited until Saturday, though she didn't come out and say "no." The regular trail riders took off as usual, and though George and Betsy Randolph stayed behind with their granddaughter Ava Grace, the couple kept the girl occupied playing horseshoes and then a board game in the living room. They wanted to wait for the real show.

Eden came to lunch wearing clean jeans and a pink cowboy shirt. Phoebe remarked how she didn't look like she'd practiced a tough riding routine all morning.

"Well, the practice is more for Berry than for me. I needed him to get used to the size and shape of the corral. We usually ride on a long track, but he's been in corrals before, so it's not completely new."

"What will you do this afternoon?"

"Rest, and so will Berry. I gave him a good

rubdown and I'll brush him just before we go on tomorrow. Mrs. Watts told me the events and prize-giving should be over by around one thirty. I'll be in the barn well before then so we can be ready."

"I'm helping organize the people who enter the events, but after the prizes are given out, I'll be free to sit down with everyone and enjoy your performance."

"And don't forget our riding lesson on Sunday."

"I won't. I've already talked to Gene, and I guess I'll be riding Applesauce. She's one of the horses they usually pair with the kids."

Eden laughed. "What a great name. I'll talk to Gene, too, and find out what kind of horse Applesauce is."

Mary gave out more details about the dudeo at supper that night.

"Those of you who are entering events should be at the barn no later than ten thirty. And I'd also suggest that if you plan to be in the audience, you get to the bleachers or the benches about the same time. People from the other ranches and around town will probably start arriving around then, and we want to make sure our own guests get a place to sit."

When supper was over Eden excused herself and walked to the barn to check on Berry-Wise. Phoebe and Mary chatted for a few minutes.

"Well, we've done all we can to get ready," said Mary with a satisfied sigh.

"It'll be fine, it's supposed to be fun, and if a few things don't go smoothly, it won't be a disaster," Phoebe assured her.

"You're right. Thank you, honey. I couldn't do this without you."

"And I wouldn't want you to!"

12

SATURDAY MORNING was glorious, with a hint of warmth to come. Breakfast was heartier than usual, and the guests wolfed down the extra platters of sausage and bacon. There was a buzz of anticipation in their conversations, and the dudes who were entered in the events hurried through their meal so they could get into their dudeo clothes. Mary had told them to wear something they wouldn't mind getting dirty, and jeans and chambray or denim shirts proved the most popular.

At eight Phoebe was at the rodeo site, putting up signs directing people to where they should gather and park. Joe was in charge of directing the vehicles to their proper places, and Sam had given him instructions the night before, with a refresher that morning.

Sam would manage the trailers which were bringing in the three roughstock horses for the bronc riding contest. They belonged to a rancher who had a large spread a few miles east of the H Double Bar. His other job was managing the wranglers who would try their hand with the broncs, and Mary was in charge of the women's barrel racing event. All of the dude events, as well as the barrel racing, would use the horses from the H Double Bar's stable. Zephyr, Pathfinder, and Hornet were the best match for that event.

The men from the Lions Club were bringing tables along with the food they planned to sell to the audience members, and they were expected around nine. Carl and Bob set up boards on top of sawhorses near the barn for the potluck that the local dude ranchers were bringing for their guests and wranglers.

Carl had the corral ready for the first event as soon as it was full light. A row of six cans with six-foot-high poles set in cement were lined up in the corral's center, twenty feet apart. He paced between the cans to make sure they were in the right place.

Phoebe was also responsible for organizing the dudes for their events. Carl made fun of the clipboard she now carried with her everywhere, but she just stuck her tongue out at him. Mary had made a few name tags, and Phoebe's read, "Dude Events Coordinator." Joe had insisted on wearing one too, and he was dubbed "Parking Coordinator." Mary and Sam's labels just had their names and the H Double Bar brand.

Eden had been at breakfast with everyone else, and Phoebe marveled at how calm she seemed. When a couple of the boys asked her what tricks she would be doing, she winked at them and said, "Just wait and see."

Cars and trucks from nearby dude ranches started

arriving around ten. Phoebe got to work gathering up the dudes, including the H Double Bar guests, and telling them how the day would go, and where they should stand when it was time for the events they'd signed up for.

The visitor seats also started filling up just after the hour, and Phoebe saw some familiar faces in the audience, including the owners of the Trading Post, Susana Lozano and Monica Baca, who had brought their husbands. Barbara Burington was sitting with police officer Steve Magly and Nora Collins. Another young woman Phoebe had never seen before sat next to Barbara. She tried to get their attention, but they didn't see her.

Phoebe could easily tell the difference between the residents and visiting dudes, and as usual, it came down to clothes. The collars of brightly colored shirts peeked out from under striped gabardine jackets, the dude uniform for the cool of the morning. Her friends, on the other hand, were in sweaters and jeans and denim jackets. Phoebe made a note to herself to include this contrast in the book she was writing...well, *trying to write*.

At precisely eleven, Sam and Mary walked into the corral, standing near the line of poles. Sam had a battery-powered bullhorn in his hand, and he raised it up to his face. The audience heard him clear his throat.

"Ladies and gentlemen, I'm Sam Watts, and this is my wife, Mary. We are the owners of the H Double Bar Dude Ranch and we are happy to welcome you to our very first dudeo. We have a very exciting program for you today, starting with our dude events: pole bending, an egg and spoon race, and steer head roping. We'll then have the bronc riding contest for wranglers, and barrel racing for our lady wranglers."

He handed the bullhorn to Mary.

"We have prizes for dudes and wranglers. And when those have been awarded, we'll move to the highlight of our day: a trick riding demonstration by Miss Eden Williams and her famous horse, Berry-Wise!"

The audience cheered. Sam and Mary beamed.

Phoebe marveled at what perfect partners they were. Their personalities were nearly opposites, and many people wondered how they managed to find enough in common to keep their marriage together. Sam was quiet, solidly dependable. Some might have called him boring, but not Mary. Phoebe knew she relied on her husband's calm center, just as he needed Mary's ample creativity and buoyant personality to bring him out of himself, and to make their dude ranch the unique place it was.

Phoebe and her late husband Jack were more alike in personality, but she had lately come to realize that the Watts's marriage was stronger than hers had ever been. *What would our life have been like if he hadn't died during the war?* The thought went through her head and out again without lingering. She preferred to share in the warmth of what Mary and Sam had, and she gazed at them with affection as they drank in the applause from the now-filled bleachers and benches.

These feelings must have shown on her face, because one of the women in line for the first event asked her, "Is that your sister?"

"No, Mary's my sister-in-law."

"It must be fun to run this place with her."

Phoebe smiled. "Yes, it is."

The clapping faded away, and Mary said, "Thank you again for coming, and let's get started."

Phoebe took in one last view of the audience as she turned around to lead the dudes out to the pole bending event, and then stopped so suddenly that a passing wrangler nearly knocked her down. She said, “Oh, excuse me,” and then looked at the seats again, scanning the crowd, where she saw a familiar hat, jacket, and bola tie.

It was Virgil.

The morning had kept its warm promise, and by noon many of the spectators took off their jackets and sweaters before they headed toward the food tables, returning with sandwiches and cups of soda or coffee. The dude and wrangler events were over, and everyone had been encouraged to get something to eat before Eden’s performance.

As they mingled, people chatted and laughed about how hilarious it was to watch the dudes, especially in the egg and spoon race. Mary had deputized Joe to clean up all the spilled eggs, and he had run into the corral and scooped up the splattered yolks with a short shovel and a bucket like a ball boy at a tennis match. When Sam questioned Mary about why she wanted the eggs removed she retorted, “I don’t care if it is just a dirt corral, I’m not leaving a mess behind.”

Jason McIntyre’s brother Matthew surprised everyone with his riding during the pole bending, coming in a close second to a girl from the Triple S Dude Ranch. Jacob Randolph’s little sister Ava Grace jumped and squealed when he won the belt buckle for the best performance in steer roping. Chris, the other McIntyre brother, came in third. A boy from Jim and Laura Stevenson’s Bar K Ranch astounded the crowd with his egg balancing and easily took first prize for the event.

None of the dudes from the Desert Grande joined the competition, but two wranglers entered the bucking bronc event. One of them was a very young man whose time on the horse was just a tick shorter than Gene Bowman's. Phoebe caught sight of Mary when that happened and saw her scowl, but it didn't last long. Lorraine was bested in the barrel race by Maggie, one of the wranglers at the Bar K Ranch. The two women were good friends, and Lorraine applauded when Sam announced Maggie's winning time.

Phoebe assumed that Mary or Sam would give out the prizes when the events were over, so she was surprised when a rodeo clown strutted into the corral dragging a large black drawstring bag. It took her a few moments to realize that it was Carl. He wore oversized jeans held up with ragged suspenders, a red-and-white polka dot shirt, and straw hat. He'd also painted his face and blacked out one of his teeth. He made funny faces at the kids when he dug into the bag to pull out their ribbons, stuffed burros, and pins, and did an exaggerated vaudeville bow to each of the winning wranglers. The crowd's laughter just spurred him on to more antics, which included doing a few trick spins with a lariat that he also had in the bag. Phoebe thought he'd missed his calling, and planned to tell him so.

Mary watched to make sure everyone was back in their seats after the lunch break, and once folks looked settled, she and Sam walked back into the corral, now cleared of poles, steer head, eggshells, and a few dropped bandannas. Sam turned on the bullhorn again, and passed it to his wife.

"Ladies and gentlemen! We hope you enjoyed the first part of our dudeo, and we want to congratulate all of the winners."

The crowd applauded enthusiastically and a few people stamped their feet, making Mary chuckle and smile before she continued.

"The H Double Bar is now proud to introduce trick rider Eden Williams and her famous horse Berry-Wise, making their first ever appearance in Arizona."

More and even louder applause followed this announcement. It was obvious that the audience had been anticipating the climax of the day's events.

"I won't make you wait a moment longer. I give you Miss Williams and Berry-Wise!"

All eyes were aimed toward the barn, but a moment later everyone turned as a horse and rider burst through the corral's far gate, which Phoebe had opened while people were getting their food.

Eden and Berry stopped in the center of the corral, and the horse reared on his hind legs as Eden took off her cowboy hat and waved to the crowd, a brilliant smile illuminated her face as the audience clapped and hooted. Her tight black riding pants were tucked into short boots, and they were paired with a deep pink satin shirt with red piping. Embroidered on the back of the shirt, in shiny black thread, were the words *Western Pride Berry Farms, Sebastopol, Cal.* She also wore a pink bandanna around her neck, tied to the side with a jaunty bow. Phoebe thought she looked like a summer rosebush. Berry-Wise had dark pink ribbons braided into his mane and tail.

The horse lowered his front legs and suddenly he and Eden began spinning in place. After a few revolutions, Eden brought him to a halt and with a swift movement she stood upright in the saddle, her feet tucked into what looked like extra pockets. Grabbing the reins, she made a slight movement and Berry-Wise began to gallop toward the open gate. But instead of going through it, the horse turned and began to run parallel to the corral. As he sped up, Eden bent over into a full backbend, keeping the position as the horse made one full circuit back to his starting point.

Plopping back down into the saddle, Eden acknowledged the cheering crowd, and with barely a beat, goaded Berry into a gallop again. The crowd gasped when she seemed to fall off the horse, but she held on to the saddle, bounced on her feet in the dirt, and then jumped back on. She did the same movement five more times as the audience continued to cheer.

Eden then rode Berry toward the corral's center again. Around her arm was a lariat and as she stood straight up in the saddle Berry-Wise began to trot around in a circle as before, while Eden twirled the rope around her head. She then made the loop wider and jumped into the air as she spun the lariat up and around her body. She finished with another flourish above her head and looped the rope over her arm.

She then slid to the ground and after whispering something to her horse, Eden and Berry-Wise together bowed to the audience.

Before the applause died down, she leaped into the saddle, stood up in the stirrups, and took off her hat again in tribute to the audience. Berry turned and galloped toward the open gate, and Eden did a final backbend, and they passed through the opening, a berry-colored blur.

As Phoebe closed the gate, Mary and Sam went into the corral, thanked everyone for coming, and asked them to give Eden another round of applause.

After the clapping finally subsided, the audience began to leave their benches and bleacher seats. Phoebe hustled toward the pathway that led past the barn and out to the parking area, to help guide the traffic. Earlier that morning Eden had asked her to keep people from coming into the barn to see her or the horse. She wanted to take some time to cool and calm him down after the performance.

Phoebe saw a few visitors looking around for Eden as they headed toward their cars, and more than a few of them asked if they could see her and Berry-Wise. Ranchers and locals understood when she told them that Eden was taking care of the horse, and the dudes tried to look as though they did.

After the crowd thinned out, Steve, Nora, and Barbara came over to Phoebe, congratulating her on the great day.

"Oh, this is Celeste," said Barbara, introducing her to the young woman she'd seen in the stands. Celeste was small and dark, with close-cropped hair and a bright orange snap-front cowboy shirt.

"I'm so glad to meet you," she said.

"Celeste is a friend from college," said Barbara. "She wanted to come for a visit and I told her this event would be the perfect introduction to Tribulation."

"Where do you live?" Phoebe asked her.

"Cody, Wyoming. I'm also a librarian, and I run the public library there."

"Lots of dude ranches up there in Wyoming," said Steve.

"Yes, and I'm embarrassed to say I've never stayed at one," said Celeste.

"Well, that can be remedied," said Barbara.

As the group continued to chat, Phoebe looked up and saw Virgil slowly heading in her direction. She waved him over, and introduced him to everyone. He seemed to take particular interest in Steve, who was holding hands with Nora.

"So, you're the famous Virgil," said Steve.

"Well, I don't know about famous," he said with

a laugh.

"All of Phoebe's friends know the part you played in what happened here two years ago, and in the book she wrote," said Barbara. "I should have you autograph the copy of *Lady in the Desert* that she gave to the library, right next to her signature."

Virgil gave a chuckle, and smiled at Phoebe just as Mary, Sam, and Joe appeared on the pathway.

"Whew!" said Mary.

"Ooh, boy," said Sam.

"She was great!" said Joe.

As the little group laughed, Barbara introduced Celeste, and Mary greeted Nora.

"It's so nice to see you again," she said.

"You too, Mary. And I'm probably going to be sticking around for a while," said Nora, glancing at Steve.

"Well, that's the kind of news I like," said Mary. "But now I have to check on Eden. Phoebe, will you come with me? Would you like to join us, Virgil?"

Phoebe glanced at Mary, who looked back at her with wide, innocent eyes.

"I'd be glad to," said Virgil.

Everyone said goodbye and made promises to get together soon.

As they walked toward the barn Phoebe said to Virgil, "I didn't know you were coming, but I'm glad you made it."

"Me, too."

"What changed your mind?"

Virgil hesitated a moment and then said, "Mary wrote and asked me to come."

When Phoebe didn't respond he said, "I hope you don't mind. She said you were disappointed that I wasn't planning to be here, and that I would enjoy the dudeo."

After a moment, Phoebe said, "Well, that sounds like Mary. I was disappointed, but now you're here and that's great."

They walked into the barn and stopped a respectful distance away from Eden and Berry-Wise.

Bob Easley had removed all the horse's tack and was using a currycomb on his back as Eden unspooled the ribbons from his mane and tail. She was talking to the horse in a low voice, and Phoebe noticed Bob was smiling now and then.

Then he looked up and saw Mary, Sam, Joe, Phoebe and Virgil. Eden's back was to the barn door and Bob touched her lightly on the arm, gesturing toward the group. She turned and gave a broad smile.

"I hope you were pleased," she said.

"Miss Williams, I've never seen anything like that," said Mary. "I guarantee our audience hasn't either. You were wonderful."

Eden looked at Joe.

"Well, did I earn a Roy Rogers today?"

Joe beamed and said, "Yes, ma'am!"

PHOEBE AND VIRGIL ARRIVED at the saloon just as Eden did, and Phoebe made introductions. As they got their drinks more guests came in, most of them gushed at Eden about her performance. Fred McIntyre asked if he could talk to her sometime about the tricks she did, because he might want to work those into one of his TV scripts.

All of the children wanted to be in her orbit, and talked to her at the same time as soon as they got close enough. She laughed, answered the questions they asked, and paid special attention to the two Graham girls and Ava Grace Randolph. Sam made a Roy Rogers and gave it to Joe to hand to her, which he did with a grin.

The children eventually wandered off toward the toy boxes and Phoebe said to Eden, "The kids are even more impressed than the adults. Especially the girls."

"I want them to know they can do whatever they want to do, even if boys tell them they can't."

"Did that happen to you?"

"Oh, yes."

Glenn and Jayne Carter walked in just then. Jayne glanced at Eden and gave the younger woman a small, quick smile. Glenn took her arm and aimed her toward the bar.

"That's quite a brooch she's wearing," said Eden, gesturing at Jayne, who wore her longhorn pin on a red-and-white plaid flannel shirt.

"I know," said Phoebe. "You'd think it would make big holes in her clothing."

She then pointed at the shiny, flower-shaped pin Eden wore on the sweater draped over her shoulders.

"I like yours, too," she said. "What is it made of?"

"It's a handmade piece. I'll tell you about it sometime. So, are we still on for our ride tomorrow?"

"Yes, as soon as we all get back after the chuck wagon lunch. Maybe two?"

"Great. Where shall we meet?"

"How about the registration office? Then we can walk to the barn together."

Later that evening after supper, Glenn continued drinking and ignored Jayne's pointed looks and sharp whispered comments in his direction. Most of the guests went into the living room to enjoy their coffee or cocktails, and the kids turned on the TV or pulled board games off the shelves. Eden, Phoebe, and Virgil continued chatting in their seats at the table. Mary and Sam told everyone good night and took a very tired Joe back to their house.

Just before nine the guests who had children got up from the couches and announced that it was bedtime.

As parents helped their kids put the games away, Glenn spoke up from one of the chairs by the fireplace, in a voice that was just loud enough for everyone to hear.

"She's a Jap."

Nobody moved for a moment, and then the parents hustled their children out the door, glancing nervously in Phoebe's direction.

Glenn had been staring at Eden and kept his eyes on her, even as Jayne tried to haul him out of his chair. Phoebe saw Eden looking back at him without any expression on her face. A moment later Phoebe got up and went over to the couple.

"Mrs. Carter, will you please take your husband to your cabin? We can't have this kind of behavior."

Glenn scowled at her, but Jayne said, "Yes, I'm sorry. It won't happen again." And with that she and her stumbling husband left the lodge.

Phoebe walked back to the table. Eden stood up and said, "Thank you. I'm going back to my room. See you tomorrow."

The main door closed behind her as she walked away, and Phoebe and Virgil were alone.

"I wonder what that was about," said Virgil.

"I have no idea. I'll tell you this, Carter has been giving Eden strange looks ever since she got here. Did he mean she was Japanese? She does look a little exotic, but Mary thought she might be part Indian. Maybe he was just drunker than usual and thinks we're still at war or something. I really don't like that man."

"I can see why. I think you might want to let Mary know what he said."

"Oh yes, she needs to know. But he'll have to do something really awful to get her to tell him to leave, because the Carters have booked their stay into early next year. I'm sure Mary will talk to them, at least."

"Well, that's enough of that. Are you staying here at the ranch tonight?"

"No, I'm staying with Frank, and I already dropped Hunter off at his place. And I should probably get going."

"Will you be around tomorrow?"

"No. Unfortunately I have to get back to Phoenix. I promised to help one of my neighbors put in a winter garden in the afternoon."

"Will you come back for Christmas?" Phoebe asked, afraid he might not be planning to come.

"I will if I'm invited."

"Of course, you're invited!" she said with relief. "I'll have Mary make it official. Come on, I'll walk you to your car."

"No, you won't, I'm walking you to your *casa*. I want to make sure you are safely home in case that Carter guy escapes his wife and starts wandering around."

They walked out the main door and toward the gravel path that led to Phoebe's little house. The small, ground-level lamps along the lodge's tiled walkways gave enough light to show them the way under a sliver of new moon. Ahead of them was the glow of the lamp on Phoebe's porch. Neither of them felt the need to speak, and neither felt any discomfort about the silence between them.

At the door, Virgil put his hand on her shoulder and said good night. Phoebe watched him walk toward the parking lot, and stayed on her porch until she heard his car start up and drive away.

The next morning before breakfast Phoebe walked up to Sam and Mary's house. When she opened the door, Mary saw the look on Phoebe's face.

"What's happened?" Mary asked.

Phoebe told her about Glenn Carter's remark and Mary's face grew grim. Sam rolled his eyes and said, "I knew he would be trouble."

"Well, that's water under the bridge. We need to talk to them now. Thank you for speaking so sharply to them, Phoebe. That was the right thing to do."

"Well, I couldn't let it go. Especially the way he was looking at Eden."

"I'll pull the two of them aside after breakfast and just drop a few words into their ears. If they take offense and decide to leave, I can't help it. They can't go around insulting my other guests, whatever he meant by it."

"That sounds good. Thanks. I'm going to go get something to eat."

"By the way, did Carl tell you about the guy he saw near the tack room the night we had the theft?" Mary asked her.

"Yes, he did."

"He talked to me after the dudeo, and said he thought that Desert Grande wrangler who won the bucking contest looked like the man he saw."

"Wow. What are you going to do?"

"There's nothing I can do, we don't have any proof that he was the thief. Anyway, since we've locked up the tack room, we haven't had a problem."

"True. Well, I'll see you later at lunch."

"Thank you, honey."

Phoebe didn't see Eden at breakfast, and the Carters weren't there either. Phoebe walked back into the kitchen, and one of the waitresses told her Eden had come in early and they'd made her a quick meal.

Helen was kneading dough for Parker House rolls. "I like that girl," she said.

Phoebe wanted to do a few things in her office,

and on her way there she stuck her head out the lodge's main door. The Carters' Buick wasn't in the parking lot.

They didn't come to the Sunday chuck wagon lunch, either. Most of the guests rode out to the picnic site, but Eden had come in Sam's Jeep along with Phoebe and Mary. After Carl arrived with the wagon, Eden helped Phoebe pull out the utensils and condiments and set them on the tables, ignoring a horrified Mary who told her that she was a guest and should not be working. When Fred McIntyre pulled Eden aside and started asking questions about her trick riding, Phoebe asked Mary if she'd seen Glenn or Jayne.

"No, and their car has been gone all morning."

"I noticed that, too. You don't think they'd skip out, do you?" "

"No," Mary said. "I asked Maryanne to check and see if their luggage was still in their cabin when she went there to clean this morning. She said it looks the same as it always has. Maybe they are just embarrassed to show their faces. If they don't come back for drinks or supper I'll start calling a few people in town and ask if they've seen them."

Phoebe and Eden sat together at lunch, and Phoebe was relieved to see that the other guests seemed to have forgotten Glenn's rudeness from the night before. Eden told her that the jeans, snap-front shirt, and boots she was wearing would be fine for their ride that afternoon. Mary overheard the conversation, and told Phoebe to also wear a hat.

"You might not think you'll need it, but the sun is still strong here, even in November. You're not used to it."

"I know, I'm only accustomed to soft California sunshine." Phoebe laughed.

"You should both take a light jacket, too. It's supposed to start getting cooler in the late afternoons."

"Yes, Mom," said Phoebe.

She helped Mary pack up the chuck wagon as usual, and Mary succeeded in keeping Eden from helping this time. Sam drove them back to the ranch, where Phoebe went to her *casa* and Eden to her shared cabin, both emerging with their cowboy hats. They walked from the office toward the barn, stopping to chat with the Grahams and their two daughters. They were on their way to the small corral behind the registration office where everyone gathered for the daily trail rides. Bonnie, the older girl, asked if Eden was going to teach Phoebe how to stand up in the saddle.

"I barely know how to sit down in the saddle," Phoebe told her with a smile. "Miss Williams is going to give me a riding lesson. If I don't fall off, I'll see you later for supper."

Both girls snorted, and the family continued on its way.

Bob greeted Phoebe and Eden when they walked into the barn, and Phoebe saw that Applesauce, a calm buckskin with a dark mane and tail, was already saddled. Berry-Wise was still in his stall.

"Which of your saddles would you like me to get for you, Miss Williams?" he asked.

"Oh, I can get it, Bob."

"It's my pleasure, ma'am," he said. "But why don't you come with me and show me what you'd like to use."

The two went to the locked tack room and emerged with Bob carrying a simple, worn-in saddle and bridle, which he then handed over to Eden. While she got Berry ready, Bob had Phoebe walk Applesauce out into the wide-open area by the barn's door. A few minutes later Eden did the same.

"Normally, I would start with teaching you how to saddle your horse," she said to Phoebe. "But let's get you comfortable on Applesauce first."

She watched as Phoebe got into the saddle and positioned her feet into the stirrups.

"Now, I want you to sit up straight, but relax your lower back. Feel yourself sinking into the saddle. And make sure you are centered. Take a look at the saddle horn. If it's right in front of you, then you are sitting properly."

Phoebe maneuvered herself again, and Eden said, "Nice job keeping your heels down in the stirrups."

"That's the one thing Sam managed to drill into me," said Phoebe.

Eden then instructed Phoebe on the best way to hold the reins. After a few more minutes, she said, "Okay, now you look relaxed. So, let's head out."

Eden mounted Berry-Wise with a grace that Phoebe envied, and both women moved their horses toward the main corral and the open gate which led to a wide desert pathway.

As they walked, Eden gave Phoebe a short lecture about how horses think, how to approach them, and how to sense their moods, which was interrupted only by the occasional reminder about sitting correctly and keeping her heels down.

They rode for about twenty minutes, and Eden then said, "We're near the chuck wagon picnic area, aren't we?"

"Yes, it's just ahead, you can see part of the *ramada* from here."

"Let's go over there and give the horses a rest."

Applesauce knew where he was, and he knew

there was always a bit of hay there for horses from the guests who rode out to the picnic grounds. He began to trot, and didn't stop until he spotted the hay that was left over from that day's lunch. He immediately put his head down, and began munching.

Phoebe got shakily down from her saddle as Eden rode in on Berry-Wise. She tied him up close to Applesauce, who ignored the other horse and kept eating. Eden made sure Applesauce was also secured to the nearby hitching post.

"You did well when he took off," Eden told her.

"Did I? I felt like I was bouncing on a pogo stick."

"You looked a little like it, too, but you kept your seat. You're better at riding than you think you are."

"Well, it helps to have a good teacher."

They sat down at the picnic tables and relaxed for a few minutes, watching the horses. Then Eden spoke.

"I want to say something about Mr. Carter's remark last night."

"You don't have to," said Phoebe.

"Yes, I do. It's important, because I have some questions about your book, and you need to know something about me first."

"What is it?"

"What Carter said about me being a 'Jap?' He was right."

14

BEFORE PHOEBE could respond, Eden asked, “Could we go back to your house and talk?”

Phoebe agreed, and after returning to the barn and handing over both horses to Bob, they walked to the *casa,* where Phoebe made two cups of coffee.

They sat together on the couch. The afternoon had turned cold, and Phoebe made a small fire in her fireplace and turned on one of the floor lamps. The soft light filled the room with a warmth that matched the flickering flames.

After taking a sip from her cup Eden said, “You did well on Applesauce. If you keep practicing, I know you’ll get better, and more comfortable as a rider. You can even graduate to a more spirited horse.”

"Thanks, that's good to hear. I did feel less nervous with you as my instructor. You can probably imagine Carl's teaching technique."

"Oh, yes."

There was a silence, and Phoebe said, "You don't have to tell me anything if you don't want to. Your background is nobody's business."

"That's true, but I want you to know something about me, because I have a favor to ask."

"Okay. Just take your time."

"Well, I'll start with my family. My father's name was Geoff Williams. My mother's name is Haru Yamagata Williams, though many people call her Helen. She was born in Sebastopol, do you know where that is?"

"Yes, it's north of San Francisco in Sonoma County, isn't it?"

"That's right. My grandfather, Kenji, was born in Hawaii, and my grandmother, Hiroko, was born on the family farm in Sebastopol. They met when Kenji moved to California to look for work around 1902. They married in 1909 and my mother was born the next year. My mother and my grandmother were born here, so they were American citizens. But that still makes me a Jap to men like Glenn Carter.

"My father, Geoff, was also born in Sebastopol," Eden continued. "His parents were John and Lizzie Williams, and they were farmers, too. They grew lettuce and strawberries, and also raised chickens and sold eggs. Dad was born in 1909. His father died young, just a year later, of a heart attack. So, my grandmother Lizzie had to raise him alone on the farm, but her sister Laura and her husband moved in and helped out.

"The farm did well. They had hired help and Lizzie also did a lot of the work while Laura looked after the baby. She didn't have any children of her own.

"Margaret Williams was Dad's grandmother, and she also lived with the family and helped with the housework. She had been a widow for a long time.

"Then, just a couple of years after my dad was born, Margaret got sick. She was about fifty, and always had some sort of lung trouble. So, she had to move to a warmer climate for her health. But everyone managed and kept in touch with Margaret by letter.

"There were a lot of Japanese families around Sebastopol, and they also had farms, mostly berries, but also apples. All the kids went to school together. Dad met Haru Yamagata when he was a sophomore and she was a freshman, and they dated all through high school."

"How did your grandmother Lizzie feel about that?" Phoebe asked.

"She was fine with it, she had grown up around the Japanese farmers and went to church with many of them. She knew Haru's parents and liked her very much. She was happy when the two of them decided to get married, that was in 1929. I was born the following year. My father named me Eden, because he said that having my mother and me meant he was living in paradise."

"Oh, that's lovely," said Phoebe.

"It was paradise for me, too. Dad and Mom worked the Williams family farm, and Grandma Lizzie helped take care of me. Her sister Laura was by then a widow, and also lived with us. Unfortunately, my mom's parents, Kenji and Hiroko, died when I was three, of pneumonia, and their farm was sold. Mom was an only child, so the Williamses were her only family, but they loved her.

"Even though I was neither white nor Japanese, very few people made remarks about me. And I frankly look more white than Oriental anyway. That helped. I went to the same schools my parents had, I had my own little chores around the farm, and life was idyllic. And then everything changed."

"Pearl Harbor," said Phoebe.

Eden nodded.

"A lot of Japanese people were shunned or even threatened in those weeks after Pearl Harbor, but that never happened to us, even when we went into downtown Sebastopol. Everyone knew my mom and dad, and most people treated the other Japanese families right, too.

"In February of 1942 we heard what the president had done, signing the executive order to send anyone with Japanese ancestry away from California and the west coast. It seemed so unreal, my father was sure it only meant people who had ties to Japan, certainly not anyone who was born here. But he was wrong.

"In early May we got the word. Anyone whose family had come from Japan, no matter how long ago, had to evacuate. Even the American citizens. They only gave us a week's notice. We didn't even know where we were going, we just had to gather at the train station in Santa Rosa. We could only carry what would fit in a suitcase.

"My father was frantic. He drove to San Francisco to talk to government officials. He told them his wife was an American citizen, married to a white man and his daughter was half white. Why should they have to go away? They told him there were no exceptions, no matter how little Japanese blood someone had, or how long their family had lived in the U.S.

"I was just twelve. My parents told me a little bit about what was happening, but I was also confused. My mother tried to keep me cheerful, and told me to pack my favorite books and to pick out the coat I wanted to bring.

"My father clung to us at the train station on our last day. Then we boarded and chugged away from my home, and from everything I knew."

Eden looked down for a moment, and then asked, "Could I have another cup of coffee?"

"Of course, I'll be right back."

A few minutes later Phoebe brought two fresh cups, handing one to Eden, and settling onto the couch with hers. Eden spoke again after a moment.

"We rode for hours but didn't know where we were, because the curtains on the windows were pulled down. When the train stopped, we were at the fairgrounds in Merced, the farming area about 150 miles east of San Francisco, you know? Armed guards maneuvered us toward some tar paper shacks they called barracks that had been built near the racetrack. We lived in those for almost four months, surrounded by barbed wire and even more guards.

"In August, after we finally got into a type of routine and had made the place almost livable, they moved us again. To Colorado. To a place called Amache.

"Turns out Merced was just what they called an assembly center. Amache was permanent. My mother and I lived in a tiny room for the next three years. And so did thousands of others just like us."

Phoebe put her cup on the coffee table and reached out to Eden, who took her hand and held it a moment.

"Was your father able to write to you, or visit?"

"He did write to us, but he couldn't make the trip to Colorado, even though they did allow visitors. He had to take care of the farm, and he also looked after the farms of two of our neighbors who were in Amache with us. He was so angry, we could hear it in his letters. He said the best way to fight the government was to protect what people had left behind. Some people in Sebastopol did the same thing, but some families lost homes or businesses when they were sent away.

"Dad had an exemption from the draft because

of the farm work, and he also had a government contract for some of our produce. He probably wouldn't have been drafted anyway because he had heart trouble. Despite that he would have fought for his country, but he would still have been mad.

"I won't go into the details of our time at Amache. But I will tell you one thing. You know that pin I wore the other night, the handmade one? A woman in camp made it from some dried beans. She polished and painted them and threaded the beans together with wire to make it look like a flower. A lot of women made jewelry. Some of the men carved wood and made decorative boxes or toys for the kids. We tried to bring beauty into our lives.

"Anyway, I was fifteen when we left there in the summer of 1945, and adjusting to life outside of a camp was hard, if you can believe it. It was all I had known, from a very young age."

Phoebe said, "I can't imagine what that must have been like. My dad and I talked a lot about the evacuation and the camps. He was outraged. We owned a small general store in San Francisco, and there was another shop a block away from ours that was run by two generations of a Japanese family. The parents and their grown children were born here, and were married.

"Dad knew them slightly, and he talked to them when the government said anyone who was Japanese had to leave the city. They told him they decided to sell the business. To a white family. Dad tried to convince them to just lease or rent the store, along with their upstairs apartment, but they said they were afraid they would lose it all. I guess they were probably right. We never saw them again."

"If they had money from the sale, I hope they put it somewhere safe where they could get it after the war."

"I wish I knew."

"Well, my parents did what they could to get us back to a normal life once Mom and I got home. And we were lucky, because my dad didn't get sent away like the other men.

"We had a school at Amache, and I did well enough that I was able to get into high school as a sophomore as if I hadn't gone away. But I also wanted to get a job, and when I was sixteen my parents allowed me to work for a few hours a week at Mr. Dennison's stable. I'd loved the farm's horses since I was little, and was so comfortable around them. I could manage them well, too. So, they said I could work for Mr. Dennison, but only if I kept up my grades. I did, of course.

"I graduated in 1947 and just a couple of months later, my father died of a heart attack. My mother always said it was because his heart got broken when we went away and it never healed."

Phoebe felt tears prickling in her eyes, and rubbed them away.

"What did your mother do?" she asked.

"She couldn't manage the farm on her own. My dad's mother, Lizzie, had died in 1944 and her sister, Laura, had moved in with a cousin south of San Francisco. Mom was very sad when Dad wrote and told her about Lizzie's death. We were still in the camp. She loved her mother-in-law, and didn't get to say goodbye.

"Mom sold the farm in 1948. We moved into a rented house near town, and she got a job working in the five-and-dime, even though we got a good price for the property. She didn't want to be idle, and she didn't want me to worry about money. But she let me keep my job, and Mr. Dennison hired me full-time at the stable. Then I started trick riding. You know the rest."

"How is your mother doing?"

"She's still working, because she doesn't want

to touch our nest egg in the bank. She has her friends, too. They go to church, they go out to lunch, and they do charity work around town. As long as she doesn't worry about me, she's fine."

"I'll bet she does worry about you, on that horse."

"Well, yes. But my father taught me to ride, and she has faith in the instruction he gave me. She misses him every day. I do, too."

"She never remarried?"

"No, and it wasn't for lack of offers. My father was her one true love. She says she's happy with the years they had."

"Wow. I wasn't that lucky."

"You're a widow, too, aren't you?"

"Yes, but that's a story for another day."

Eden smiled. "Okay. Besides, I want to tell you why I came to Tribulation. I told you about Margaret Williams,. She was my father's grandmother, my great-grandmother. She had to leave Sebastopol when my dad was two, because she had weak lungs. Her doctor told her she needed to move to a drier climate, so she moved to Arizona. To Tribulation."

Phoebe's jaw dropped.

"You're kidding. Why did she move here?"

"She had an old friend from her hometown, I think it was somewhere near San Jose, who had moved to Arizona and now ran a boardinghouse in Tribulation. She wanted Margaret to stay with her while she got better. Margaret had a little money, but she also told her friend she would help with expenses and even do some housework to earn her keep.

"After a couple of years in Tribulation she developed tuberculosis, and spent about six months in a sanatorium near Tucson. Then she moved back to her friend's place because the doctors told her she needed to stay in the dry air of Arizona. They said she could return to California if she wanted, but she would have to be very careful with her health."

"And did she?"

"No."

"Because she was too worried about getting sick?"

"Because her grandson married a Japanese girl."

It was almost time for cocktails, and the sky was growing dark, so Phoebe turned on the other floor lamp in her living room. The two women had decided to stay in the *casa* and keep talking instead of going to the saloon. Phoebe made her usual Four Roses and water, and Eden asked for a Coca-Cola. She took a sip, and then wrapped both hands around her glass.

"I didn't know much about Margaret until after Mom and I got home from Amache. Margaret died in Tribulation in 1943, when we were in the camp."

"She never came back to California?"

"No. After her death, someone gathered up her effects and sent them to my dad. There was a huge box full of the letters that my grandmother Lizzie had written to her for over thirty years. I found them after Dad died."

"Had your parents ever talked about her?"

"Yes, Dad said that his grandmother was still alive but she was sick and lived in Arizona, so I just accepted that. After I found Lizzie's letters, I took them to my mother.

"They were chatty and fun, full of details about the farm, about my dad, how he was doing in school, that kind of thing. I asked Mom if she had any of Margaret's letters. She said no, and tried to get me to believe that they had been lost, but I always knew when she wasn't telling me the full truth. Then I finally got it out of her.

"Margaret had moved to Sebastopol when she was in her twenties and a new bride. She apparently never showed any prejudice against the Japanese families that lived all around her and her husband John. After she moved to Arizona, Lizzie wrote her at least once a week. She also sent photographs, and when my dad learned how to read and write, she had him write little boy notes to her. Later, Lizzie wrote Margaret about Haru and that she and my dad were getting married. She sent her an invitation to the wedding, too.

"She didn't hear from Margaret for a long time, and even wrote to the friend who ran the boardinghouse, asking if something had happened to her. Then, after the wedding, Margaret wrote a horrible letter to Lizzie and my dad.

"It was short but to the point. She did not believe in race mixing and didn't want anything to do with her grandson or his new wife."

"Oh, how awful," said Phoebe.

"It didn't really bother my parents because they didn't know her. But I guess Lizzie was deeply hurt. Margaret had been a loving mother-in-law to her and a doting grandmother before she moved away.

"That didn't stop Lizzie, though. She kept on sending letters, and gave Margaret every detail about my parents' lives, about my birth, even about the government sending Mom and me away during the war. Margaret never wrote her again. But Lizzie mailed letters regularly until the day she died."

Phoebe said, "Even though she hated the fact that her grandson had a Japanese wife, Margaret didn't destroy the letters."

"I know, I always wondered about that. Maybe she had a little bit of heart that wasn't eaten up with hatred. But maybe she just couldn't throw anything away."

"Do you still have them? The letters?"

"Yes, I still reread them now and then. My grandmother Lizzie loved my mom, and me, and it's wonderful to feel that love in what she wrote."

"I'm glad you have that. And I have to say, you don't seem bitter, after what happened to you."

"I am sometimes, on the inside. But like I said, my family didn't lose its home or business like so many others did. I try to count my blessings. And besides, I won't let anyone take away the good life I have now."

"Do people ask you if you're Japanese?"

"Yes, though sometimes people ask me if I'm part Indian. I think a lot of people assume that I am. But when they ask I tell them that my mother's grandparents were born in Japan and the Hawaiian Islands, but that I was born in California, which makes me an American. Most people give up after they hear that."

"But not everyone?"

"No. I don't waste my time with them. But when I'm on my horse, I'm a cowgirl like all the others at the rodeo. I like to think that when those people with small minds see me that way, maybe they can change."

"I hope so."

"Anyway, I'd like to try my hand at barrel racing and compete for the Girls Rodeo Association, but I'm still working and can't devote the time I need to get good enough to qualify. I set up a racing practice area on Mr. Dennison's ranch about a year ago, and Berry-Wise is getting the hang of the barrels, but we have a long way to go. And I don't want to ask so much of him. Trick riding is easier to practice, it gets me noticed, gets me in the doors at the rodeo. I'm twenty-four and may only have a few more years to try to become a rodeo star. I might need to get another horse. But one way or another, I'm determined to make it happen."

"I know you will," said Phoebe.

They sipped their drinks for a few moments, and then Phoebe looked at her watch.

"Whoa, it's time for supper. Why don't you come back here after we eat and continue with your story? You still haven't asked me about that favor."

15

MARY RAISED HER eyebrows in question at the two of them as they walked into the lodge, the last to arrive for dinner. Phoebe smiled and nodded, signaling that everything was all right. The waitresses set down platters of pork chops, bowls of mashed potatoes, and larger bowls of steaming hot string beans with cheese sauce. Guests passed the salad bowl and cruets of variously colored dressings, and grabbed rolls from the baskets that lined the center of the tables.

Eden chatted with Jason McIntyre, and Phoebe looked around, spotting Glenn and Jayne Carter at the next table, talking to some new guests who had arrived the day before. They were also from Nevada, and the two men were talking with great animation while their wives tried to converse around them.

Relieved that Carter wasn't staring at Eden again, Phoebe started talking with another new guest who was sitting next to her, a lively woman who was staying at the ranch with her sister. They had come to celebrate her fortieth birthday.

Phoebe and Eden left the lodge after dessert was served, taking slices of chocolate cake with them back to the *casa*. They ate in Phoebe's kitchen.

"I don't think we need any more coffee, do you?" Eden asked her when they finished eating.

"Not me, I'd like to sleep tonight. Would you like a drink?

"No thanks, but you go ahead."

Phoebe poured a small bourbon, and they retired to the living room. She had already turned on the lamps and built up the fire again.

"Where were we?" asked Eden.

"You discovered the letters that your grandmother sent Margaret when she lived in Tribulation and…"

Phoebe stopped, her eyes widening.

"Wait a minute. Did you say Margaret moved to Tribulation when your dad was two? That would be 1911, right? But that means…"

Eden finished her thought.

"It means Margaret Williams lived in Tribulation the same time Ellender did. The woman who wrote the diary you found. The woman you wrote your novel about, Ellender, might have known my great-grandmother."

Eden grinned at the expression on Phoebe's face.

"This is amazing. And I think I know what you want to ask me. You want to know if Ellender mentioned Margaret in her diary," Phoebe said.

"Yes. I hope you don't mind."

"Are you kidding? Of course, I don't mind. This is so exciting. I love anything related to Ellender. I've read the diary all the way through a few times of course, though I don't remember the name Margaret Williams. Ellender dropped a lot of names and maybe it will be in there. I took notes about the diary, but I didn't make a full typed transcript. I probably should have, but for some reason I felt as if I never wanted to see Ellender's words other than written in her own hand."

"I can see how you'd feel that way. And I also know it will take a while to look through it, which is why I feel this is a big favor."

"It won't be big if we both look at the diary."

"You mean you'd let me look at it? I know you keep it wrapped up and safe in a special suitcase or something."

Phoebe smiled.

"True. I do that to keep it safe, yes. But I also want to show people how precious it is. Not everyone understands that, but I think you do. So, how did you hear about my book in the first place?"

"A friend of mine who lives in San Francisco went to one of your talks. I think it was at a bookstore. Even though you gave the town a different name in your novel, you told the story of the real diary and Tribulation at your lecture. I'd told Maggie, my friend, about Margaret's letters. When you said Tribulation, she got so excited, and wrote to me about your book. I bought a copy and read it over the summer. I was thinking about how to get in touch with you when I saw the ad for the H Double Bar dudeo. I hoped you would be here, but if you weren't, I was going to ask the owners to help me get in touch with you."

"Well, thank Maggie for me. Do you want to see it? The diary?"

"Now?" Eden's voice betrayed her excitement.

"Sure, why not now?"

Phoebe went into her bedroom, and came out with

the briefcase. She opened it, unfolded the embroidered pillowcase inside, and handed the diary to Eden.

She hesitated a moment and then gently took the book with both hands, placing it on her lap.

"What do you think?" asked Phoebe.

"It's beautiful," said Eden. Her hands were shaking a little.

"Let me show you where 1911 starts." Taking the volume, she put it on her own lap, turned some pages, and then gave it back to Eden.

"Here it is. Did you say she went to a TB sanatorium after a couple of years in town?"

"Yes, I think she left in early 1913, and then came back six months later."

Eden turned the pages for a moment and then said, "I'm feeling a bit overwhelmed. And tired. Could I look through the diary another time, maybe tomorrow?"

"Sure, I understand, believe me. I'm feeling overwhelmed, too. This is exciting."

Eden closed the book and gave it back to Phoebe.

"I have some paperwork to do tomorrow morning, but why don't you come down here after breakfast? I'll leave the door unlocked, and you can let yourself in. I'll leave the briefcase under my bed," Phoebe said.

"You take a lot of care with it, don't you?"

"Well, I had a problem with a guest a couple of years ago, so I'm not taking any chances."

"Tell me about that sometime."

"I will. By the way, I think you should tell Mary your story. Not necessarily everything, but tell her about your family background. Then she'll be armed against people like Glenn Carter. You won't find a better defender than Mary Watts. Especially if you come back for another dudeo."

"Okay, I think that's fair. I'll talk to her tomorrow."

"Do you think you can come back again if we put on more dudeos?"

"I'd love to, but it depends on my work with Mr. Dennison and the other rodeos I'm attending. I want to work on a few more tricks, and practice my barrel racing."

"Well, I hope you can. Especially if you find out more about Margaret."

"That, too."

Phoebe walked with Eden on the gravel pathway toward the flickering glow of the lodge's lamps. They said good night and Phoebe watched the proud young woman walk with purpose toward her cabin.

After breakfast the next morning Phoebe sat at the dining table with a cup of coffee, while Eden took Mary aside. The other guests were getting ready for the morning's trail ride, so the lodge was empty and private.

They sat on the couch talking softly then Mary smiled and patted Eden's knee. They both got up, Mary left and Eden pulled up a chair next to Phoebe.

"How did it go?" Phoebe asked.

"Great. You were right, she was glad I told her about my family. I suddenly feel like I have a shield around me or something."

"That's Mary, she mothers and protects all of us. Do you want to go down to my *casa* now?"

"Yes, now would be perfect."

"I have some work ahead of me so you can read undisturbed. I'll come see how you're doing, and if you need more time, that won't be a problem."

"I don't know how to thank you."

"Just find Margaret! That's all the thanks I need."

"Before I go, there's something else. Last night, on the way back to my cabin, I ran into Glenn Carter."

"Oh, no."

"He was drunk, though not as much as he was the other night. He asked me what I was doing here with the real Americans."

"What did you do?" Phoebe was horrified.

"I've learned that you can't reason with unreasonable people. I just stared at him, I didn't say a thing. He just got more and more angry, and frustrated because I wouldn't respond. Then he made a rude noise, turned around, and walked off toward his cabin."

"Did anyone hear this, or come out to help?"

"We were right by the door to the place I'm sharing with Carrie, it's pretty isolated. She was out on a date. So, nobody heard anything, but it's fine."

"Did you tell Mary?"

"No. I know the Carters are guests she needs to keep, and she would probably throw them out if I told her. Maybe he finally got it out of his system. And besides, I'm leaving on Wednesday."

"That's very generous of you," said Phoebe.

"It's not a big deal. I've dealt with worse."

"Ugh. I'm sorry."

"Don't be. It's done. And I'd much rather think about the diary," said Eden.

"If you find something, please come and tell me right away."

"I will!"

Phoebe's office chores didn't take as long as she thought they would, and about an hour later she took the typed menus down to Mary in the registration office.

"I see Eden talked to you this morning," she said.

"Yes, thank you for suggesting that. What an extraordinary young woman. Especially given what she went through. You know, there was one of those camps here in Arizona."

"Jack told me. What was it called...Poston?"

"Yes, south of here, on the Colorado River. It was on Indian land, too, on a reservation. The government gave the Japanese the same excuse they gave the Indians for rounding them up. It was for their 'protection,'" Mary said. "What a load of…well, it was wrong. I hope someday people will realize how wrong it was."

"I hope so, too. But I'm glad that Eden has been able to put it behind her."

"Oh, she hasn't, honey. Why do you think she works so hard on her job, and on her riding? She has something to prove. And to rise above."

"She did say something like that to me."

"Well, I told her she is welcome to stay here as long as she likes. After that performance she gave, she deserves more than just a few days of room and meals. And feed for Berry-Wise," Mary replied. "I also told her about a conversation I had with Jayne Carter earlier this morning," Mary continued.

"What about?"

"She apologized for Glen's hostility toward Eden. It seems his brother was killed in the Battle of Okinawa during the war. He never got over it and pretty much blames anyone who's remotely Japanese for his brother's death. Even all these years later."

"Well, that's sad, but it's no excuse for his behavior. Though it seems like he only gets that way when he drinks," said Phoebe.

"Mrs. Carter said the same thing. I told her I understood, but that it wasn't fair to my guests to have to endure his outbursts. She was very humble and contrite about the whole thing."

"I've never seen that side of her. Well, maybe that will be the end of it."

"I think it will. That woman has some steel in her, I think she can keep her husband in line. But with Eden leaving, I guess we won't have to deal with it. And she won't either."

"Eden said she's heard stuff like that before."

"I'm sure she has," said Mary with a grim smile.

"I like her a lot. I wish she could stick around, but she said she has to be back at her job on Monday."

"Yes, she told me that, too. Well, I said that we really want her to come back if we have another dudeo."

"So that's really happening? I thought it was just a joke to irritate Thelma Powell with," said Phoebe.

"I admit that was the original idea. But look at the crowd we got on Saturday, I think we could do even better next fall with more time to plan. It was a lot of work, but we could make a dudeo a regular thing. Nobody else in town has anything like it."

"That's for sure, though I wouldn't put it past the Desert Grande to copy it, and on a larger scale."

"I'll worry about that later," said Mary.

"Eden said if she doesn't have work duties, or isn't at another rodeo, she'll be glad to perform again."

"Fingers crossed."

Phoebe walked down to her *casa* and knocked at the door before opening it, to let Eden know she was back.

Eden looked up at her from the couch, a smile lighting her face.

"Phoebe, I was just about to come to the lodge."

"Did you…?"

"Yes. I found her. I found Margaret."

Phoebe sat down on the couch and Eden handed

her the diary, pointing to the page with an entry from September 14, 1912.

> *The musical evening in aid of our suffrage efforts last night was a big success! I think all of Tribulation turned out to hear our talented ladies, and at 25 cents a ticket we raised 72 dollars! That will help us pay for the handbills we plan to give out when we make the trip to Phoenix next month.*
>
> *Miss Martin played the piano, Miss Armstrong the violin, and Miss Cabot sang some lively tunes. I'm glad she got over her shyness about singing in public. I think everyone has heard her voice as she helps her father around the livery stable.*
>
> *Mrs. Ellis was in charge of the table at the entrance, taking in the entry fees. Mrs. Williams sold the baked goods some of us provided. Since I can neither play an instrument, sing, or bake, I presided over the drinks sales. I also kept an eye on the men who were sneaking stronger libations into their glasses of punch. But no one gave us any trouble, and we received many compliments about how much people enjoyed the evening.*

"What do you think?" asked Eden.

"Well, Williams is a common name," said Phoebe. "But it's certainly a possibility."

"Mrs. Ellis ran a boardinghouse, didn't she?"

"Yes, she did."

"I found something else, later on in 1914. It's when Emory Summerfield had his accident and went back to stay with Mrs. Ellis at her place."

Eden took the diary back, turned a few more pages, and then handed it to Phoebe.

"I think this is more promising," said Eden.

October 5, 1914 - I visited Mr. Summerfield again today. Mrs. Williams was in a chair in his room reading Tom Sawyer, picking up where I'd left off on Friday. He was awake and smiling, and I can see he is recovering quickly now that his fever has gone. He said he was lucky to have two ladies willing to read to him, and who both do it so well. Mrs. Williams said that he was a difficult patient and only Mark Twain kept him quiet. We all laughed at that. She then left us to go back to her room. I'm glad there is someone else here to keep an eye on Mr. Summerfield, so Mrs. Ellis doesn't have to worry about him all on her own.

"Margaret lived in a boardinghouse in Tribulation," said Eden. "This really could be her, don't you think?"

"I'd forgotten about this diary entry. And there's another way to find out more. When did she die, do you have any idea?"

"In 1943, but I don't know the exact date."

"The library has old copies of the local paper, the *Mining-Register.* I know they have the 1940s. You could look through them and see if her obituary is in it."

"That would be great! When could I go?"

Phoebe looked at her watch. "It's almost lunchtime, you could go this afternoon. I want to make sure my friend Barbara, the librarian, will be in to help you. Give me a second, I'll call her."

Phoebe sat on the bench of her telephone table and

dialed the library. After a few minutes of conversation, she hung up and turned to Eden.

"Barbara won't be in this afternoon, she has to go to Phoenix for a library meeting of some kind and won't be back until this evening. But she said to come over tomorrow at ten if you can. She'll be glad to help you."

"That's wonderful, thanks. I'll do that."

"In the meantime, I can write to Virgil and ask him about Margaret."

"Why Virgil?"

"Oh, I guess I didn't tell you. He was Ellender's husband. He also lived in Tribulation the same time Margaret did. Though he left town for...."

Phoebe stopped when she saw Eden's face.

"Are you okay?" Phoebe got up from the bench and went over to the couch.

Eden had turned her head to stare at the fireplace mantel, where Phoebe kept the photo of Ellender and Lucy Jane. Then she looked at Phoebe and began to smile.

"Oh yes, I'm fine. I'm just a little stunned. I met someone who could have known my great-grandmother."

"It's possible, though as I started to say, he was away during World War I and left Tribulation after Ellender and her daughter died of the flu in 1918. He stayed away for a few years. When he came back, he worked on nearby ranches, and only came into town for supplies or to see friends.

"He had started working in the general store in 1914, and it looks like Margaret was in town then, after her time in the TB sanatorium. Maybe their paths did cross. And the store is still here, by the way. It used to be called Campbell's, but now it's Barton's. I have some postcards with photos of what it used to look like." Phoebe went to her desk and pulled out three sepia-colored cards with images of a rickety-looking wooden storefront with a plank walkway in front. She handed them to Eden, who looked them over closely.

"Margaret must have shopped there," she said.

"Very likely. It was the biggest store in town."

At that moment, they heard the clanking ring of the iron triangle, announcing lunch.

"Come on, I'm starving," said Phoebe. "Let's get some food. I'm going to take you somewhere after we eat."

"Where?"

"It's a surprise."

16

THEY ATE A QUICK lunch with the few remaining guests, and after they finished Phoebe told Eden, "Grab a jacket and put on boots or shoes that you won't mind getting dirty. I'll meet you at my car in five minutes."

Back at the *casa*, Phoebe put on a grubby pair of cowboy boots and grabbed her dad's old corduroy jacket. Afternoons were chilly now.

Eden was waiting for her by the Nash, and Phoebe saw she wore a barn coat that looked just like the one Mary had.

Phoebe drove them through the center of town and a few minutes later made a turn onto Cemetery Road, which led to the city's graveyard. The main gate was closed, as usual, but Phoebe knew it wasn't locked.

She maneuvered the car into the nearby parking lot, and looked at Eden as she turned off the ignition. Her eyes had grown large.

"We're going to look for Margaret's grave?" Eden said. Her surprise was obvious.

"Yes. Is that okay with you?"

"Oh yes, thank you! Where do we start?"

After they both got out of the car, Phoebe said, "As far as I know, there aren't any maps to show us where people are buried. It's a pretty big cemetery, and it's old, going back to the time of the Butler brothers. But let's look for burials or markers that look kind of new. I think they expanded this place in the 1930s, so people who were buried in the 1940s are probably in that area."

Phoebe started walking with Eden at her side. After a trek over a small hill, they saw a collection of marble monuments, markers, and small fenced places.

"I think this is it," said Phoebe. "Let's split up and each take a section."

"Okay."

Phoebe wandered around the graves, now and then bending over to read the markers. Just as she started seeing more dates in the 1940s, she heard Eden exclaim, "She's here!"

Eden was gesturing at Phoebe from about fifty yards away. "I can't believe it," Eden said. "Look."

She pointed to a small bronze marker set into the soil, almost obscured by weeds.

MARGARET WILLIAMS
1860-1943
Rest in Peace

"Not much of a tribute, is it?" Eden said.

"Well, she probably outlived everyone she knew."

The women didn't speak for a long time.

"Thanks for bringing me here," said Eden. "I didn't even think of looking for her grave."

"Finding Ellender's grave helped me learn more about her," said Phoebe. "And I still visit her."

"Can I see it?"

Phoebe was touched."Yes, I'd love to show you."

Eden said, "Wait just a minute."

She pulled a few weeds away from Margaret's marker, then brushed away the dirt and rocks that had settled there.

"Okay," she said.

They walked back toward the main gate, and then headed in the direction of the enormous Leroy Butler monument, which dominated the cemetery's design. Phoebe steered them right toward a group of mesquite trees, and then to a small clearing beyond them. Next to a large boulder was a marble slab, also set into the ground.

Eden squatted down to read what it said.

Ellender Freeman, 1890-1918
Lucy Jane Freeman, 1910-1918
Beloved wife, beloved daughter
Never Were Any More Loved

"Oh, how sad," said Eden. "I know the story from your book, but seeing it here is just…I think the correct word is 'poignant.'"

"Yes, that's it. Thank you."

The marker was clean, though a few weeds were beginning to sprout in the dark soil around it. Phoebe leaned over, pulled them out, and tossed them toward the mesquite grove.

"I plant a few annuals here in the early spring, though they're gone now," Phoebe said. "So, I just keep it looking neat through the winter. I was here during the summer two years ago and actually kept a few Shasta daisies alive by bringing a Thermos of water here now and then."

"That's lovely," said Eden.

Phoebe looked at her watch.

"Let's head back, I need to do a bit of paperwork before cocktails. How about if I meet you by your car around nine forty-five tomorrow morning? I'll write down directions to the library for you."

"Great, thanks. And thank you for helping me find Margaret here. I'll never forget this."

Phoebe wrapped herself in her dad's jacket again before she met Eden in the parking lot the next morning. Every day started off chilly now. Eden was already standing next to her car, dressed in slacks, a white shirt, and a green sweater. She'd pinned on her flower brooch, and Phoebe noticed how pretty it looked against the sweater's dark emerald shade.

She gave Eden her notes about getting to the library, and she roared away in the Oldsmobile. Phoebe then headed to her office in the lodge. Eden didn't turn up for lunch, but Phoebe took this as a good sign that she was finding success at the library.

The ranch wasn't full, which was normal for the first week after Thanksgiving. One couple, Anya and Wim, had come from Holland, and were spending a month in Arizona, including five days at the H Double Bar. They were retired and had enjoyed Thanksgiving with their grandchildren in Scottsdale.

There were also a couple of archaeologists in residence. Phoebe had met them two years ago when they'd stayed at the ranch, and she was happy to see them again. Paul and James both taught at the University of Southern California and always had stories about their adventures out in the desert, which kept guests enthralled. Paul's clothes were just as wrinkled as ever, though James was tidier, and managed not to look as though he pulled his shirt out of an archaeological dig that morning. Everyone sat together at the same table and enjoyed Helen's lunch of tomato soup, cold cuts, and salad.

Glenn and Jayne strolled in a few minutes after everyone started eating. Glenn had taken the car and left the ranch in the morning, but he had come back in time for both of them to go on the morning trail ride. They sat down and the waitress brought over their soup bowls.

"You are an excellent rider, Mrs. Carter," said Anya, as she assembled a ham and cheese sandwich.

"Well, thank you. The wranglers do a good job helping us novices get used to being in the saddle."

"You didn't look like a novice to me," said James, to Jayne as he reached for more salami.

"My wife is a sharp little cookie," said Glenn. "She picks up things quickly."

James looked like he wanted to say something else, but then changed his mind.

Paul spoke up as the conversation began to lag.

"Anybody shoot at you this year, Phoebe?"

Phoebe rolled her eyes, and when they looked startled, she told Anya and Wim the story of her encounter with a murderer during her first season at the ranch. Glenn's eyes never left her face as she spoke.

"It's been boring here, sorry to disappoint you," she said to Paul, finishing up.

"Well, the year isn't over yet," he said.

"You're just jealous," Phoebe retorted. "You want someone to pull a gun on you, so you'll have a Wild West story to tell your students."

"You bet we do!" said James.

Dessert that day was apple pie, straight out of the oven, along with vanilla ice cream. As everyone was finishing up and pouring coffee, Mary walked into the lodge with a tight smile on her face.

"Hi everyone, hope you enjoyed your lunch. Phoebe, may I borrow you for a moment?"

Phoebe knew her sister-in-law, and could tell something was wrong.

"Sure. 'Bye everyone, see you at cocktails."

She followed Mary out the door and they walked toward the registration office. Although there was no one around, Mary spoke in an almost-whisper.

"Some of our cattle are wandering around down on the highway."

"What? How did that happen? Nobody ran into them, I hope."

"No. Luckily Jim Stevenson saw them before that could happen. He parked his truck on the side of the road and directed traffic, and tried to shoo the steers back in our direction. Someone else stopped and Jim asked him to come to the ranch and tell us. Sam grabbed Carl, Bob, and Gene and they just rode down there."

"Do you know how many there are?"

"The man who came here…oh dear, I forgot to get his name…he said he counted six on the road, but he could see other animals in the distance heading that direction. He said it looked like part of the fence was down. Sam and the boys should be able to at least keep more of them from escaping. I'm waiting for one of them to come back and tell me what's going on. I guess Jim is still down there with them."

Mary sat down in the chair in the registration office and sighed. Phoebe took the other chair and pulled close to her.

"How many more incidents like this are we supposed to put up with?" Mary said wearily.

"You think it was deliberate."

"Of course, I do. It's that Desert Grande again, sabotaging our business."

"I'll admit this looks suspicious, but we don't have any evidence it was someone from that place."

"I know it in my bones, and I'll prove it somehow."

They sat in silence for a few minutes, and then Phoebe heard a car coming down the long driveway. She looked out the window.

"Oh, it's Eden, she's back from the library."

"Why did she go to the library?"

"It's a long story, her great-grandmother lived in Tribulation forty years ago, and might have known Ellender. So, she's been looking through the diary. I sent her to the library to see if she could find out more."

Mary smiled, not grimly this time.

"How wonderful for her! Go on and talk to her, I'll manage the cattle escape problem."

"Are you sure? I can stick around."

"No, that girl needs you. Go on, scoot, I'll talk to you later."

Eden was smiling as she got out of her car, and waved at Phoebe as she walked in her direction.

"So, were you successful?" said Phoebe.

"Yes, I can't wait to tell you. Do you have some time now?"

"I do, I just finished lunch. Did you have anything to eat?"

"I ate at The Wild Burro, and then took some time to walk around town. I went to Barton's, too, and bought some of those postcards."

At Phoebe's *casa*, they sat on the couch, and Eden pulled a small notebook out of her purse.

"I always carry pen and paper with me, in case I get ideas for new tricks, or hear something about an upcoming rodeo."

"I do the same thing, though all my notes are about books or articles I could try to write."

"I have been meaning to ask you what you are working on now. I saw the paper you have in your typewriter. Are you writing another novel?"

"I'll tell you about that later. I want to hear about what you found."

"Okay. To start, Miss Burington was so nice, and she knew just what to pull out for me to look at. She brought out a cart with these big, heavy books. They were all bound-up copies of the newspaper, the *Mining-Register*, just like you said.

"I told her Margaret Williams died in Tribulation in 1943, but that's all I knew. She said I had a lot of work ahead of me, because I would have to go through every issue. But they always put the obituaries in the same place in the paper, so I knew which page to turn to each day. Miss Burington said that in the early years the paper only came out once a week, but by the late 1930s it was a daily. Of course, there were some issues with no obituaries. I had to go through almost the whole year, but I found her. In October."

Eden turned the pages of her notebook.

"I copied it down. She died on October 6 of heart failure, which I guess just meant old age. She was eighty-three years old."

"That's pretty good, considering that she'd had TB. I guess Arizona was good for her," Phoebe said.

"I know. Anyway, here's what the obituary said. It's…well, surprising."

Eden cleared her throat and read aloud.

Margaret Williams, of Tribulation, died yesterday morning of heart failure, at the age of eighty-three. Originally from California, Mrs. Williams was a widow and moved to our city for her health in 1911.

She first lived with the popular Mrs. Ellis at her boardinghouse, and after her death, Mrs. Williams took over the establishment and managed it until her own passing.

She leaves behind a daughter-in-law Lizzie Williams, a grandson Geoff Williams, his wife Helen, and great-granddaughter Eden, all in California.

Services will be held this coming Saturday, October 9, under the auspices of the Order of the Eastern Star.

"She told people she had a married grandson and a great-granddaughter? You thought she had cut all of you out of her life," Phoebe said.

"That's what my mother told me. She had no idea Margaret even considered them family anymore. I wonder what this means?" asked Eden.

"It sounds like she must have been reconciled to the facts at some point, that her grandson married a woman with Japanese ancestry."

"But she never said anything, not to us anyway. Mom said there weren't any letters from Margaret. She would have told me if there were."

"Let's think about this. Someone sent your parents all the letters that Lizzie wrote to Margaret for decades. So, she kept them. She could have thrown them away, or burned them, but she didn't. That means she wanted to know about your dad as he was growing up."

Eden's face grew hard. "She knew that Mom and I were at that camp. She knew it for a whole year. But she never wrote Lizzie about it at all."

"Yes," Phoebe agreed. "But the war had just started and there was so much hysteria. Maybe it could have jeopardized her position in town if people knew she had a Japanese granddaughter-in-law."

"I suppose. I wonder who gave the information about her to the newspaper? Isn't that usually a family member?" Eden asked.

"Typically, I guess. But Margaret must have had friends in town. And she was probably close enough to them to talk about her family in California. She might not have mentioned that her grandson's wife was named Haru, though."

"Lizzie used the name Helen in her letters. It's what all of Mom's white friends call her."

"That makes sense. But this is big news, Eden. It means Margaret cared about all of you. Maybe she was thinking about reconciling with your father before she died. Or maybe she couldn't write after all those years of silence because she was too proud. Whatever the reason, what's important is that she knew your name, she knew you, and she's there with your family, on the page of this newspaper. That's something permanent, something to hold on to."

Eden's eyes were swimming, and she reached out for Phoebe's hand.

"I didn't think of it that way. Thank you." She wiped away the tears falling on her cheeks.

"No wonder you're such a good writer," Eden said, pulling a handkerchief out of her purse.

"Thanks," said Phoebe. "I hope I am."

"Your book was a big success, wasn't it? I sure enjoyed it."

"I'd say it was moderately successful, and I guess that's pretty good for a first novel."

"So tell me what you're working on now."

Eden took a final dab at her eyes and put her notebook on the coffee table, prepared to listen to Phoebe.

"Well, I'm trying to write a novel about what it's like to live on a dude ranch. I have made-up characters, but I based them on the real people I've met here over the last couple of years. The book is turning out to be more like individual short stories. The only thing they have in common with each other is that they are all set on a dude ranch."

"That sounds interesting."

"I hope so. I sent three chapters off to my publisher in Los Angeles a few weeks ago, and I'm just waiting to hear what he says."

"I'd like to know what happens. Will you write to me?"

"Of course! And I'll let you know what Virgil says after I hear back from him. I'll send him a letter later today and we'll see if he knew Margaret."

She thought for a moment, and then said, "Would you like me to have Virgil write to you directly? Then you'll have his address."

"That would be wonderful, thank you," said Eden, beaming.

"Are you still leaving tomorrow?" Phoebe asked.

"Yes, right after breakfast. What about you? You live in San Francisco but just work here during the season, is that right?"

"Yes, though I'm finding that I'm torn between the two places. San Francisco was always home, but I love being here in Arizona, at the ranch. I never thought I would enjoy the tourist business, but it's fun. My work for Mary doesn't take all of my time, so I can also do some writing. And I do meet some interesting people. Like you."

"Thanks. I'm glad I met you, too."

The two women exchanged addresses, then Phoebe told Eden about the escaped cattle, and they chatted and speculated about Margaret again until it was time for cocktails.

The next morning, Bob helped Eden hitch the horse trailer to the Oldsmobile. He had already loaded the tack, and Joe put her suitcase in the car moments before she brought Berry-Wise from the barn. Eden walked the horse into the trailer while Carl, Gene, Lorraine, Mary, Sam, and the new guests watched. The morning was cold, and steamy puffs of air burst from Berry's nose, matching the visible breath of all the people around him.

"I wish I'd seen her do those tricks," said James.

"Then you'll have to come back next fall," Mary suggested with a smile.

Eden heard this exchange and she smiled, too.

Once Berry-Wise was safely loaded, Eden walked up to Mary and held out her hand.

"Thank you so much for hosting me, it's been a wonderful experience."

Mary took both of the girl's hands in hers, then pulled her into a fierce hug.

"I will write and tell you the date of the next dudeo, and I hope you'll be able to return. We will put you up as we did this time. Anyway, we will figure out those details. Have a safe drive back to California, dear. We'll miss you."

Eden waved to the assembled crowd, winked at Joe, and turned to Phoebe, and hugged her, too.

"I'll write to you as soon as I hear from Virgil,"

she said. “And keep in touch, okay? I’d like to know how your rodeo career is going.”

“Thank you, I will.”

Eden got into the car and drove slowly on the graveled lot, down the long driveway, and was soon out of sight.

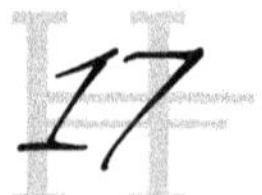

PHOEBE DASHED OFF a letter to Virgil just before lunch. She told him about Eden's great-grandmother Margaret, asked if he remembered her from his early years in Tribulation, and gave him Eden's address. She put the letter in her purse instead of the outgoing mail basket in the registration office. She needed to go to Barton's to do some grocery shopping and Sam had asked her to also pick up some nails at the hardware store, which was right next to the post office.

As she walked to her car, she heard Mary calling her name.

"Honey, can you come here for a minute?"

Mary was standing in the door of the office, and Phoebe veered off to talk to her.

"What's up?" she asked.

"Look at this," Mary said, handing her a large, cream-colored envelope with the Desert Grande Guest Ranch brand stamped on the back. Phoebe thought the intertwined D and G looked like medieval calligraphy, not a western brand. She opened the envelope and took out a heavy card.

You're Invited
to
The Desert Grande Guest Ranch
Christmas Open House
Saturday, December 18, 1954
1:00 p.m. to 6:00 p.m.
RSVP

"Another open house?" asked Phoebe.

"I know, they must have a budget just for parties."

"There's another small card and envelope in here…oh, it's for the RSVP."

"Yes, and I want you to drop it off to them in person after you finish your errands today."

"Why not mail it?"

"Because if they are already advertising an open house, that probably means their place is decorated for Christmas, and I want to know what they're doing."

"So, I'm your spy," Phoebe said with a grin.

"Yes."

"Okey dokey. Fill it out and I'll take it with me."

Mary put the ranch's name and the number of people attending on the RSVP and handed it to Phoebe.

"I'll be back in a couple of hours and give you a full report," she said.

Phoebe thought about Eden as she drove into town, and hoped that Virgil would be able to tell her something about Margaret. She marveled at how many friends she made every time she came to Tribulation, adding to the family she already had in Sam, Mary, and Joe. Barbara Burington, Jim and Laura Stevenson, and Steve Magly were on that list. There were rumors that Steve's girlfriend Nora Collins would soon be wearing an engagement ring, and that meant she would be added to the little group of people Phoebe spent her off-hours with. Eden was also a new friend, and that thought made her happy.

She dropped her letter in the slot at the post office and walked into the hardware store run by a man named Ralph Hardie. There were two stores in town but she liked going to this one because of the name: Hardie's Hardware. Frank Douglas, the friend Virgil sometimes stayed with in town, was coming out as she entered, and they talked for a few minutes about Virgil and his dog, Hunter.

"I'm going to steal that dog someday," said Frank with a laugh.

Phoebe approached the counter, where Mr. Hardie himself could always be found.

"Good afternoon, Miss Kelley," he said. "What can I get for you today?"

"Hi, Mr. Hardie. Well, I'm shopping for Sam. He needs a couple of boxes of fence nails."

"I heard about those cattle getting through your fence down by the highway," he said. "What happened?"

Phoebe did not tell him what Sam reported after he and the other men rounded up the escaped livestock and returned to the H Double Bar. The animals hadn't knocked down the fence. Someone pulled a couple of sections down. On purpose.

"Who knows?" she replied. "But the fence is easily fixed, Sam just needs the nails."

“Glad to hear it. Nails are over on aisle three, at the end.”

After leaving the hardware store, Phoebe pointed her car toward the Desert Grande. As she parked, Phoebe could tell that the ranch was already prepared for the holidays. The roofline had multicolored lights from one end to the other, which were turned on and shone brightly in the gray gloom of early December. The giant logs which held up the porch roof were encircled by white lights, and a wreath of holly, pine, and red berries was nailed to the big front entrance door. Phoebe touched it before she turned the door handle. *Artificial.*

An enormous Christmas tree, probably ten feet high, dominated the open space by the registration desk, and caught her eye as soon as she walked in. It was also covered with lights, accompanied by dripping tinsel and plain red glass ornaments of various sizes. A pointed gold star topped the tree.

Phoebe peeked into the cocktail lounge which, at that hour, only had a bartender and a few tired-looking guests sitting at small tables covered with red-and-green tablecloths. The only other festive item in there was a string of lights around the mirror behind the bar.

Her mission completed, Phoebe went over to the registration desk and waited behind a couple checking in. The process seemed more complicated than it was at the H Double Bar, and took longer, so her eyes and her attention wandered. She then heard raised voices coming from behind a door at the back of the lobby. Even from a distance Phoebe could see the door’s large PRIVATE sign in bright gold lettering.

The couple in front of her finally finished the paperwork at the desk and moved away, looking for someone to help them with their luggage. Just as Phoebe walked up to the desk, she heard a door slam, and looked up to see Jayne Carter as she tore out of the private office and strode right past without seeing her.

Jayne was wearing a silk scarf over her hair but Phoebe could see that her face was red and her expression was furious. She had her purse with her, as usual, but she squeezed it against the front of the coat as if she was afraid of losing it. Phoebe glanced back at where she'd come from, and saw Thelma Powell closing the door.

The young woman in charge of the registration desk said, "Can I help you?"

Phoebe was startled but quickly recovered.

"Oh, yes. Thank you. Would you please give this RSVP to Miss Powell?"

"I'll be glad to. We look forward to seeing you."

Phoebe left the lobby quickly and scanned the parking lot but didn't see the Carters' car. She got into her Nash and drove to Barton's general store, her mind buzzing with possible reasons for what she'd just witnessed.

Why would Jayne be meeting with Thelma Powell? And what were they arguing about? I don't think she saw me.

Phoebe was so distracted that she forgot to buy coffee along with her other groceries, and didn't notice until she got back to her *casa*. She swore, sighed, and then looked at her watch. There was time to go back into town, but she didn't feel like it, and she had enough coffee to keep her for another day. She could go up to the lodge and get a cup from the always-full urn on the sideboard if she got desperate.

Both Glenn and Jayne Carter were at cocktails that night. Phoebe was relieved to see that Jayne didn't act any differently toward her.

But she was torn about whether she should tell Mary about what had happened. She didn't mention it when she got back to the ranch, though she did give Mary a full report about the underwhelming Christmas decorations at the Desert Grande.

Mary chuckled and said, "An artificial wreath? Well, that's not a surprise. The woman has no taste."

"I thought you said she had great taste in clothes."

"She does, I'll give her that. But décor? Not at all. Our Indian rugs and other decorations are simple but much classier than what she's displaying."

Phoebe didn't want to spoil Mary's good mood. She would tell her about Jayne and Thelma later.

But first, she wanted to do a little snooping.

Phoebe stacked four typed pieces of paper into a tidy pile, then took them from her desk over to the couch to reread. She hadn't written to Katie in a while, and had a lot to say. After a short but comprehensive description of the dudeo, Phoebe spent most of her letter writing about Eden, her search for Margaret Williams, and Glenn Carter's reaction when Eden showed up at the ranch. She summarized the episode of the broken fence and cattle escape, then moved on to Jayne Carter and her apparent association with the Desert Grande.

> *I don't know what's going on with the two of them. Glenn has such a complicated personality; all affability at cocktails and around the supper table, then sheer hatred toward Eden. I never saw Jayne express much emotion, except that day when she bolted out of Thelma Powell's office.*

Virgil asked me not to meddle in other peoples' lives (given what happened the last time) but I'm going to see if I can get to the bottom of this Desert Grande business.

In her last letter, Katie had asked Phoebe how the novel was progressing. She left her response for the final, shortest paragraph.

I sent off three chapters of my novel/short stories (I still don't know what it is) to Mr. Mackenzie, at Mackenzie & Bedford. I haven't heard back yet, so I'm not doing much with the thing. He might ask me to do something completely different. I'll let you know.

Phoebe didn't tell Katie how she would figure out the "Desert Grande business," because she hadn't come up with a plan. But it was on her mind.

One night after supper, Phoebe went up to Mary and Sam's house for a nightcap. As they sat in front of the fire, Mary told Phoebe that she'd been up in the attic looking for Christmas decorations and found boxes of old papers and photos about the H Double Bar when it was the McFarland family cattle ranch.

Mary and her brother Jack, Phoebe's late husband, had grown up on the ranch, which their parents had purchased in the late 1920s. Mary and her husband Sam lived at the ranch after they were married and Mary helped manage the place while Sam served in Europe during the war. The elder McFarlands died just as the war ended, and Sam and Mary turned the H Double Bar into a dude ranch after he was discharged.

“I’d forgotten all about that stuff,” said Mary. “Maybe there’s something in there you can use for *Trail Notes*. I haven’t gone through it. What do you think?”

“It’s worth a look,” said Phoebe.

Mary sent out *Trail Notes* to all former guests every month, as well as to a few businesses in big cities. Organizing the articles (and writing most of them), typing everything up, and sending the pages to the printer in Phoenix was Phoebe’s job. It was a cheerful summary of what was happening on the ranch, and included a few recipes, some photos, and a story from Tribulation’s past. This last portion was also Phoebe’s responsibility, and thanks to the library’s healthy local history collection, she had no trouble finding things to write about.

“I’ll have Sam get the boxes down and bring them to your office. I think you have room on that big table you have in there,” said Mary.

“And there’s plenty of space underneath it, too. I can’t wait to see what’s in that collection!”

As they finished their drinks, Mary told Phoebe that most of the regulars who stayed at the ranch over the holidays had made reservations.

“That’s good news. See, you didn’t really have to worry.”

“I always worry. We still have two empty cabins for December, and we’re usually full. Two couples haven’t made their usual reservation, but I think we’ll be okay.”

Sam brought six bulging boxes to Phoebe’s office the next day. Phoebe despaired at the collection of papers, folded newspapers, scrapbooks, loose photos, and photo albums. She decided to go through one box at a time and look for anything that might be suitable for *Trail Notes*.

She was still plowing through the first box the next day when she heard a knock at the door and Mary poked her head into the office.

"Here's a letter from Virgil," she said, handing Phoebe a small envelope.

"You didn't have to bring it to me," Phoebe said.

"I know, but I'm anxious to hear if he remembered Eden's great-grandmother. Open it, and let's see. You don't have to read me anything that's too personal."

Phoebe rolled her eyes. "He's not going to say anything like that."

She cut the flap on the envelope and took out a single sheet of paper.

Dear Phoebe,

Great to hear from you, and how interesting that Miss Williams had a relative in Tribulation. Unfortunately, I don't remember Margaret Williams. I do recall a number of middle-aged women at Mrs. Ellis's boardinghouse, but I don't think I ever knew all of their names. And even if they shopped at Campbell's when I worked there, I wouldn't necessarily have learned their names, either. Tribulation was a small town, but the population was spread out and grew and contracted over time.

I will write to Miss Williams, too. Thanks for putting us in touch.

And please thank Mary for her invitation to stay at the ranch over Christmas. It looks like I'll drive down the afternoon of Christmas Eve and stay over until the 26th, if that's convenient. Would you please let her know?

Virgil

"That's a shame," said Mary. "I'm sure Eden will be disappointed."

"I know. I'll write her tonight."

After supper and drinks that evening, Phoebe sat down to compose a letter to Eden. She went through three drafts before settling on the right words. She hated giving bad news.

New guests checking in to the ranch during the first couple of weeks of December were greeted by cheerful Christmas decorations, not only in the lodge, but in their cabins.

All of the cabins had a small table by the front window, and Mary covered each one with a green-and-red plaid tablecloth, along with a large bowl filled with small golden glass balls, each painted with desert plants or animals: a cactus, a roadrunner, a saguaro flower. Next to the bowl was a small red or white poinsettia. She also tacked a bright red ribbon on the doors. A string of lights hung from the roof of each cabin, and it was Joe's job to plug them in each evening at dusk.

The lodge itself was resplendent. Sam and Joe had spent hours putting up lights on its roof, as well. Mary's plaster saguaro cactus "Christmas tree" had been set up in its place of honor by the fireplace. Phoebe, Mary, and Joe had hung lights, glass ornaments, tinsel, strings of popcorn and cranberries, and a sprinkling of fake snow over its "arms." The dining tables had red-and-green striped tablecloths accented with glittering gold threads, the main door was surrounded with colored lights both inside and out. All the orange-and-black Thanksgiving-themed rugs in the living room had been replaced with some in colors of deep red, emerald green, and gold. The fireplace mantel also sported lights and a collection of plaster animals: cows, horses, mules, sheep, and chickens. The stack of sheet music on the lodge's piano was now mostly Christmas carols. Joe had tried to put red ribbons around the necks of the ranch cats, Bea and Sabine, and now had a large Band-Aid stretched across the top of his right hand.

Phoebe also allowed herself some time to practice her horsemanship. She still rode Applesauce, and by the second week of December she was saddling him on her own, though she noticed Bob always watched her out of the corner of his eye. She joined in the trail rides and even took the horse out by herself a couple of times.

"You might be ready for Bingo," Carl said to her one day.

Bingo, a bay with a star on his forehead, was larger than Applesauce, and although he was just as placid, Phoebe knew from some of the guests' stories that he also had a mind of his own.

"Thanks for the vote of confidence, but I think I'm going to stick with what I know for a while."

"Okay, but you just tell me when you're ready to trade up, and I'll watch to see how you do."

Trail riding gave her a lot of time to think, and one day Phoebe came up with a way to investigate the Carters' strange activities. She put her plan into action the morning of the Desert Grande's Christmas open house.

She knew that all of the guests planned to attend, because Mary and Sam were ferrying people over there in the ranch's two station wagons. Glenn also offered to take a couple of people in his car, which meant that he and Jayne would be away from the ranch.

As everyone assembled in the parking lot just before two, Phoebe left her office and walked over to talk to Mary.

"I'm going to be a bit late to the open house."

"Why?" Mary asked, surprised.

"I just noticed some errors in the *Trail Notes* piece I wrote about Eden, and I have to retype two entire pages. I want to stay here and get it fixed."

"Can't you do it this afternoon or tomorrow?"

"No, I'm worried that if I leave it too long, I won't have time before everything goes to the printer on Monday. Then it's off my mind. I'll just be a little bit late, and I'll drive myself."

"Okay," Mary said with a smile. "I appreciate your devotion to duty. Lock the registration office door when you leave, will you? I'll leave it unlocked in case someone calls or shows up while you're still here, though we're not expecting anyone. I'll put the sign on the door saying we'll return by five."

The ranch's staff members were also going to the open house. Carl and his wife Susie planned to drive over from their little apartment in town, and though Bob originally said he didn't want to go, Mary persuaded him by saying the ranch had to present a united front. Mary asked the staff to leave the same time as the dudes because she wanted to arrive as a group. She'd considered giving everyone name tags but Phoebe had talked her out of it.

A few minutes after the two ranch wagons and Glenn's Buick had disappeared from sight down the long driveway, Helen the cook, waitresses Carrie and Maryanne, and housekeeping staff members Maria and Olive walked out of the lodge together and got into Helen's spacious Oldsmobile. Shannon and Sandra went with Bob in his battered red pickup. Phoebe waved as they all drove away.

She walked over to the registration office and opened the door. Mary kept a master key to all the cabins in the bottom drawer of the desk, and Phoebe found it easily. Clutching the key, she left the office, glancing at the driveway to make sure no one was heading her way. She then sprinted to the Carters' cabin, inserted the key, and went in.

18

PHOEBE AND KATIE had seen plenty of movies where people sneaked around rooms looking for clues or damning evidence, and she smiled as she envisioned how Katie would play "film director" if she were there. She took a quick mental inventory of what the cabin's interior looked like, and then got to work.

She started with a quick look through the bureau drawers, opening them up and lifting each shirt, blouse, sweater, and, unpleasantly, piece of underwear. She took a moment to stick her head out the door to listen for cars but heard nothing.

Next were the bedside tables, and here she was rewarded. One drawer had a matchbook from the Desert Grande. She knew the Carters hadn't gone to the Labor Day open house, so they couldn't have picked it up then.

Besides, Jayne smoked so much she would have used up the matches within a week. Only two were missing, so someone must have brought the matchbook back recently.

Her final stop was the closet. The pockets of the coats and shirts were a bust, and just as she was about to close the door she looked up at the shelf. A single pillow and a folded blanket took up its full length. Remembering how she used to hide Ellender's diary when she stayed at motels on her many drives to Arizona, Phoebe pulled down the pillow. She grinned when she saw the small, unmarked cardboard box hidden behind it. After taking another moment to listen out the door, she picked the box off the shelf. It weighed nothing but rattled in her hands. She lifted the corner of the lid slowly.

Bullets! They were short and squat and deadly-looking, eight in all.

Phoebe stared at the contents for a moment, and then decided it was time to go. She put everything back exactly as she'd found it, and took a final look around the room to make sure. She checked the door twice to be certain it was locked.

As she was about to leave, Phoebe noticed that the door to the cabin next to the Carters' was ajar, which she hadn't noticed before. It was occupied by a retired couple, Harry and Carolyn Fairfax, who were planning to check out just after Christmas. She walked over, slowly pushed the door open a few more inches, and heard a strange sound which she couldn't immediately identify. Just as she realized what it was, she saw its source: a rattlesnake was coiled on the rug by the bed.

She slammed the door shut and took off, returning the key to the registration office. She ran to the *casa* and changed quickly into black slacks and a deep red sweater, tying the white scarf with horses and cacti design around her neck. She'd bought a camel's hair swing coat at

Goldwater's during a trip to Phoenix the previous year, and she grabbed it as she picked up her keys and purse and tore out the door.

She gunned her Nash down the driveway and onto the main road, hoping she wouldn't get pulled over. Even in her haste to get to the Desert Grande she couldn't stop thinking about what she'd found. Not to mention what she didn't find: a gun. She also knew she couldn't tell a soul. Not yet, anyway.

Phoebe walked through the main door of the Desert Grande and dropped off her wrap at the coat check, trying look casual as she went into the bar, looking around for either Sam or Mary. She saw Mary talking to a cluster of H Double Bar guests and made her way over with a forced smile saying, "May I steal you for a moment?" She took Mary's arm and almost dragged her into a quiet corner where they could talk.

She told her about the snake in the Fairfax cabin, and Mary blanched, looking around for Sam. She saw him across the room and waved him over. He saw the look on her face and joined them.

"How did you notice the door was open when you were working on your office?" Mary asked.

Phoebe had anticipated the question and was ready with an answer.

"I realized one of my good pens was missing. I remembered I'd had it with me when I went on a walk the other day on that side of the ranch. I went over there to look for it."

This seemed to satisfy Mary. Sam left the bar.

"I need a drink," Phoebe said, and she and Mary returned to the crowd. Phoebe ordered a double bourbon and listened to the chatter around her while looking for the Carters. She saw them sitting in the corner with a couple who had just checked in to the ranch. Glenn and the man, a salesman named Bill Foster, were talking quietly, and Phoebe was startled to see Jayne smiling and waving her hands as the talked with Foster's wife, Edith.

"Feeling better?" Mary asked her.

"Yes, thanks. Will Sam be okay?"

"Oh yes, he's dealt with a lot of snakes over the years. But I want to know how it got in there. I always tell guests how important it is to keep their doors closed. I'll say something to everyone tonight to remind them."

"Good idea. So, what do you think?" Phoebe asked, gesturing around the room.

"Well, the decorations are cheaper-looking than you described. The food and liquor are good, of course. That's one of their specialties. I've been talking to some of their guests."

"Spying again?"

"Well, I'm trying to be subtle about it."

"I'm sure you are. What have you found out?"

"A very nice woman told me about what is planned for Christmas dinner."

"How did you get that out of her?"

"It was easy, I said I was a local dude rancher, and was looking for tips on how to please my guests."

Phoebe nearly choked on her Four Roses.

"Mary! Suppose that woman tells Thelma Powell what you said?"

"So what if she thinks I'm trying to get good ideas from her? That will throw her off guard."

The buzz of conversation suddenly got louder, and heads turned toward the bar's entrance. Thelma Powell began to walk through the crowd, greeting the guests she knew, and thanking the newcomers for visiting. She was beautifully dressed, as usual. She wore a red skirt decorated with dozens of small white stars, which billowed out from her cinched-in waist and swirled as she moved. It was topped with a white silk shirt and wide black belt, and instead of her Acme boots, Thelma wore smart black heels. The one concession to western style was the large turquoise ring on her right ring finger, and her only other jewelry was a pair of simple pearl earrings.

Phoebe glanced sideways at Mary to get her reaction to Thelma's outfit. From her expression she appeared uninterested, but Phoebe knew better. As Thelma worked the room, Phoebe saw her looking at Mary, too, but other than a quick nod as their eyes locked, she made no attempt to talk to her. Before she moved on to visit with another cluster of guests, Thelma also looked at Phoebe, and for a second, Phoebe sensed hostility there, but then it was gone.

A young couple from Colorado, Chuck and Jan Hamilton, rode back to the ranch in Phoebe's car. She asked them what they thought about the Desert Grande.

"Well, the lodge is sure spectacular," said Chuck. "But the place feels more like a hotel than a dude ranch."

"I wonder what the rooms look like," said Jan.

"Did you talk to any of their guests?"

Chuck said he hadn't but Jan had.

"What did they say?" Phoebe asked her.

"I heard an older couple mention their home in Grand Junction, which is about fifty miles from where we live in Cedaredge. So, I started chatting with the wife.

"She told me they go to a lot of dude ranches for vacation. Her husband is retired. They like the Desert Grande a lot and said they would come back. I guess the food is really good. I told them where we were staying, and she said they've heard of the H Double Bar but never stayed there."

"Did she say what they heard about it?"

"No. Why do you ask?"

"Oh, no reason, it's just good business to know

what people think about the ranch," Phoebe explained with a smile.

Sam presided over cocktails that evening as though nothing had happened, but Phoebe could tell that Mary was still worried.

To distract her, Phoebe told Mary what Chuck and Jan said.

"I don't think they came away from the open house wanting to stay at the Desert Grande," said Phoebe.

"That's what I was hoping for," said Mary. "I knew it was a bit of a risk to take my guests over there, but I knew most of them would see the difference. They'd see that we are a real dude ranch. I need to find out more about their meals, though."

"How are you going to do that?"

"I'll think of something."

As the guests were finishing their supper that night Mary stood up and got their attention.

"Hello everyone. I hope you all had a good time at the Desert Grande open house. We're all dude ranch friends here in Tribulation."

Phoebe knew that wasn't easy for her to say.

Mary continued, smiling. "I just want to remind all of you about keeping the doors to your cabins closed at all times. The local wildlife likes to pay us more visits as the weather gets colder, and we don't want you to find an unwanted critter in your room."

Carolyn Fairfax spoke up when the other guests looked either amused or startled.

"We are very careful," she said. "We went to a dude ranch in Wyoming once and forgot about closing the door. We came back after supper and there was a weasel running around the bathroom."

As the other guests laughed, Mary glanced at Phoebe, trying to keep alarm off her face. Then she pulled herself together.

"I'm glad to hear it. Everyone follow Carolyn and Harry's example, and we can keep the wildlife outside where it belongs."

As soon as supper was over, Mary took Phoebe aside, away from the guests.

"They did not leave their door open," said Mary, with accusation in her voice.

"What else could have happened?"

"Someone found a way to get into their cabin and put the snake in there."

"But…why? They don't seem like the kind of people who have enemies," Phoebe said.

"They don't, but I think we do. Just look at everything that's happened here. Glenn Carter's accident, the cattle getting loose, the thefts. Something is going on."

"I think you're right. And we need to figure out what it is," said Phoebe.

"We'd better," said Mary.

A week before Christmas Phoebe went to the registration office to get her mail, and as she was going through the letters and packages, Jayne Carter walked in.

"How can I help you?" Mary asked.

"Would it be possible for us to extend our check-out date?"

"Of course, let me look into that for a moment. I'm sure it won't be a problem."

Mary flipped the pages of her reservation book.

"I see you originally planned to depart on January 8. When were you thinking of leaving?"

"Is Friday, March 11 a possibility?"

After another look at her book Mary said, “That will be fine, we’ll hold your cabin until then. Thank you, Mrs. Carter. We are so pleased you’re enjoying your stay.”

With a strange smile Jayne said, “Yes, thank you.”

Mary asked her to fill out a new registration card, and handed Jayne a pen. Just as she began to write, the women heard Phoebe give a sharp exclamation.

“Oh, damn.”

She was holding a letter in her hand, and as she made a face and looked up, she saw both women staring at her.

“Oh, I’m sorry. It’s just…well, news.”

“What’s happened?” asked Mary.

Jayne moved away from the desk but didn’t leave the office.

“Mr. Mackenzie, my publisher, you know. Um… he turned down my novel.”

“Oh, honey, I’m sorry.”

“Some Christmas present,” said Phoebe.

“Did he say why?”

Before she could answer, Jayne said, “I’ll go tell my husband we have changed our reservation. Thank you again, Mrs. Watts.”

She walked out the door, and when she was well away, Phoebe said, “I wish she hadn’t heard that.”

“Don’t worry about it, I’m sure she doesn’t care.”

“Thank you very much!” Phoebe had to laugh.

“You know what I mean. Anyway, what did Mackenzie say?”

“He said the story wasn’t ‘western’ enough, that the dude ranch activities weren’t compelling.”

“Well, that’s just silly. What are you going to do?”

“I don’t know, I need to think about this for a while. Anyway, I’m surprised that the Carters want to stick around.”

"Me, too, but I'm not going to ask them why."

"Have you noticed that Jayne takes that purse with her wherever she goes? Is she worried it will get stolen if she leaves it in her cabin?" Phoebe asked.

"I noticed that, too. Well, some women feel more secure with a purse on their arm."

"It looks heavy, you'd think she would want a break from it now and then."

Phoebe put aside Mackenzie's letter and picked up an envelope at the top of her pile.

"This looks like a Christmas card, and it's from Eden. I hope she wasn't too upset that Virgil didn't know anything about her great-grandmother."

"Virgil will be here in a few days, that will cheer you up," said Mary.

Phoebe walked back to the *casa*. She made a cup of coffee and sat on her couch to open the rest of her mail. Katie's Christmas greeting included a long letter about the people in Phoebe's neighborhood that was so funny she laughed out loud. That helped her feel a bit better, so she opened Eden's card next.

> *Dear Phoebe,*
>
> *Thank you for your letter, and for asking Virgil about Margaret Williams. I'm not surprised that he didn't remember her, but it's good to know, anyway.*
>
> *Things are quiet on the rodeo circuit here, so I'm spending more time with my mom, and doing some extra training with Berry-Wise.*
>
> *I hope you have a wonderful Christmas and New Year.*
>
> *Eden*

Phoebe was happy about Eden's stoic acceptance of the news, but she still wished she could help her.

She finished her coffee and opened an envelope from her friend Lois back in San Francisco. Lois had gotten married the previous year and sent out photo Christmas cards to everyone. Phoebe gazed at the snapshot of the couple with their new baby and got an idea.

As the holiday approached, Phoebe helped out with the grocery shopping and she also picked up some of the guests at the train station. She could have squeezed in a trail ride, but she wanted to spend time in her office.

Lois's card, with its family photo, had made Phoebe wonder if the boxes of old stuff from Mary's attic might have photos of the people who lived in and around Tribulation. There were probably a lot of shots of the ranch itself, but maybe the McFarlands had taken a few snaps in town, too. Could they have also taken a photo of Margaret Williams?

On the afternoon of the twenty-third Phoebe had a couple of hours to herself, and she pulled out the box she had started to look through a few days earlier. It didn't have photographs at all, so she set it aside. Two more boxes held old newspapers, books about animal husbandry, and Sam's letters to Mary from his time overseas. Phoebe got excited when she saw a pile of loose photographs wrapped in tissue paper underneath the letters, but they were only pictures of people in early twentieth century clothing in a place that didn't look like Arizona.

She hit paydirt with the fourth carton.

Two photo albums filled up the entire box, and as Phoebe pulled them out, the black, nobbly cover of the larger one fell off onto the floor. She picked it up, gently placed both albums on the table, to turn the pages.

The first album had McFarland family photos,

and Phoebe smiled at the shots of a young Jack. He had never taken to cowboy or western life, even as a boy, and looked uneasy as he sat on a black horse that was too big for him. Mary, on the other hand, posed tall in the saddle and looked as though she was about to spur her bay into a dead run.

Phoebe looked carefully at every photo, just to be sure she wouldn't miss anything, and then picked up the other album.

It also had family shots, but Jack and Mary were older, and they were now shown at places like the high school football field, and with friends in front of the drugstore on Center Street. After she went through about four pages, the photos switched from the McFarland kids to the town itself.

Phoebe saw many familiar buildings: the post office, Campbell's general store that was now Barton's, and the block where the souvenir shop, two restaurants, and a car dealership were now. The photos were probably from the 1920s, and back then the buildings housed a saloon, a women's clothing store, and a barber shop. They showed people walking past the various businesses, or standing in doorways. Phoebe took a moment to admire what the women were wearing.

The photographs on the last few pages had views from a hill outside of town, and pictures of homes around Tribulation. Phoebe could see a sign in the window of a large house with a wraparound porch, but she couldn't read it. She rooted around in her desk drawer and found a magnifying glass, and held it over the photo.

The words were blurry, but she could just make them out.

Mrs. Ellis
Rooms
Inquire Within

Phoebe gasped.

It was Mrs. Ellis's boardinghouse, where Margaret Williams had lived.

She looked quickly through the rest of the album but there weren't any more images of the house.

It was a terrific discovery, but she still felt deflated. She had so wanted to find the woman herself. But she gently pulled the photo off the page and put it into an envelope. She returned everything back into the boxes and rearranged them under her office table.

Looking at her watch she figured she had just enough time to go into town to drop off the photograph at the drugstore. It would just take them a day or two to make a copy for Eden.

19

VIRGIL ARRIVED on Christmas Eve, just after lunch. Phoebe had been watching for his car, and when she saw him pull into the parking area, she went out to greet him.

"Did you get Hunter settled over at Frank's?"

"Yes, he was a happy dog."

They went into the registration office, where Virgil said hello to Mary, and Phoebe got the key to his cabin. She walked him there and opened the door, and then watched as he set down his suitcase and took off his coat.

"Have you had any lunch?"

"I had a snack before I left, but I am a bit hungry."

"Let's go over to the kitchen. Helen's busy with the Christmas Eve supper, but I'm sure we'll be able to find something for you."

Virgil greeted the staff, and Phoebe quickly grabbed bread, bologna, and cheese, while trying to stay out of everyone's way. She made a sandwich, took a bottle of Coke from the refrigerator, and went with Virgil into the dining room. While he ate, she nibbled on an oatmeal cookie from the plate on the sideboard.

Phoebe filled him in on the latest activities at the ranch, including the Desert Grande open house. He chuckled as she described the decorations.

"I'll bet Mary felt good about that. She sure knows how to make a ranch look like Christmas," he said.

She also told him about finding the photograph of Mrs. Ellis's boardinghouse, and then said, "Wait a minute, I'll be right back."

She went into her office and returned holding a black-and-white snapshot.

"Look at this. It's Campbell's general store. Is this what it looked like when you worked there?"

Virgil took the photo in his hands and studied it for a moment. Phoebe noticed that he had a cut near his left thumb. He worked on his car a lot, and helped his friends now and then with gardening and small construction jobs, so she was used to seeing his hands looking like they'd been beaten up. Her eyes lingered on them as he gazed at the picture.

"Do you know when this was taken?" he asked.

"No, but from the clothes the women are wearing in some of the other ones, I'm thinking it was the 1920s."

"That makes sense. The store did a remodel about that time, after I stopped working there. But it's still the same old place."

Virgil smiled, and Phoebe knew he was remembering that he met Ellender at Campbell's.

Phoebe let the moment linger, then glanced at her watch.

"Do you mind if I take off? I need to do some work in the office before cocktails. See you at five?"

"Sure. I'll go down to the barn and see Carl and Bob. Have you gotten any new horses since I was here last?"

"Yes! Sam bought a beautiful young pinto a few days ago. He told Joe he's just a new horse for the trail rides, but it's actually Joe's Christmas present. He is going to be so thrilled. That kid's a real cowboy."

"Isn't he lucky? I'll ask the boys if I can take a look at him. I promise not to spill the beans."

After Virgil left the lodge, Phoebe returned the photo to the box it came from, and sat at her typewriter to prepare the menu and place cards for both the Christmas Eve and Christmas Day suppers.

Mary believed in holiday tradition, so she always served the same food on the twenty-fourth: prime rib, scalloped potatoes, mashed potatoes and gravy, Parker House rolls, baked beans, green salad, and red and green Jello salads. Apple and pumpkin pie with homemade vanilla ice cream were the usual dessert items, along with chocolate cake with White Mountain frosting. She always put tall glasses filled with candy canes at the children's place settings, but no kids were in residence at the ranch this year. There were three older couples, including Chuck and Jan from Colorado, a newly-married couple, two young women who were expert riders and roomed together and, of course, Glenn and Jayne Carter. Mary loved seeing the candy canes on the table, so she set them out anyway.

Phoebe sat with Virgil next to the single women, Kay and Linda, who told them they had been friends since grammar school in upstate New York and had learned to ride when they were teenagers. They were roommates in Buffalo, where they both worked as secretaries in downtown offices. Phoebe told them about her efforts on horseback, and they offered a few pointers. She also saw Virgil glancing now and then at Glenn Carter.

Mary sat at the piano after supper and played Christmas carols, while nearly all of the guests clustered around and sang along. Phoebe and Virgil joined them, and everyone stole looks at him when they heard his strong, baritone voice.

Virgil walked her to the *casa* when the other guests began to trickle back to their cabins. It was nearly ten, and the temperature had dropped so much and so fast that Phoebe started shivering as soon as they left the lodge. Virgil took off his suede jacket and put it around her shoulders, holding on to her for a long moment.

She returned it to him as they arrived at the porch of her *casa*.

"Thanks. *Brrrrr.* Mary told me it snows here sometimes. I wonder if we'll get some?"

"It never snowed when I lived here, but it's certainly possible."

Phoebe started shivering again.

"Okay, time for you to go in." He put his hand on her shoulder, which was his usual way of saying goodbye.

"Come on down tomorrow before breakfast and I'll give you your present."

"And I'll bring yours," Virgil replied.

Phoebe was dressed and had a fire going by eight on Christmas morning. She had also turned on the heater in the *casa* while she showered and got ready, as the temperature had dropped even further the night before. When she looked out her front window, she could see blades of frost on the cactus near her porch.

She wore black wool pants, a white-and-blue cable knit sweater, and the scarf Virgil gave her last year, along with her turquoise roadrunner earrings. She had placed two wrapped boxes on the coffee table in the living room, and took a moment to straighten the ribbons on the larger one. She had already opened Katie's gift: a silver concho band for the Stetson she'd given Phoebe for her birthday.

Phoebe had called Frank a couple of weeks earlier to ask his advice about a present for Virgil. She knew he had some tools that were getting pretty old, and asked Frank if she should get him new ones.

"Oh, no. Don't do that. He loves those things, and if he wants to replace them, he'll decide when the time is right. But I know he does need a new chisel. He loaned his to some guy who moved out of state and didn't bother to give it back when he left."

Frank told her the right style and size to buy, and she'd picked it up at Hardie's Hardware. But she thought a chisel was a little impersonal, even if it was practical. So, she also got an enlargement of the picture she'd taken of Virgil standing in front of his Buick with Hunter's head poking out the window. She put it in a simple frame she found at the drugstore.

As she was fussing with the ribbons, she heard a knock at the door.

Virgil was wearing his usual white shirt and roadrunner bola tie, with black slacks and his best black cowboy boots.

Phoebe gave him a quick hug when he came in and said, "How about an Irish coffee to start the day?"

"That sounds great."

She made the coffee and brought the two mugs into the living room. Virgil was sitting on the couch, and Phoebe saw a small package with bright green ribbon on the table next to the other presents.

They clinked glasses and said ,"Merry Christmas."

"You go first," said Phoebe, handing him the larger box.

His eyes lit up when he saw the chisel.

"How on earth did you know that I needed this?" he asked, grinning.

"I asked Frank," said Phoebe, and Virgil laughed.

"Now the other one," Phoebe said.

When he saw the framed photo, Virgil smiled and reached out to squeeze Phoebe's hand.

"Thank you, I don't have any pictures of Hunter. This is wonderful."

He put the picture on the table and then handed the green-ribboned present to Phoebe.

"Your turn."

Phoebe's mouth dropped open when she parted the white tissue paper inside the box, and pulled out a silver hair comb decorated with various sizes of turquoise stones. It glowed in the firelight.

"Oh, Virgil. It's just beautiful...is this like the one Ellender had?"

"Yes, I had this made from what I remembered about it. I know she wrote about the comb in her diary, and I thought you'd like it."

Ellender had lost her prized silver comb when she had to fight for her life, as well as the life of her daughter. Phoebe knew it was out in the desert somewhere, and she thought about it sometimes when she was on a trail ride.

Phoebe's eyes pricked with tears, which caused Virgil to say quickly, "Put it on and let's see how it looks."

She got up and went to the mirror hanging on the wall near the front door. She gathered up some hair on the side of her face and inserted the comb to hold it. The turquoise seemed to float among the parted strands, and brought out the blue of her earrings.

She turned to Virgil and smiled.

"I love it," she said.

Virgil's voice croaked for a second when he said, "You look lovely."

Phoebe smiled and felt herself start to blush, and sat back down on the couch.

"This means a lot to me, you know," she said.

"I hoped it would. You are…um…well, you care so much for Ellender, I wanted to give you something that she loved."

For a moment, Phoebe felt sad and, strangely, a little jealous. But she dismissed the thought, and said, "I'm starving, shall we get some breakfast?"

Virgil looked relieved, and said he would take his presents back to his cabin and meet her in the lodge. They walked out together, Phoebe putting on her camel hair coat against the frosty air.

"Will you exchange presents with Mary and Sam today?" Virgil asked.

"Yes, we always do that after supper. That way they can have the morning to themselves, as a family. I'm really pleased with what I got them this year, and I always buy the gifts in California. Mary is getting a string of pearls I found in a little shop in San Francisco's Chinatown. Sam loves to read Steinbeck, so I got him a first edition of *Grapes of Wrath* from a used bookstore near my house. And I got Joe a Lone Ranger lunch box. He loves that television show."

"You're a great gift-giver. I sure like my presents."

"Thanks. I like mine, too."

Phoebe went into the lodge while Virgil headed for his own cabin. All the guests were at the tables eating eggs, toast, bacon, and cinnamon rolls. Virgil came in a few minutes later, just as Mary walked through the back door and wished her guests a Merry Christmas.

There was only a single afternoon trail ride on Christmas Day, so that the wranglers could have the morning with their families. Carl was coming in later, but the two seasonal wranglers would not return until the next day.

Bob had gone to Phoenix on Christmas Eve to be with his sister, his nieces, and a few cousins, but he was due back around lunchtime. Mary told him that Carl could handle the ride on his own, but he said he wanted to help out. Mary knew he couldn't stand to be around large family gatherings for very long, and the job was his escape hatch. She let him think he was doing her a favor.

Virgil greeted Mary, and said that after breakfast he was going to Frank's house to spend the morning with him and his wife Sarah.

"I'll be back in the early afternoon," he said.

"So, we'll see you at cocktails then?"

"Yes, and thank you again for hosting me."

"Don't be silly," said Mary, as she sat down next to Phoebe.

Virgil smiled and sat on Phoebe's other side. He finished his breakfast quickly, said goodbye to both women, and left the lodge.

Phoebe turned to Mary and asked, "How did Joe like his present?"

"For once in his life he was speechless," she said. "He's still down at the barn getting acquainted with the horse. Sam will take him out a little later for a ride."

"Did he come up with a name yet?"

"I think he has, but he hasn't told us."

Mary then spied the comb in Phoebe's hair.

"Wow, that's beautiful," she said. "Did Virgil give that to you?"

"Yes, I just love it. He had it made. It's a replica of the one Ellender had."

Mary's eyebrows shot up. "That's interesting."

"Why?"

"He had something made specifically for you. And it looks just like the comb his late wife owned. I think that's *interesting*," Mary emphasized.

"He knows how I feel about Ellender. It was very thoughtful of him."

"So, you don't think this says anything about how he feels about you?"

"We are very close, we have Ellender in common."

Mary sighed. "Well, if you can't see it, I'm not going to try to convince you."

With that, she touched Phoebe on the arm, got up, and walked out the lodge's main door leaving Phoebe behind to shake her head and finish her breakfast.

She went back to the *casa*, turned on the radio, and pulled out the thirty typed pages of her new novel. She read them straight through, then dropped the papers on her lap. *This is good western stuff, Mr. Mackenzie.* She decided to write a chapter about Eden, so she grabbed a pad of paper and a pen and began to make notes. She was so engrossed she nearly forgot to go to lunch, and was reminded only by her growling stomach.

She went right back to work after wolfing down a ham sandwich, chips, and handful of peanut butter cookies, and came to a good stopping point just as it was time for cocktails. Virgil was already in the saloon when she got there. He was talking to Joe, and Phoebe could tell that the subject was the new horse, whom Joe had named Buster. She walked over to join the conversation, and listened to every detail about Joe's first ride. She saw Virgil glance at the comb in her hair and smile to himself.

Supper on Christmas Day was always an elaborate buffet set out on the sideboards under the lodge's front window. Guests filled their plates from platters of turkey, mashed potatoes, maple-glazed sweet potatoes, cornbread muffins with cheese and chilis, green beans with pearl onions, and stuffed bell peppers. If they had room, they could choose from two kinds of pie, chocolate cake, a chocolate Yule log, and Christmas cookies for dessert.

Around eight, as everyone got up from the tables, some of them groaning, Phoebe said to Virgil, "I'm heading up to Mary and Sam's house for the rest of the evening. Would you like to come?"

"Thanks, but I'm going to Bob's cabin for a nightcap. Will you see me off in the morning?"

"Sure, what time are you leaving?"

"After breakfast, if Mary doesn't mind giving me one more meal."

"Of course, she doesn't. Let's eat together, say seven-thirty or so?"

"Okay."

Virgil squeezed her shoulder and left the lodge, and Phoebe headed to her *casa.* She picked up three wrapped presents, took a flashlight from a drawer in the kitchen, and went up the pathway to the Watts's house.

She knocked on the door, and heard Mary shout out for her to come in. They were in the living room, and Sam got up to make her a bourbon before they started to exchange presents.

Mary cooed over her pearls, and both Joe and Sam beamed when they opened their gifts. Joe gave Phoebe a new pen, which was his traditional present and which always pleased her. Mary's gift was an amber-colored Bakelite pin in the shape of a horse's head, from which dangled two cowboy boots and a horseshoe with metal studs. She pinned it to her sweater and Mary clapped her hands in approval.

Sam had made her a portable writing desk out of mesquite wood. He loved woodworking and harvested downed pieces of mesquite from the desert floor whenever he could. The desk had a slanted, polished top with a hinge which, when opened, revealed a large storage area inside. The smooth, reflective surface brought out the wood's unique irregular grain.

"Oh, Sam," she said. "It's just beautiful."

"And practical," he replied. "It's small enough that you can carry it from room to room if you want. Even put it on your lap."

"I helped!" said Joe.

"Yes, he did," said Mary.

"Thank you all so much. I love my presents."

"We do too, honey. Merry Christmas."

An hour later, Phoebe followed Sam as he carried her new desk down to the *casa* and put it on the coffee table. After he left, Phoebe gathered up paper and pens, pencils, and a small notebook, and stored them inside the desk. Then she picked up the pages of her novel and her new pen, sat on the couch with the desk on her lap. The papers fit perfectly on the slanted top, which also had a strip of wood along the bottom to keep them from sliding off. Phoebe shuffled them around, making notes here and there. A few minutes later she grinned, sighed with happiness, and put the desk back on her coffee table.

As she went to change into pajamas, she thought she heard yelling coming from the direction of the guest cabins. It suddenly got louder, and then turned to screams. She threw on her coat and ran out the front door. As she passed the fence in front of her *casa*, she saw a glow in the distance. *FIRE.*

PHOEBE STARTED RUNNING faster and as she approached the lodge, she saw a group of guests gathered by the main door. Some were in pajamas and robes, while others were still in the clothes they'd worn to supper. Mary was walking around them like a border collie, maneuvering everyone to stay together and talking to them in a quiet voice. Virgil was with her, exchanging comments with a couple of the men.

When Mary saw Phoebe, she motioned her over and said, "There's a small fire in the toolshed next to the tack room. Sam and the boys have it under control, and we have also called the fire department."

Her face belied the calm tone of her voice, which startled Phoebe who realized she'd never seen Mary look scared before.

Virgil came to stand next to Phoebe.

"Can I do anything to help?" Harry Fairfax asked Mary. Chuck Hamilton chimed in with the same question.

"Thank you both, but we'll be fine, and I don't want to put you guests in any danger. The firemen should be here soon," she said.

On cue, the sound of a siren filled the air and a red truck with wildly flaring lights pulled into the parking lot. A man got out of the cab, went straight to Mary, asked about the situation, and then started barking orders at the other firefighters.

Phoebe looked up just then and her stomach clenched. The glow had been replaced by flames, now licking the night sky. She was pretty sure the toolshed was far enough away from the lodge for it not to be any threat. Mary began moving everyone toward the lodge, and then turned to Phoebe.

"Honey, will you make some coffee and see if there are any rolls or pastries or anything we can serve? This is going to take a while."

"Yes, of course."

"I'll go with you," said Virgil. "Unless you need me out here, Mary?"

"Thank you, but I think we're doing okay. Just let me know if anyone looks too worried," said Mary.

"I will. Is Joe at home?" Phoebe asked.

"Yes, he's safe up there for now, but I'm going to go and check on him."

Mary sprinted out the back door. Phoebe got the guests seated and quickly made a pot of coffee, also heating up water for a couple of guests who asked for tea. Helen always had cookies ready to serve, so she put a selection onto a plate while Virgil made a pile of toast and cut slices of ham.

"You know your way around a kitchen," said Phoebe with a smile.

"I had to learn, being on my own for so long," said Virgil. "Turns out I like to cook."

They took the plates of food into the dining room and set them on tables. The guests were quiet, but didn't seem overly concerned. Roommates Kay and Linda stood by the windows trying to get a glimpse of the activities. Chuck and Jan looked like they were having a fine time, and ate heartily. Glenn and Jayne Carter sat off by themselves, both looking grim.

"Is it always this exciting around here?" asked Harry Fairfax.

"Not like this," said Phoebe. "We like to reserve the thrills for the trail rides."

About half an hour later, just before eleven, Mary came into the lodge and told everyone that the fire was out, and they could go back to their cabins.

"I'm afraid some of your rooms might smell a bit like a campfire," she said. "If you can, leave your windows open the rest of the night. The screens will keep out any insects, and your heaters should keep the rooms warm. Then we'll open all your windows tomorrow and let in some fresh air while you're on your ride or having meals. Also, we will refund all of you for one night's stay for the inconvenience."

The announcement perked up the weary guests, who got up from the tables and left the lodge, all of them saying thank-you to Mary. Even the Carters.

After they were gone Phoebe turned to Mary and said, "That was smart."

"Yes, it was," said Virgil.

"Well, it's the right thing to do. We can't have those people go home and tell their friends they got rousted out of their rooms and still had to pay for the privilege."

"What's happening now?" asked Phoebe.

"The fire is out but the men are staying around for another hour or so to watch for hot spots or whatever they're called. The flames could flare up again."

"Do they know how the fire started?"

"One of them said they thought they smelled gasoline, which we kept in there," said Mary. "The can must have gotten knocked over or something."

"How much damage was done?"

"The shed is completely destroyed and, well, so is part of the tack room."

"Oh, no," said Phoebe. "What did you lose?"

"The wall closest to the shed burned completely, along with the bridles and blankets that were hung on that side. The firemen got here in time to keep the flames from spreading to the other side where all our saddles are. We are very lucky. If we'd had wind tonight, it could have sent the fire toward the barn, or even the cabins."

"Oh my god," said Phoebe.

"We're insured, of course, and can pay to replace everything. But we need that stuff now, so I'm going to call Jim Stevenson in the morning and see if he has some tack we can borrow."

"I'm so sorry about this, Mary," said Virgil.

"Thanks for helping Phoebe keep an eye on the guests. Did anyone seem like they were scared, or angry, or anything?"

"Not really, but the Carters looked pretty upset," said Phoebe. "I wonder why?"

"No clue. I'm going to check on Joe again. He's so excited about all the shenanigans I doubt he'll sleep the rest of the night."

When she was gone Phoebe said to Virgil, "I guess you won't get a lot of sleep either before your drive home tomorrow."

"That's not important. I just wish there was more I could do."

"I know, but I think Mary and Sam have things in order."

"Okay. Well, let me walk you to the *casa* and then I'll turn in. Are we still meeting for breakfast at seven thirty?"

"Let's make it eight," said Phoebe with a tired sigh.

Most of the guests were late for breakfast the next day, too. Carrie, the waitress who lived at the ranch, also looked bleary but she brought out the plates with her usual bright smile. Helen was aghast when she arrived at the ranch that morning from her apartment in town and heard the news about the fire. Her solution to most problems was baked goods, so she made a double batch of her cinnamon rolls and spread glazed frosting on half of them.

Phoebe and Virgil arrived at the lodge at the same time, and sat down at the far end of one of the tables.

"How are you this morning?" Virgil asked.

"Okay, I guess. I managed to get some sleep. How about you?"

"Oh, I'm fine. Have you seen Mary?"

"Yes, I went over to the site of the fire a few minutes ago, and she is there talking with Sam about rebuilding. She already called her friend at the Bar K and he's bringing over some tack for today's trail ride."

"It's wonderful the way all the ranches pull together," said Virgil, who had given his plate to Maryanne and asked for seconds on bacon.

"I know, it's a very special kind of business," said Phoebe. "Well, except for the Desert Grande, of course."

"That place doesn't sound much like a dude ranch to me."

"That's what Mary says. She is sure they are behind some of the mishaps that we've had around here."

"Why would they do that?"

"To put her out of business? Who knows."

"Have you had any more trouble here with that Carter fellow?"

Phoebe hesitated a moment, then made a decision.

"Well, not exactly trouble, but I did find out something about the both of them."

She told Virgil about seeing Jayne at the Desert Grande, and about what she found when she searched the Carters' cabin.

His reaction surprised her. She had never seen Virgil look mad.

"Phoebe, what were you thinking? First of all, that was completely illegal, and what if they came back early and found you? That could have been a disaster for Sam and Mary and their business. And dangerous for you. That Carter guy has a temper. He could have hurt you."

Phoebe was shocked at his scolding tone, and then she got angry.

"Don't lecture me, I was very careful, and I can take care of myself."

"Just because you survived the last time a man threatened you, doesn't mean it won't happen again."

A guest at the H Double Bar had been killed two years ago, and his murderer pulled a gun on Phoebe when she confronted him. She got away, but had nightmares for a long time.

"I'm worried about you," Virgil continued.

Phoebe saw a couple of the guests looking their way and lowered her voice.

"Well, you don't have to be," Phoebe retorted.

"I know you love Mary and Sam, but does your loyalty to your late husband mean you have to put yourself in danger for them?"

Phoebe gaped at him.

"What the hell are you talking about?"

Maryanne brought Virgil's bacon at that moment, saw the look on his face, and Phoebe's, and set the plate down quickly.

When she had scurried away, Phoebe continued.

"First of all, I am not loyal to Jack. He died ten years ago and I've moved on with my life. I come here because Mary is like my own sister, and her family is my family. The Desert Grande is a real threat to their business and I will do whatever I can to protect it."

"You're being reckless, Phoebe. Please don't do anything to get yourself hurt."

"I am not reckless, I know what I'm doing."

"I don't think you do." Virgil stood up. "And it's obvious that I can't talk you out of any course you plan to take."

He put his napkin on the table next to the untouched plate.

"I think I should go. Please thank Mary for her hospitality. And please take care of yourself."

Before Phoebe could respond Virgil left the table and she watched him walk out the lodge door. She sat at the table for a few more minutes, then got up and looked out the front window. Virgil's car was gone.

She left the lodge and went back to her *casa*. She lay down on the couch, covering herself with the multicolored blanket draped over the back, and willed herself to sleep.

She woke up two hours later, and made a sandwich instead of going to the lodge for lunch. She spent the afternoon reading, and didn't feel like going to cocktails and supper, but thought she should make an appearance. And she wanted to see how Mary and Sam were doing. Mary was behind the bar at the saloon.

"Sam's still going through the rubble and figuring out how much lumber we'll need to rebuild. He doesn't think it will cost as much as we thought, though the big expense will be replacing the tack. But it can't be helped. Anyway, a contractor is coming out here tomorrow to look at everything."

"Was Jim able to loan you what you needed?"

"Yes, thank goodness for Jim and Laura. We'll be fine, and I'll go into town and pick up new tack in a day or so."

"Oh, good."

"Where's Virgil?" asked Mary.

Phoebe didn't meet her eyes.

"He had to leave, but told me to thank you for hosting him."

"Why didn't he say goodbye?"

"I don't know, maybe he couldn't find you."

Mary caught Phoebe's tone.

"Okay, what's up?"

"Nothing," said Phoebe.

"Did you two have a fight?"

"There is no 'you two.' He just had to get home, that's all."

"Whatever you say."

The next day was Monday, and all of the guests except for the Carters and Jan and Chuck left the ranch, thanking Mary for a good time, a little excitement, and a free night's stay.

Phoebe walked down to the registration office just in time to say goodbye to Kay and Linda, who were leaving on the train. Bob took them to the station in Sam's Jeep, because Sam was talking with the contractor and couldn't be spared. The two women said they would try to come back next year, and Mary beamed at them.

Phoebe checked her mail. Nothing from Mr. Mackenzie, but she didn't really think he would write a letter saying he'd changed his mind about her book. There was nothing for her at all, which was also not surprising, since all her friends had just sent her Christmas cards.

"Anyone checking in today?" Phoebe asked Mary.

"Not until Thursday. Three couples are all arriving then. We won't have a full house for New Year's Eve, but I'm happy with the numbers we had for Christmas. Despite the flashy Desert Grande, we're doing okay, though of course, we can always do better."

"I wonder what they're doing over there for New Year's Eve?" Phoebe said.

"I've been thinking about that myself. If they were having another open house we would have heard something by now. How can I find out…oh, wait...I have an idea."

"Uh-oh," said Phoebe with a laugh.

Mary made a face at her and then said, "I'm going to write Thelma Powell a thank-you note for inviting us to the open house and you can deliver it."

"Isn't it a little late for that? The open house was over a week ago."

"I'll tell her that we've been so busy I didn't have time to write earlier."

"Well done. That's both polite and a subtle hint that they haven't done anything to affect your business."

"I'll write it when I've finished going through the mail. Can you take the note up to them this afternoon?"

"Sure."

Phoebe almost told her about seeing Jayne at the Desert Grande the last time she went over there, but decided not to ruin Mary's good mood.

When she finished composing a short letter on the ranch's branded stationery, Mary put the slip of paper into an envelope and wrote Thelma Powell on the front. She handed it to Phoebe and said, "Keep your eyes open."

After lunch Phoebe dressed in black slacks, a crisp white cowboy shirt with pearl snaps, and her best boots, topped with the camel hair coat. Just before leaving she went into her bedroom and opened her jewelry case. She pulled out a sterling silver star covered with blue rhinestones, which had belonged to her mother, and pinned it onto the coat near her left shoulder. For a moment, Phoebe considered putting the silver comb in her hair, but returned it to the case. She got into her Nash and drove out to the Desert Grande.

The parking lot was pretty full, but the lobby was quiet, with a few guests sitting in chairs by the fireplace. Phoebe went up to the main desk and noticed a large, colorfully printed card propped at the far end. Before she could get close enough to read it, the young woman behind the counter said, "Good afternoon, ma'am. How can I help you?"

"Hello. I'd like to leave this note for Miss Powell."

Before she could reply Phoebe heard a voice speak behind her.

"I'll take it."

Phoebe turned around. Thelma Powell stood with her hand held out and a false smile on her face.

"Oh, hello Miss Powell," said Phoebe, trying not to look startled.

"You have something for me?"

"Yes, my sister-in-law, Mrs. Watts, asked me to

bring this over for you."

Thelma took the envelope without looking at it.

"Thank you. How are things at your ranch? I hear you had a fire the other night."

"Yes, we did. But it was very minor, and we only lost a shed and a few pieces of tack."

"Well, that's good news," Thelma said. "Were your guests affected at all?"

"Not a bit, in fact they enjoyed the excitement," said Phoebe. *And it's none of your business.*

"Good," said Thelma. "Well, I must get back to work. Thank you for coming by, Miss Kelley."

"You're welcome."

Phoebe waited until she saw Thelma walk into her private office, and then casually stood by the sign, which said:

New Year's Eve
at the
Desert Grande Guest Ranch
Casino Night
Prizes include:
A week's stay at the Desert Grande
Fine wines and liquors
Boots
Cowboy Hats
Indian blankets
Come to the cocktail lounge at 8:00 p.m.

Mary won't be happy about this.

But Mary laughed when Phoebe told her about the Desert Grande's plans.

"Where does she think she is, Las Vegas? Nobody goes to a dude ranch to pretend they are in a casino. That just proves they aren't a dude ranch at all."

"I actually saw Thelma Powell, and gave her your note myself."

"I'll bet she wasn't happy to see you."

"She tried to find out how bad things were here after the fire but I told her that it was nothing, and the guests weren't affected at all."

"I bet that stopped her in her tracks," said Mary. "Our guests will have real fun at our New Year's Eve."

"Did you hire that cowboy singer you were talking about? What's his name again?"

"Romaine Lowdermilk. He has a dude ranch up in Cave Creek, north of Phoenix. He knew my mom and dad well, so I thought I'd take a chance and ask if he would come and entertain our guests on the thirty-first. He doesn't do much of that anymore, but he said he'd love to."

"He's really famous, isn't he?"

"Well, he founded one of Arizona's first dude ranches, over there in Wickenburg, the Kay El Bar. He would entertain his guests by singing, doing rope tricks, and then the radio people started hearing about him. He sang on the radio for years, and he writes music and articles for magazines. He's a lovely man, and he's busy with his own ranch, but he's coming here out of respect for Mom and Dad. I think he's about Virgil's age. Which reminds me, did you ask him to come down for New Year's Eve?"

"Um...no."

"Why not?"

"You can't keep putting him up here for free every few weeks. That's too much to ask," said Phoebe.

"And that's not the real reason," Mary replied.

"I don't think he'd come, so I didn't invite him."

"I'm sorry to hear that, I think he'd enjoy seeing Romaine perform."

"Well, it's too late now."

"*Humph*."

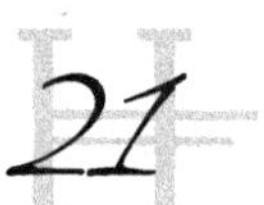

WITH NO GUESTS AROUND for a couple of days, and little paperwork to do, Phoebe spent time doing some shopping in Tribulation, and made a plan to see Barbara Burington.

She had hoped to see Steve Magly, too, but, as everyone had predicted, he and Nora Collins had gotten engaged. The two of them were spending the New Year's holiday in Phoenix, where her mother was now living, and they'd left two days ago.

Phoebe and Barbara met for lunch at The Wild Burro on Tuesday. They exchanged presents, and Phoebe was thrilled with the beautiful leather notebook Barbara gave her. She'd bought her friend a small souvenir San Francisco tray made of black lacquer. Barbara had only been to the city once but had loved it.

They talked about Eden's quest to find her great-grandmother, and Barbara was fascinated.

"I'll take a look at our local history materials when I get back to the library after lunch," she said. "I can probably find something about the woman suffrage campaigns in town back in 1911 and 1912, at least. Maybe there will be a membership list or something."

"That would be great, I know she'd appreciate that," said Phoebe.

"What's Mary planning for New Year's?"

"A singer named Romaine Lowdermilk is coming to perform."

Barbara's eyes got big.

"You're kidding. I heard him sing on the radio, he's wonderful. Your guests will be thrilled."

Phoebe also told her about going out to the Desert Grande to check up on what they were doing.

"I agree with Mary. Only a real dude rancher would hire a cowboy singer. Anybody can put on a casino night but why for New Year's Eve?"

"I'll tell her you said so. Are you doing anything to celebrate?"

Barbara glanced at Phoebe for a moment and then said, "Yes, my friend Celeste is coming from Cody to stay with me over the holiday."

"What fun. I'm sure she'll enjoy the weather down here. And how nice to see your friend again."

"Yes. She's…she's special and...very important to me." Barbara stared straight into Phoebe's eyes. "I believe you know what I mean."

Phoebe was about to say something trite, and then she saw the intensity of Barbara's expression—a question, a little hope, and more than a little fear. She knew instantly what Barbara was trying to tell her, and reached out to take her hand.

"I do know what you mean." She smiled. "And I'm happy for you."

Barbara squeezed Phoebe's hand, and said simply, "Thank you."

Then Phoebe got an idea.

"Would you and Celeste like to come and see Lowdermilk's performance? I can't offer you dinner, but I know Mary would be pleased if you popped in to see him perform."

"Hey, thanks. I'll ask Celeste, but I'm sure she'd love that."

"I'll call and let you know what time to come by, probably around eight."

"We'll be there."

About four forty-five on the afternoon of December 31, Mary and Phoebe sat in the registration office, taking occasional looks out the window. Five minutes later a sleek black Buick pulled into the ranch's driveway. A white-haired, handsome man stepped out of the car, wearing a blue-and-white checked cowboy shirt, black gabardine pants and boots, and a blue silk scarf held around his collar with a slide shaped like a bucking bronco. Mary ran out to greet him, and the man gave her a bear hug.

"Miss Mary, look at you!" he said. "You are the image of your dear mother."

Mary grinned and said, "And you are the image of the man I remember from my childhood."

"Oh, stop your flattering. And who is this?" he said, looking at Phoebe, who had come out of the office.

"This is my sister-in-law, Phoebe Kelley. Phoebe, this is Romaine Lowdermilk."

"I am so happy to meet you, Mr. Lowdermilk."

"You don't need to call me Mister," he said, shaking her hand.

"Let's get you checked in," said Mary. "And then we'll head to the saloon."

"I like the sound of that," said Lowdermilk.

"How is Jean?" Mary asked.

"She's doing just fine, she decided to stay home and let her husband be the star for the evening."

After taking Lowdermilk to his cabin and getting him settled, Mary brought him to the saloon, where the guests were already gathered. A couple of them gaped when they saw the singer, and scooted over to be introduced to him.

He told stories all through the cocktail hour and supper, and kept people laughing so much they could barely finish eating. Barbara and Celeste came into the lodge as dessert was being served. Mary greeted them with a huge smile and aimed the women toward the sideboard and told them to get whatever they wanted for dessert. They filled their plates and sat at the dining table next to Phoebe.

A few minutes later, Lowdermilk left the lodge and Mary made sure everyone had brandies or other after-dinner drinks. When he returned, he was carrying a well-worn but still shiny guitar. He'd changed into a bright gold satin shirt with black smile pockets, and switched to a black silk neck scarf.

Mary gathered her guests and the two visitors into the living room, and they settled themselves onto the couch, the armchairs, and the one rocking chair by the bookshelves. Phoebe pulled a chair out of the dining room for herself, and settled next to Barbara. Joe sat cross-legged on the floor next to his dad.

Lowdermilk walked into the open area between the door and the fireplace, began to strum the guitar softly, and then broke into a loud and raucous cowboy ditty that had everyone clapping.

He performed familiar songs like *Home on the Range, I'm an Old Cowhand,* and *Tumbling Tumbleweeds,* and encouraged everyone to chime in when they knew the words. He also sang *Old Corral*, a song he wrote but never got credit for. After singing about ten songs in a row (Phoebe lost count), he motioned to Mary, who reached into a trunk next to the fireplace and pulled out a huge lariat. Lowdermilk took it from her, moved away from the seated guests and whirled the rope into a huge circle.

Using the slack end of the rope he made the circle wider and made it spin just above the floor, jumping into and out of the circle as it turned. Then he jumped into the center himself and raised the rope above his head, making it twist up and down around him, from the floor almost to the ceiling. And just when everyone thought he was finished, he did the same movement again, only this time from side to side. He was the still center in the midst of the lariat, which seemed to have a mind of its own, and he only moved to jump out of its way.

He then surprised everyone by roping a laughing Mary as she stood off to the side near her guests. He gave Mary a kiss on the cheek, released her from the lariat, and returned it to her.

Mary sat down at the piano, Lowdermilk took up his guitar, and they started to play *Auld Lang Syne.* After hearing the first few notes, the guests stood and sang along, and there were more than a few moist eyes when he made the final, gentle strum.

When the moment was over, Mary got up from the piano bench.

"Thank you, Romaine, for that tremendous performance. I thought I knew a lot of cowboy songs, but you have me beat!"

"Well, I've been at it longer than you, Miss

Mary," he said. "And thanks, folks, for giving me such a warm welcome."

Everyone applauded again, and Mary handed him a small bourbon, telling her guests that they could get what they desired from the drinks cart by the sideboard in the dining room. Lowdermilk chatted with people for about twenty minutes, and then they began to head off toward their cabins. Barbara and Celeste thanked Mary and left, giving Phoebe a wave as they went out the door.

Mary walked over to Phoebe, who was standing by the fire.

"Romaine is coming up to the house for a visit and to have a drink before he turns in. Would you like to join us?"

"I'd love to. That was quite a performance, and I guess you planned those rope tricks in advance."

"We did, but I didn't know he was going to include me in the show," said Mary with a laugh.

The singer told even more stories at the Watts house, and just before midnight, Lowdermilk said he was going to head back to his cabin so he could call Jean as the New Year turned. He said good night to everyone, giving Mary another kiss on the cheek, and asking her to say goodbye to Joe, who was sound asleep on the couch.

As the clock chimed twelve, Sam, Mary, and Phoebe toasted the New Year with their drink glasses nearly empty.

"Well, I think that was a successful evening," Mary said.

"Your guests will remember tonight for a long time," said Phoebe.

"Yes, they will. Thelma Powell can give away all the cowboy boots and liquor she wants. Nobody at the Desert Grande will remember their New Year's Eve."

Phoebe laughed and told everyone good night. Sam picked up Joe, still limply sleeping, and took him into his room.

As she stepped onto the lighted porch of her *casa*, Phoebe turned off her flashlight, and then heard the phone ringing. She dashed through the door and picked up the receiver, but there was only a dial tone.

She shrugged, and wondered who would be calling her this late.

Virgil's face popped into her mind at that moment. *Well, that's just silly*. She got ready for bed.

New Year's Day at the ranch was always quiet. Many guests slept in, nursing the aftereffects of Mary's excellent liquor, except for weary parents whose children were ready to jump back into their activities. If the dudes wanted to ride, one of the hands would lead them in the afternoon, but no one on the adults-only guest list this year signed up. Mary gave Carl, Bob, and the other wranglers the day off, except for their regular duties in the barn, and asked Helen to prepare a comforting breakfast of biscuits and gravy, eggs, bacon, sausage, and her famous cinnamon rolls.

Phoebe had slept well, though just before she woke up, she dreamed that she chased Virgil down the driveway of the ranch with a letter in her hand, desperate to get it to him before he reached the highway. He was driving his old truck, and Hunter had his head out the window, laughing. Sitting up in bed, she shook her head to clear the cobwebs and made a quick cup of coffee, before walking up to the lodge to enjoy breakfast with the others.

Mary passed through the dining room on her way to the registration office, offering New Year greetings to everyone. Phoebe knew she hadn't had a chance to open the latest batch of mail, and since none would be delivered today, she would spend time catching up. After finishing her second helping of bacon, Phoebe said goodbye to her table mates and walked down to the office.

Mary was behind the desk with a pile of letters and empty envelopes in front of her, and she beamed at Phoebe when she walked in.

"Honey, look at this. Eden Williams wants to come back and perform here again, isn't that great? She said she could come in February or early April, but I don't know if either of those would work. We can't pull a dudeo together by next month, and April is near the end of the season for all the ranches, and sometimes we're not full."

Phoebe thought for a moment and then said, "What if she came in February and we put on an exhibition instead of a dudeo? We could ask her to do a longer demonstration of trick riding and invite the locals and the guests at the other ranches to come and just watch her."

"That's a great idea, let's look at some dates."

The two women flipped the pages of Mary's large desk calendar.

"We should do this on a Saturday, of course, when the kids aren't in school. So far it looks like all of them are free. Let's give Eden her pick. Would you write to her, I'm sure she'd love to hear from you. Do it now, and then run into town to mail the letter so we have enough time to find out what she wants to do and get things organized, okay? I'll buy some supplies for posters and flyers this week."

Phoebe sat in Mary's office chair and wrote a short note to Eden on H Double Bar stationery. As she was about to go back to the *casa* to get her car keys, she said to Mary, "Someone better tell Glenn Carter that Eden is coming back."

"Oh god, that's right. Well, I'll tell Mrs. Carter, she'll keep him in line."

"Good idea."

"Will you invite Virgil to the exhibition?"

Phoebe started rearranging papers on the desk.

"Probably not."

"Why?"

"Well, we had a disagreement when he was here last and we're...um...not really speaking."

"What did you argue about?"

Phoebe wondered how much to tell Mary. Only Virgil knew about her search of the Carters' cabin.

"I told him we were worried that the Desert Grande was responsible for some of the accidents around here and I was going to look into it."

"And he was afraid you'd get hurt," Mary said. "Just like you did the last time you got involved in something mysterious?"

"I don't want him to interfere in my life."

"He's a man and he cares about you. We really need to have a talk about men one of these days."

Before Phoebe could respond, Mary had changed the subject.

"I keep forgetting to tell you about something," she began. "The Carters have been having their mail forwarded here because they are staying such a long time. Jayne told me they have a friend who collects their letters and then sends them here once a week. I think you've seen the big envelopes that come in for them, I guess they are filled with the Carters' correspondence and bills. Anyway, the flap on the one that was delivered last week had come loose and I spilled the contents all over the floor. When I was picking everything up, I noticed that all the Carters' mail had a Las Vegas address, not a Carson City one."

“Well, that’s strange, I thought that’s where they lived. They talk about it now and then.”

“I know, and that’s the place where I sent their registration confirmation. Well, maybe it’s their second home or something, and they have another residence in Las Vegas. Who knows? It seems like it might be a strange place to live.”

Phoebe agreed, and then left the office before Mary could ask her about Virgil again.

EDEN'S REPLY to Mary's invitation arrived the following Monday, and she suggested Saturday, February 19 as the day for her exhibition at the ranch. If that suited their schedule, she would arrive on the Thursday before. She also asked if she could keep her departure date open, and said she would be happy to get a hotel room in town if there was no room for her at the ranch. If so, could Berry-Wise stay in the barn?

"What a nice girl," said Mary, after reading the letter aloud to Phoebe. "Of course, she can stay here, she can room with Carrie again. There's still a free bed in that cabin. I need to let her know that's okay, so I'll send her a telegram instead of waiting for the mail. Would you go into town and take care of that? I have two couples checking in later today."

Eden responded by telegram the next day, so

Phoebe, Mary, and Sam started preparing for the show. Mary had already talked to the store owners on Center Street about putting posters in their windows, as she had for the dudeo. They all agreed, and said they would also talk to the tourists about her event.

Mary decided to do something grander than her handmade posters from last year. The office of the *Mining-Register* newspaper had a commercial print shop, and she and the owner, Mr. Brayton, designed a beautiful handbill. She gave him a photo she had taken of Eden standing on Berry-Wise's back, which he printed in the middle of the announcement in large, black lettering.

TRICK RIDING EXHIBITION!

Miss Eden Williams and Berry-Wise
return to
The H Double Bar Dude Ranch
Saturday, February 19, 1955
1:00 p.m.

RESIDENTS • DUDES • TOURISTS • FAMILIES
ALL ARE WELCOME!

She also wrote invitations to the owners of Tribulation's dude ranches, inviting them and their guests to the performance. Phoebe helped by addressing the envelopes.

"I can tell when you are writing to Thelma Powell," she said to Mary.

"How?"

"You have a slight smile on your face, and you are thinking that she won't have anything like that for her dudes this spring."

"You know me so well." Mary laughed.

"When you're done with those, I'll take them to the post office. Are the posters ready?"

Mary looked at her watch.

"Brayton said they would be ready today at three. If you pick them up, then we can start handing them out at the businesses on Center tomorrow."

A few days later, nearly every storefront in Tribulation had a poster either in its window or taped behind the cash desk. Susanna Lozano and Monica Baca asked for two copies, so they could put them in both places at the Trading Post.

January was windy, cold, occasionally rainy, and sometimes too blustery for trail rides. Phoebe found small icicles hanging from the ocotillo and wire fence near the *casa* most mornings, and Sam replenished the pile of firewood on her patio every couple of days.

All but two sets of guests were regulars who knew that the weather could be iffy that time of year. These were mostly older couples who were happy to sit by the fire in the lodge, play cards, and enjoy the never-empty coffee urn and daily supply of snacks on the sideboard. Bea and Sabine, their fur now winter-thick, spent most of the day sleeping by the fire instead of on mousing duty.

The Sunday chuck wagon lunch was postponed in the winter months, but Sam had built a small replica of the wagon which he installed in the far corner of the dining room. He and Mary filled it with the supplies they usually took out to the picnic site, and served the same foods, so that guests could still have the experience. Given the chilly weather, Helen also added a couple of hot dishes to the usual sandwiches and salads.

Mary took the two younger couples to Phoenix in the ranch's station wagon one afternoon to go shopping for western wear. They also signed up for a tour of the old Maybelle Mine site, now run by a company looking to make some tourist dollars.

Mary had bullied the owners into giving her the same tour discount they gave to the Desert Grande. She drove the guests out there and then picked them up two hours later, enjoying their enthusiasm about the old shacks, shafts, and long rooms with mysterious iron equipment. No one complained about the weather.

Glenn and Jayne Carter spent a lot of time in their cabin, but did come to the lodge sometimes to join the fireside quiet time or card games in the late afternoon. Glenn continued to go on trail rides, and Bob had decided he could graduate from placid Huck to livelier Rockhound, a friendly gray. Jayne did not ride again.

Before the posters were printed, Mary had taken Jayne aside to tell her Eden was returning to the H Double Bar the following month. She let that information sink in, knowing that Jayne would understand what she was really saying: *make sure that your husband doesn't cause another scene.*

Mary spent a few afternoons writing letters to some of her regulars, letting them know that Eden Williams would be back at the ranch in February, and was pleased to get reservations from two families. They wouldn't be able to stay long, because they had to take their kids out of school, but they wanted the children to see the exhibition. Four couples also reserved cabins.

The December issue of *Trail Notes* had included Phoebe's article about Eden and Berry-Wise, with a hint that the cowgirl would return soon to the H Double Bar. Mary always kept a pile of the newsletters on the coffee table in the lodge for guests to take back to their cabins.

"Your story really helped get the word out about Eden," said Mary one morning as the women had coffee together on the living room couch. "Maybe you should have taken that PR job with the travel agency."

"What, are you sorry I'm here?"

Mary slapped at Phoebe's knee.

"Of course not, don't be silly, I'm simply paying you a compliment."

"I know, thanks. I wouldn't have had as much fun at the agency as I'm having here."

"I'm glad to hear it," Mary said with a grin.

"You know I love coming here."

"Yes, but you can't keep living in two places."

"Why not?"

"Well, how are you ever going to meet someone if you keep moving around?"

"Oh Mary, I've met men in San Francisco, but they just didn't do anything for me."

"That's because you've met someone here."

"Don't start with Virgil again," Phoebe said with an exasperated sigh.

"Okay, but you know I'm right."

"He hasn't written or called me."

"Do I have to write to him again like I did last time, and invite him to the exhibition?"

"Please don't. I don't know what's going on with him, or with me. I hate that we argued, but he shouldn't have told me what to do."

"I know. No woman likes that. You just have to work with what you have."

"Sam doesn't boss you around."

"That's because he knows me, we know how to best work together, we understand each other's strengths and weaknesses. But that took time. And we were living in the same state." Mary gave Phoebe a wink when she said it, then she smiled and stood up to go. "You'll figure it out. You'll figure him out. I have faith in both of you."

Mary visited Tribulation's store owners regularly throughout the rest of January and early February, to find out what people were saying about the exhibition. She always brought a handful of posters with her, in case anyone wanted to replace a well-worn piece. The owner of the barber shop asked for a new one because someone had stolen the poster he'd put in his window. "I think it was a kid," he said. "Everybody loves the picture of that trick riding girl."

She also received thank-you notes and RSVPs from the local dude ranches. Except the Desert Grande. By February 16, all expected guests had checked in, and Mary had everything ready for Eden's arrival the following day.

In her telegram, Eden said she would probably get to the ranch around one that afternoon. Mary and Phoebe went to the registration desk right after lunch and Joe hung around with them, watching for the arrival of both the woman and her horse.

Right on schedule, Mary heard the rumble of wheels on the gravel drive. She poked her head out of the office door and Joe bolted past her. Mary and Phoebe joined him while he fidgeted in the parking lot waiting for Eden to get out of her car.

Most of the guests were on their way to their cabins to change clothes for the afternoon trail ride, but when they also saw the car and its trailer, they veered off as one, and stood together by the office.

Eden pulled her Oldsmobile into the lot and got out of the car with a smile on her face, walking up to Mary with her hand extended. Mary gathered her into a powerful hug, welcoming the startled young woman. Eden turned to Phoebe, who gave her a quicker embrace, and she then stuck out her hand to Joe, who shook it with enthusiasm. As she had done the previous fall, Mary invited the guests to follow Eden down to the barn to meet Berry-Wise.

"You know the routine," Mary said to Eden, after the horse was in his stall. "Cocktails at five, supper at six. Do you need anything?"

"No, thank you so much. I'll get Berry settled and then go to the cabin."

"Carrie is looking forward to seeing you again," said Mary.

"Oh, that's great, I love talking with her. And I have some ideas for my performance, but I need your permission."

"Really? Well, come see me before five and you can tell me what you have in mind."

Phoebe got to the saloon early that night to observe Glenn Carter's reaction to Eden's return and was ready to intervene. She felt protective of the young woman, though she knew Eden was ten times tougher than she was.

Some of the guests were early, too, and Phoebe smiled when she saw them watching the door for the trick rider's entrance. When Eden came in, she was practically swarmed by the women, who all exclaimed at her beautiful black wool skirt and red sweater, and then started asking her questions about the upcoming performance. Eden expertly dropped hints but gave nothing away about what she planned to do.

The Carters were the last to arrive, and they got their drinks and talked with one of the men as though Eden wasn't in the room. Phoebe caught Mary's eye and raised her eyebrows. *So far, so good.*

The next day was Friday, and Eden planned to spend the morning before the performance exercising and rehearsing Berry-Wise. She and Phoebe had breakfast together first, and Phoebe told her that Carl and the younger wranglers would be working today to clear the windblown mesquite leaves and errant pieces of paper out of the corral. They would also clean off the benches and bleachers which Mary had kept up after the dudeo.

The weather was sunny and no rain was in the forecast, but it was still chilly, and in her jeans, a man's sweatshirt, a bandanna, and with her hat pulled low on her head, Eden looked like one of the ranch hands herself.

As the women took the last sips of their coffee, Carl came into the lodge and motioned to Eden, who smiled at Phoebe and said, "There's my helper." And with that cryptic remark, she left the table and went out the main door.

Mary came in a moment later.

"Eden says that if people want to meet her and Berry-Wise after the show she would be glad to make herself available."

"Really? She didn't do that last year."

"I know, but I think she is finally realizing her appeal and wants to use it to her advantage. She's a very smart girl."

"I agree. So how shall we handle that part of the program?"

They talked for a few minutes, and then each of them began their day.

23

VISITORS BEGAN ARRIVING at the H Double Bar around twelve thirty on Saturday afternoon and Joe took up his "Parking Coordinator" duties again, happily sporting the name tag he had kept on the bulletin board in his room. Phoebe's only task was to guide people to the seating area beyond the barn. She had also been counting heads as they went by and she motioned to Mary, who was walking toward her.

"I think we have more people than last year, I'm glad you borrowed those extra chairs from the Presbyterian church. How did you know we'd need them?"

"I just had a feeling about it. I know people talked a lot about Eden's performance at the dudeo, and those who missed her would want to see it this time."

Sam appeared at Mary's side just then and said, "It's almost one."

He was carrying his bullhorn, and when he and Mary walked into the corral, the crowd applauded. Stragglers hurried toward the open chairs, and Phoebe was relieved to see that a couple of them were empty. She didn't want anyone to have to stand through the whole thing, especially the ranch's guests. Glenn and Jayne Carter were in the stands, though Glenn didn't look happy about it. Phoebe was disappointed that Thelma Powell hadn't shown up, though she wasn't surprised. *I wonder if any of the Desert Grande's dudes are here?*

Sam welcomed the crowd and handed the bullhorn to Mary, who introduced Eden Williams and Berry-Wise by saying, "Thank you all so much for coming. Those of you who saw Eden's performance last fall will be thrilled by the new tricks she has brought to show us this year. And if this is your first experience with the talented woman and her horse, prepare to be dazzled!

"The H Double Bar is pleased to be the only ranch in Arizona to host this duo, and we plan on many more visits in the future. Be sure to stick around after the performance to meet our stars. And with that, I give you Eden Williams and Berry-Wise!"

Mary gestured to the far side of the corral and its open gate, then she and Sam walked quickly toward the side closest to the barn where Bob was waiting to let them out.

The audience stopped buzzing, and the silence was soon broken by a rumbling of hooves, as Berry-Wise galloped into the corral, with Eden standing in the saddle. The horse stopped in the center and Eden lowered herself down, posing upright in the stirrups, waving her hat in the air while the people in the stands shouted and clapped.

Eden wore her black pants tucked firmly into boots, along with a red-and-black plaid flannel shirt embroidered with the berry farm's name on the back. A white chiffon scarf was tied around the collar and held with a silver slide, and a black Stetson sat firmly on her dark hair. The ribbons in Berry-Wise's mane and tail this time were a mixture of red and black, which made his powdered-sugar coloring even more distinct.

Eden performed the tricks she had done the previous year: spinning in place, jumping on and off Berry's back as he ran, and a handstand, which she maneuvered after tossing her Stetson into the corral. She then leaned out of the saddle, grabbed her hat, and plopped it on her head without a pause, and then did a few moves with her rope while trotting around the ring.

Gathering her lariat into a tight circle, she next galloped toward the seating area, and tossed it into the crowd. Kids and adults scrambled to catch it, and Phoebe watched a teenage girl get hold of the rope and keep it by elbowing a young boy, obviously her little brother.

Eden had trotted off while this was happening, and when she saw the commotion in the stands die down, she and Berry began galloping again in wider and wider circles. She suddenly leaned off the side of her saddle, aimed her head toward the ground and raised her arms. Her left leg stayed on the horse while she raised the other leg straight in the air. The crowd had gone quiet, and just when it seemed Eden couldn't hold the position any longer as she circled the corral, she pulled herself into the saddle in a fluid, effortless-looking movement. She made another circuit and then did the trick again on the horse's other side.

As people clapped and stomped their feet, Eden pointed Berry-Wise toward the open gate and galloped away. Phoebe, along with everyone else, thought the demonstration was over, but a moment later she heard another loud noise and saw Sam's Jeep pull into the center of the corral with Carl at the wheel. He was dressed in his rodeo clown costume, and sat in the driver's seat with a grin on his face as he waved at the laughing audience members. Just as Phoebe wondered if Carl was going to do some of his own rope tricks, she was astonished to see horse and rider tearing into the corral straight toward the Jeep. She gasped along with the audience as Berry leaped into the air and over the car while Eden raised her hat in the air, smiling as the horse's hooves easily cleared Carl's head.

As Berry-Wise landed, Eden aimed him toward the side of the corral by the seating area. She stopped at the rails, hopped off the horse, spoke a few words to him, and the two bowed deeply, acknowledging the noisy standing ovation before them.

After nearly a minute of applause, Eden got back into the saddle, leaned over into a backbend, and Berry-Wise trotted toward the far entrance, with Carl and the Jeep following behind.

Mary and Sam hurried into the corral again, and Mary spoke to the crowd.

"Well, wasn't that something? We hope you enjoyed the performance today. If you'd like to meet Eden and Berry-Wise, please form a line by the far end of the corral. They will be back in just a few minutes. And thank you again for coming!"

Phoebe walked quickly through the corral to the open gate as people started lining up, kids bumping each other for a good place. Her job was to make sure Eden wasn't mobbed by fans, and to keep the crowd under control.

More applause broke out when Eden appeared leading Berry-Wise. She walked the horse a few steps into the corral and then nodded at Phoebe, who asked the individuals, couples, and families to take turns speaking to Eden.

She noticed that quite a few of the girls, and even some of the mothers, had small notebooks with them, and they all asked Eden for her autograph. For a moment she looked flustered, blushing as the first few girls held out their books. But it didn't take long for her to handle the requests as if she'd been signing her name for years. Berry-Wise gazed around placidly and accepted all nose and neck rubs as his due.

One of the final people in line was Chris Kaplan, a reporter for the *Tribulation Mining-Register*, who asked Eden a lot of questions about where she lived, where she trained, her background, and where her next performance would be. Phoebe worried that he might dig too deeply into Eden's parentage, and was relieved when he didn't.

Phoebe pointed Kaplan and the last few visitors toward the parking lot, and once they were gone, Eden and Carl took Berry-Wise back to the barn, and Phoebe arrived a few minutes later. Mary and Sam were talking with Eden while Carl and Bob unbraided the ribbons from the horse's mane and tail.

"Oh, Phoebe, there you are," Mary said as Phoebe came into the barn. "I was just telling Eden how much fun it was to surprise everyone with her new stunts."

"Well, I was surprised, that's for sure. How did you think up that idea to jump over the Jeep?"

"I got it from Bonnie Gray, she was a trick rider back in the 1930s, and she used to jump her horse, King Tut, over a car."

"That was really spectacular." Turning to Carl Phoebe said, "So, did you tell Susie what you were planning to do?"

He grinned. "She's my wife, she knows what to expect by now. But yes, I told her. She just rolled her eyes and told me I was a lunatic. But she didn't say no."

"Did you work on those two new tricks just since your last trip here?" Phoebe asked Eden.

"Oh no, I started practicing those with Berry last summer. But we just weren't ready until now. I'm glad everyone enjoyed them."

"I'm thrilled that the H Double Bar was the first place you showed them off. Well, I need to go check on Joe, I want to make sure he gets everyone into the right car," said Mary.

Sam went with her, and Phoebe watched Eden, Carl, and Bob rub down Berry-Wise and get him into his stall. Buster, Joe's new pinto, whinnied at him from across the barn.

"Those two have become buddies," said Carl.

"I noticed that," said Eden.

"How can you tell?" Phoebe asked.

"Well, whenever Joe takes Buster out of his stall, he wants to walk over to Berry. So, Joe lets him, and they touch their noses together. I've heard Berry whinny when Buster comes back to the barn, too," said Carl.

"Have you seen him do that before?" Phoebe asked Eden.

"Oh yes, Berry has a good friend back in Sebastopol on Mr. Danielson's farm, a great big palomino named Starlight."

"I never knew horses made friends," said Phoebe.

"They're herd animals, they need each other. Just like people."

Eden walked over and gave Buster a rub while Berry watched her.

Phoebe looked at her watch and said, "I'm heading up to the lodge to get some coffee."

"Me too," said Eden, and thanked the three men for their help with Berry.

As they walked Phoebe asked, “How long will you be here?”

“Mary told me I could stay as long as I liked, which is very kind of her, but I don’t want to overstay my welcome. I did want to ask you something, though. I’d like to go back to the cemetery and see Margaret’s grave again, so can you give me the directions to get there?”

“Sure, that’s a lovely idea. Do you need to go back to the library, too?”

“No, Miss Burington wrote to me over the holidays and said she didn’t find anything else about Margaret in their books or old records.”

“She loves helping people track information down, she’s a born librarian.”

“I can tell. I thought I’d go to the cemetery on Monday. Oh, that reminds me. Thank you for sending me the photograph of Mrs. Ellis’s house. I’m so happy to have that.”

“I wish I could have found more photos for you.”

“Please don’t worry, I’m thrilled with what you found. So, I want to take Berry out for a short ride tomorrow, do you want to come with us?”

“Yes, I’d love to,” Phoebe said enthusiastically. “You can tell me if I’ve improved my riding skills. I’m still on Applesauce, but Bob says I’ll be ready for another horse soon.”

“Don’t let him put you on an animal until you feel ready. No one else can tell you when you are feeling confident enough.”

“Thanks, that’s good advice. I was beginning to crack under the pressure.”

Laughing, the two women walked into the lodge and sat down at one of the tables with mugs of coffee and a plate of cookies.

The next day was Sunday, and with the continuing good weather, Mary and Sam were able to hold the chuck wagon lunch outdoors again. Once everyone was back at the ranch, Phoebe and Eden got ready for their ride. Eden praised Phoebe's progress.

"It's up to you, but I think you can start riding a livelier horse."

"I have been thinking about it, and if you think I'm ready, then I guess I'll give it a try. Would you help me choose the right horse?" Phoebe was pleased.

"I'd love to, but do you think Carl or Bob would rather choose it for you? I don't want to step on their toes."

"Oh, don't worry about that. They think the world of you."

"Well, let's make it a joint decision, and look at the horses when we get back."

"Sure. A few of them are out on the afternoon trail ride, but we can see who's still around."

Carl was leading the ride that day, so Eden and Phoebe talked to Bob when they got back to the barn.

"Phoebe is ready for another horse, Mr. Easley," said Eden. "Do you have any recommendations?"

"I've been thinking the same thing, Miss Eden," said Bob. "I have a few ideas."

Bob and Eden walked slowly down the stalls, petting the occasional horse, and talking with their heads together. They also walked outside to the largest corral, where a dozen horses milled around, taking in the soft early spring air. Phoebe trailed behind, trying to catch what they were saying, but she knew whichever horse they chose would be the right one.

Twenty minutes later they were back in the barn,

and Bob led a small bay mare with one white sock out of her stall.

"I think Lark will be perfect for you," he said.

"I agree," said Eden. "She's gentle but has a sprightly step and might occasionally challenge you."

"Well, *that* sounds terrifying," Phoebe laughed.

"I know, but she's not going to throw you and then stomp you into the ground or anything. She will help you improve your seat and your grasp of commands."

"Okay, I trust both of you," said Phoebe, and walked over to Lark to stroke her neck.

Bob walked down the aisle to a small room and came out with a currycomb, which he handed to Phoebe.

"Give her a nice rub and get acquainted," he said.

"We'll watch to make sure she really likes you," said Eden.

Phoebe smiled, took the comb, and reached out to her horse.

On Monday morning Phoebe walked into the lodge for breakfast and immediately knew something was up. The guests were all talking loudly together, and Jan Harrison walked over to Phoebe with her eyes wide.

"Did you hear what happened last night?"

"No, is something wrong?" Phoebe was holding her breath, anticipating bad news.

"Well, not any more, but I heard the horse that Mr. and Mrs. Watts gave to their son got out of the barn."

"Oh no, is he…"

"They found him, he was just wandering next to the corrals this morning."

"Oh, thank god. Thanks for telling me. Will you excuse me, I want to check in with Mary."

Phoebe hurried to the registration office, where Mary was talking on the phone.

"Yes, thanks Steve. I'll see you in about an hour."

She hung up and looked at Phoebe.

"You heard?"

"Yes, what happened? Is Buster okay?"

"He's fine, but I've asked our vet, Dr. Wellik, to come by and look him over."

"Tell me what's going on," said Phoebe.

"When Bob got up this morning, he found Buster ambling around outside the barn, and the door was open. So was Buster's stall door. Luckily, he's a homebody and stuck around, though we don't know when he got out. Or how."

"What about Berry-Wise, is he all right?"

"Yes, he was safe in his stall. Bob also went to the far corral to check on the other horses, and all of them are there. It's just Buster."

"Does Joe know?"

"No, Bob found him early enough, before Joe left for school. I've asked the guests not to say anything, and they've been lovely about it," Mary said with a sigh.

"I'm beginning to think you're right. Someone must be responsible for all of these 'accidents.'" Phoebe's thoughts skimmed through a dozen possibilities.

"It has to be Thelma Powell, she's trying to drive us out of business," Mary said with conviction.

"But why? And how can she manage when she's over at the Desert Grande all the time?"

"She probably has someone coming over to do her dirty work. Remember what Carl said about seeing a stranger here the night of the fire?"

"What are you going to do?"

"We're going to be more vigilant. And I just called Steve Magly."

24

THE YOUNG POLICE OFFICER arrived at the H Double Bar just as Dr. Wellik was leaving, and the two men waved at each other from their cars. Magly parked and walked into the registration office where Mary and Phoebe were waiting.

"Good morning, ladies," he said. "Tell me what's going on."

Mary gave him a quick rundown of the strange events of the past few months: the cut mark on Glenn Carter's cinch, the Jeep's flat tire, the missing tack and the toolshed fire, Glenn's spooked horse, the cattle on the roadway, the rattlesnake in the Fairfaxes' cabin, and Buster escaping out the open barn door.

"Steve, if only a couple of these things happened, I wouldn't give them a second thought. But add everything up and I smell sabotage."

"I'm inclined to agree with you, Mary, though I don't know as I'd use the word sabotage," Steve said. "Maybe they are just pranks that got out of hand."

"Pranks?" said Phoebe. "Who would be mean enough to endanger Joe's horse? That goes way beyond a practical joke."

"Are you sure none of your cowboys left the stall or barn door open?"

Mary just stared at him for a moment then said, "Of course not, what are you talking about? My men wouldn't do that."

"Okay, okay, I know, but I had to ask. Here's what we're going to do. Write down in detail everything that's happened, with the dates if you have them. Bring that to me at the station and I'll open an incident file. In the meantime, you might consider asking your hands to keep watch at night. Have you done anything else to prevent these kinds of activities?"

"We're now locking the tack room, and Sam has removed anything flammable from the ranch."

"Are you worried about your safety at home?" Steve asked.

"No, it seems only the ranch is being targeted. And anyway, Sam has his twelve-gauge."

"Well, I know he'll be slow to use it, but I'm glad you're not too worried."

He asked a few more questions and before he left Mary said to Phoebe, "Stick around, will you? Let's get all of this down on paper, and then will you type it up for Steve?"

"Sure, and I'll take it to the station this afternoon."

Steve thanked the two women and got back into his patrol car.

"Do you think he'll be able to do anything?" Phoebe asked Mary.

"I don't know, but I feel better that he'll have the whole story," she said.

"Me too. Okay, let's make some notes, and I'll take the pages down to my office."

The list of accidents looked even worse on the page, and Phoebe was very careful to include every detail as she typed. Before returning to her office, she went looking for Eden, and found her in the barn by Buster's stall, talking to Carl and Bob.

"Hi, Phoebe," she said. She looked serious, but not worried.

"I'm so sorry if you were concerned about Berry-Wise," she said. "Is he okay?"

"Yes, he's fine. His stall wasn't tampered with. It seems whoever did this was after Buster."

"At least he wasn't hurt, though. Dr. Wellik said he was fine."

"Yes, I looked him over, too," said Bob, his voice low and harsh. "I'd like to horsewhip whoever did this. The pony could have hurt himself in the dark, or wandered into the desert. I'd like to...."

He couldn't finish the sentence.

Eden touched his arm and said, "I know. But Buster is fine, and let's give him a little extra attention. Though I'm sure he just thought he had an adventure."

Phoebe left them to fuss over Buster, walked to her office in the lodge, and started typing.

She didn't see Eden for the rest of the day, but she was in the saloon that evening, and Phoebe asked if she had gone back to the cemetery.

"Yes, it was actually nice to be there. I'm feeling differently about Margaret. I told my mom about your diary and about the obituary after I left the ranch last year, and she was very happy. She only wished my dad could have known that Margaret thought about the two of them, and about me, at the end of her life."

"I know. I hope it's enough."

"It is."

They sipped their drinks, Eden having her usual Roy Rogers.

"So, what are your plans?" Phoebe asked.

"I'm leaving tomorrow. I've been corresponding with Virgil, I think you knew that. I'm going to visit him in Phoenix before I drive home. He has a friend who has a horse property, where I can let Berry stay. It will just be for a day or so."

"Oh. Well, that will be great. Maybe he can tell you more about Mrs. Ellis."

"I thought he might be here for my exhibition, but I guess he was busy."

Phoebe didn't say anything for a moment.

"Is something wrong?" Eden asked.

Phoebe looked around, then lowered her voice.

"No, not really, but we had a disagreement during his last visit, so we haven't chatted for a while."

"What happened?" Eden said.

Phoebe thought for a moment before answering, and then said, "Why don't you come down to my place after supper. I'll tell you what's been going on."

Only a few people knew about the incidents that were happening on the ranch, and only Virgil knew how far Phoebe had gone to figure out why. She trusted Eden about horses, and knew she could trust her about people, too. So, when they got settled on her couch in front of the fire later that evening, Phoebe told her about the accidents, seeing Jayne Carter with Thelma Powell, and her search of the Carters' cabin.

"My god, Phoebe," said Eden. "I knew a couple

of strange things had gone on here, but this sounds like a pattern to me."

"Exactly. I don't think Steve Magly agrees, but Mary and Sam are doing everything they can to stop it. They've also told Carl and Bob to keep their eyes open."

"With them on alert, I'm sure things will get better," Eden said firmly. "And I think I agree with Mary about the Desert Grande being at the bottom of all of this. Though Jayne seems an unlikely saboteur. Maybe Jayne and Thelma knew each other in Nevada. Didn't you say that's where Miss Powell was from?"

"That's what I heard. But there was also that guy lurking around before the fire."

"You took a chance searching Glenn's cabin. But I don't blame you for wanting to. And just think, if you hadn't been there, you wouldn't have seen that snake, and someone might have really gotten hurt."

"Thank you. I wish Virgil agreed with you. That's what we quarreled about."

"Oh, he was just being protective, right?"

"Yes. But I don't need protecting. I can take care of myself."

"We all can, but not everyone believes it," said Eden with a laugh.

"That's for sure."

"Virgil is very fond of you," Eden said.

"Well, I'm fond of him, too, which makes this rift between us really awful."

"I think he might be in love with you."

"Oh no, not you, too," said Phoebe. "That's what Mary thinks."

"I saw how he looked at you when I was here last fall. Can I ask how you feel about him?"

"I…I don't know, I do care about him. Mary thinks I haven't found a boyfriend in San Francisco because I want to be in Arizona with Virgil. Maybe I do, I don't know. But he never remarried after Ellender died, I think he's still mourning her, she was his great love. I just know I'm unhappy that we aren't speaking and I don't know how to fix it."

"I don't either, but maybe I can figure something out after I see him this week."

"Oh, don't say anything, please."

"I won't, I'll just be...*observant*."

"Okay." Phoebe smiled and reached over to give Eden's hand a grateful squeeze. "So, while we're on the subject, you said something about a boyfriend in one of your letters. Mike is his name, right?"

"Yes, Mike Ozawa, though his given name is Masao. His family was at the camp called Manzanar, in southern California, but they moved to Sebastopol after the war. They opened an appliance store in town, and Mike and I met in high school after we both got back from the camps. He works for his dad, but he's also studying over in Berkeley to become a lawyer. He was outraged at what happened to all the Japanese families, and decided to enter the law to make sure nobody has to go through something like that again."

"He sounds like a great guy."

"He is. And he doesn't try to get me to stop riding and do something safe, either. That's my favorite thing about him."

"You're lucky, I'm happy for you."

"I think you'll be even happier when I tell you that we're engaged. We're getting married when he graduates next year."

"Oh Eden, that's wonderful!"

"Thank you. My mom is over the moon, she loves Mike. We don't have a date yet, but I'll let you know, I'd love for you to come."

"I'll be there! Be sure to tell Mary, she loves hearing about people getting engaged and married."

"Thanks. You know, I'm sorry to be leaving tomorrow, I really like it here. Mary and Sam have created something very special. I don't think they have to worry that the Desert Grande will lure their guests away."

"That's what I've been telling Mary. That place is a novelty. Anyway, I hope you'll come back again, too."

"I want to, and it sounds like Mary will throw another dudeo next fall. As soon as you come up with a date, write to me and I'll make sure I'm free. Berry likes it here, too."

"Well, he has his buddy Buster, doesn't he?"

"Yes, he does. We're both lucky to have found new friends."

Eden left the next morning before the first trail ride, so that the guests could say goodbye to her and to Berry-Wise. Mary handed her an envelope before she got into her car. Eden opened it to find a $10 bill and started sputtering that she didn't need it, but Mary was firm.

"Honey, take it, you earned it, and it will buy you a couple of tanks of gas for your long drive home. Or put it in your wedding fund."

"Oh, thank you, Mary."

"You've been generous with us, and we want you to come back."

"You know I will."

Mary squeezed her hand, Eden took a last look at Berry in his trailer, started her car, and drove slowly down the drive.

The rest of February continued sunny, and was warm enough that Mary was able to plant new geraniums and herbs in the tall clay pots on the lodge's walkway.

Nights were still chilly, and though she didn't really need it, Phoebe continued to light a fire in her *casa* in the evenings. She felt a little lost with Eden gone and also being out of touch with Virgil. She decided to take her novel apart and write separate short stories instead, and discovered that she really enjoyed the work. If Mr. Mackenzie didn't like it, she was convinced she could find herself another publisher.

Mary and Sam always closed the H Double Bar around the middle of April and started planning for it in early March: final wages for seasonal staff, accommodations for Bob during the summer, and the transfer of their livestock up to Wyoming. Phoebe's task was to do all the final bookkeeping and correspondence, and get the summer issues of *Trail Notes* put together. Some of Mary's regular guests booked for late March and early April, as they liked to visit when winter was over and before the hint of summer heat that sometimes came with spring. Phoebe remembered that Glenn and Jayne Carter would be leaving soon, and wondered what life would be like on the ranch without them in those last few weeks.

Phoebe was in the registration office with Mary on the first Monday in March when the door slammed open and Jayne stumbled in. She wasn't in her usual skirt and sweater, but had thrown on a pair of jeans and a flannel shirt. She carried her purse as usual, but she held it against her chest as though worried someone would take it from her. Her face mirrored her frantic voice.

"He's gone, I can't find him," she said.

Mary got out of her chair and went to Jayne, taking her arm in an effort to steady her.

"Okay, Mrs. Carter, who's gone?"

"Glenn. It's Glenn. I got up this morning and he wasn't there."

"Are you sure he isn't out for a walk?"

"No, he wasn't there all night, his bed hasn't been slept in."

Jayne seemed to realize how this sounded and continued, "I went to bed early and took a sleeping pill, I slept the whole night."

"All right, let's not panic. I'll get Sam and we'll start a search."

"Call the police!"

"Well, let's do something right away, we have men who can ride out immediately to look for him, and I'll send Sam in the Jeep."

"I'll ride out with you, just get me a horse."

Before Mary could respond to this comment, Phoebe said, "I'll go, too, I can ride Applesauce."

Jayne turned on her with a look so vicious that Phoebe took a step back.

"You? You think you're a cowgirl because you work here and you finally learned how to ride a horse? You're just playing at it. You sit at your typewriter and then you go home to your soft life in San Francisco thinking you're tough because you spent a few months on a ranch. That Japanese girl is more of a cowgirl than you'll ever be. And you can't even sell your stupid western novel to anyone."

Shocked by Jayne's attack Phoebe immediately turned on her. "At least I try to be part of what's going on here. All you've done for months is sneer at the guests and let your husband insult good people like Eden. You're...."

"Enough," Mary said sharply. She was surprised by Phoebe's uncharacteristic harsh response. She stepped between the two women with a look that immediately stopped all conversation.

"Mrs. Carter, although it's obvious you know more about horses than you let on, I cannot permit you to ride out in the state you're in. Please go back to your cabin, or go to the lodge and get some coffee. My husband and my staff will take care of this."

"I don't care what you think, I want to find Glenn."

"I know that, but I must insist that you wait at the ranch. I will make sure you are informed about everything that happens."

Jayne seemed to waver, and then turned abruptly and stalked out the door.

Mary turned to Phoebe and said, "Honey, will you…" Then she saw Phoebe's face."What's wrong?"

"What she said to me...that was terrible, I'm...."

"Phoebe, she's distraught and doesn't know what she's saying. Let's talk about this later, okay? We need to get out there and find Glenn."

Phoebe took a breath. "You're right. How about if I go in the Jeep with Sam instead of riding?"

"Is that because of what she said?"

"Well, a little. Anyway, it will be faster."

"Okay. I'll call the house and get Sam down here. You go to the barn, tell the hands what's happened, and have them head out on their horses. I'll meet you there."

Phoebe walked quickly, not wanting to alarm the guests milling around outside the lodge or heading back to their cabins after breakfast. She gave a stiff smile to a few people and then hurried through the barn door to find Jayne Carter arguing with Bob.

"I need a horse. Now. I need to go out and find my husband!"

"Ma'am, I can't let you…" Bob was saying.

Phoebe stepped in. “Mrs. Carter, Mary asked you to stay in your cabin.”

“Don’t tell me what to do.”

“Give her a horse.”

They turned to see Mary standing in the doorway.

“Mrs. Carter, I will let you ride on one condition. You say to all of us here that you are doing this of your own accord, and anything that happens while you are riding will be on you, and not the responsibility of the ranch. Do I have your word?”

“Yes, I agree, let’s go, please!”

“Bob, put her on Arrow,” said Mary.

He didn’t look happy about it but he said, “Yes, Mrs. Watts.”

He went out to the corral and came back with a stocky black quarter horse. He saddled Arrow, put on the bridle and handed the reins to Jayne. She vaulted into the saddle with her purse still looped onto her arm. As she settled herself, the purse fell onto the ground and landed in front of Phoebe.

She heard a slight clunking sound and then Jayne said, “Give that to me.”

Phoebe handed the purse up to her, wondering why it was so heavy, and then Jayne turned the horse toward the barn door. Once in the yard she kicked Arrow into a canter and took off.

“I knew it,” said Mary.

“What?” asked Phoebe.

“She’s a horsewoman. And a good one. Well, I guess she won’t hurt herself out there. I just hope she doesn’t get lost. Come on, here’s Sam.”

Phoebe and Mary got into the Jeep and Sam pointed it toward the open desert.

25

IT DIDN'T TAKE LONG to find him.

Sam started driving the Jeep in a grid pattern around the ranch property and after about twenty minutes he noticed some of their cattle milling around in a group, staring at the ground. He drove over, scattering the animals, and saw Glenn lying in a shallow depression in the soil.

Sam jumped out of the Jeep and ran over to him. He knelt down and then stood up quickly.

"He's dead."

"Oh, damn. Can you tell what happened?" Mary asked, her shock evident.

"Not really, it looks like he's been chewed on by vultures or coyotes. We need to leave the body here and call the police. I'll stay with him. You go back to the ranch and call Magly," Sam told her.

Mary and got into the driver's seat. As they drove, Phoebe said, "I wonder where Jayne is."

"She rode off in the opposite direction, so I hope she didn't find him like this."

Just before they got back to the ranch, they saw Jayne, still on Arrow. She rode up to the Jeep.

"Glenn. Where is he?"

"Mrs. Carter, I'm sorry to tell you this, but we did find Glenn, and unfortunately he has died," said Mary.

Jayne looked like she was about to slide off her horse, but said, "Where? I need to go to him."

"No, you don't, I am going to insist this time. Sam is with him, we are calling the police, and you can ask them about what to do next."

For a moment Jayne looked defiant, and then defeated. Without a word, she turned Arrow around and headed toward the ranch.

"Whew, that was close," said Mary, and then drove into the parking lot. She and Phoebe went to the registration office and Mary called Steve Magly.

He arrived ten minutes later, talked with Mary for a moment, and then got back into his patrol car. He called for one of the police force's Jeeps to join him at the ranch and told the dispatcher to also send an ambulance. While he waited, Mary gave him detailed directions to where Sam was waiting.

Once the additional officers and ambulance crew arrived and had taken off, Mary and Phoebe sat in the office, staring into space and not speaking. Then Mary stood up.

"I'm going to check on Mrs. Carter. We'll have to tell the guests tonight, I'll do it at cocktails, as everyone should be there."

"What do you want me to do?" Phoebe asked.

"It's almost lunchtime, go up and see how the guests are, and see if anyone has heard about this."

Lunch was just being served as Phoebe got into the dining room, and she tried to keep smiling as she ate and chatted with a couple from Texas. A few people asked why the police had come by that morning, and she told them that Mary would tell them what was going on later. And that there was nothing to worry about. Everyone seemed satisfied with that explanation.

After eating, Phoebe went to her office to do some work, wanting to keep busy even as she puzzled over what happened. How did Glenn die? Why did he go out to the desert in the first place, and apparently at night?

But her mind kept going back to what Jayne Carter had said to her, had accused her of. Being a phony, and being a lousy writer.

Was it true? Did other people see her that way? Was she just deluding herself about her work at the ranch, about her stories? And what did Virgil think?

She put her head in her hands, and then raised it quickly when she heard a knock on the door. Mary walked in, looking grave.

"Hi honey, are you okay?"

"Yeah, I'm fine. What's going on?"

"The police took Carter's body to the hospital morgue and Steve wants to take statements from people. He's talking to Jayne now. She's much calmer than I expected her to be. I said she didn't have to come to meals, that I could have Carrie bring her some food on a tray for the time being and she said that was fine, though I'm not sure she'll eat anything. Steve wants to talk to you, me, and Sam at two. Can you come to registration?"

"Sure. I'll see you there."

The ranch was quiet when Phoebe headed for the

office later that afternoon. Nearly all of the guests were on the afternoon trail ride, which was a relief. Steve and Mary were talking quietly when she walked in, and he asked her to take one of the chairs behind the desk. Sam stood in the corner with his eyes on his wife.

"Hi Phoebe. Mary and Sam have given me the details about what happened this morning, and I want to hear your version, as well," said Magly.

Phoebe told him about Jayne bursting into the office, the tussle over her wanting to ride out to find Glenn, and how she, Sam, and Mary had eventually found his body.

"Okay, thanks. We won't know how Carter died until we get a coroner out here from Phoenix to do an autopsy, though Dr. Calhoun took a look at him and thinks he was shot."

"Oh my god," said Mary.

"Could he tell what caliber of bullet was used?" asked Sam.

"No, and I wouldn't tell you if I knew," said Steve. "I think you understand."

"Oh, of course," said Sam.

"I need to be on my way. I told Mrs. Carter to stay here for the time being. I assume that won't be a problem?" Magly asked.

"No, they were booked to stay here for a few more days anyway. I'm not going to kick her out if she's here longer than she expected."

"She's pretty upset, and also seems very angry. When people have a loss like this, they sometimes do stupid things."

Magly glanced at Phoebe, who gave him a quick glare, and then he got back into his car and took off.

Mary scanned the crowd in the saloon that night, making sure that all her guests were there. She raised her hand and her voice and said, “Ladies and gentlemen, may I please have your attention.”

Conversation stopped immediately, and there was no sound but that of ice tinkling in glasses as people sipped their drinks.

“I have some unpleasant news I need to share with all of you. Mr. Glenn Carter, who has been a guest here since last fall, died after leaving the ranch to take a walk last evening. We don’t have any other details, but his death is being investigated by the police. Mrs. Jayne Carter is in her room and she will likely stay there for the time being, and my staff will see to her needs personally.

“I know this is a shock and you have a lot of questions. We do, too, but as yet we don’t know anything more. We also are sure there is no danger to any of you. It seems Mr. Carter went for his walk late last night, and likely got lost in the desert. While we want our guests to appreciate the beauty of our Sonoran landscape, we also want to emphasize that it can be dangerous if you are out there on your own.

“If you have any concerns, please talk to me, Sam, or Phoebe anytime. Thank you.”

Mary’s announcement had drawn a few gasps from the guests, and everyone looked shocked, but nobody seemed scared or troubled. As conversation started up again, Phoebe drew Mary aside.

“You did that well. No one looks like they need to talk to you or ask questions. At least not now.”

“This is a new batch of guests, I don’t think they had time to get to know the Carters, so it’s not a real personal loss. I just hope they feel safe here.”

“I’m sure they do,” said Phoebe.

“I’ve told the staff to keep their ears open during

meals, in case people start rumors or talk about being worried. Would you do the same?"

"Of course."

"I asked Helen to prepare a few special extras for supper tonight."

"Do you know what she's going to make?"

"No, but I got the impression that most of it will be desserts."

"That will make everyone feel better."

Over the next two days, Phoebe heard very few people talking about Glenn's death, and Carrie and the other waitresses said the same.

Mary had asked Carrie to take food to Jayne at each meal and told her to report back on her actions and her state of mind. She spoke to Mary when she and Phoebe were in the office talking about *Trail Notes*.

"Mrs. Carter just sits at the desk in her room, smoking and going through papers," Carrie said. "At least that's what she's doing when I go in there. Olive said Mrs. Carter leaves her cabin when she's making the bed and cleaning, but she just sits in the chair outside her room and goes right back in when Olive is finished. And she's always wearing that ugly pin, that big longhorn."

"Her husband gave that to her. She probably wants to keep it close to remember him. Well, that's mostly good news. Thank you, Carrie."

"It sounds like she's taking things well," said Mary, after Carrie walked away.

"I don't know," said Phoebe. "She was so upset at first, and now she's calm? That doesn't seem right to me."

"At least she's not upsetting the other guests. I'm concerned for Jayne, but I also have others to think of."

"I know. I wish Steve would tell us the results of the autopsy," said Phoebe.

"You asked him about that yesterday, didn't you?"

"Yes, I saw him in town. He was vague but said the autopsy had been done and now it was just a matter of doing the paperwork."

"Ugh. I hate waiting," said Mary.

She didn't have to hate it long. That same afternoon, Steve's patrol car rolled into the parking lot. He found Phoebe in her office in the lodge and asked where Mary and Sam were.

"They're both at the house. They want to be there when Joe comes home from school, at least for a few days. They told him about Carter and they just want to make sure he's okay. He is, apparently, because he wants all the gruesome details."

"Well, I have some of those to report. Can we go up there?"

"Sure, come on."

They walked up the path to the Watts house. Mary settled both of them on the couch, while Sam stayed with Joe in his bedroom.

"I'll get right to the point," said Magly. "Dr. Calhoun was right. Carter was shot, right in the heart. Just one shot, and he likely died instantly."

"And the gun?" asked Mary.

"A .38 revolver," said Steve. "We are in the process of doing ballistic tests to see if we can identify the gun, but I'm not hopeful. We had to send everything to Phoenix, because we don't have the right equipment here. If I hear anything, I'll let you know."

"Do you know when he died?" asked Phoebe.

"Yes, around eleven the night he disappeared, Sunday the sixth."

"So he was out there all night. How awful."

"Yes, Mary. I need to see Mrs. Carter and tell her what's happening."

"Does she still have to stay here?"

"I'd prefer if she did, but I don't have any evidence to hold her. Didn't you say the couple was planning to leave soon?"

"This Friday, actually. Will you tell her she is welcome to stay longer if she wants?"

"All right. But if she does want to leave, I'll get her address so we can question her more if necessary."

They talked for a few more minutes and Phoebe and Magly left together.

"Why don't you think Jayne's a suspect?" she asked him as they walked toward the lodge.

"I didn't say that."

"What?"

"I said I didn't have evidence. We looked at her clothes, and the only pants and shoes that looked dirty were the ones she wore when she went out on the horse to look for her husband. But she could have chosen those to wear because they were already soiled from being out in the desert with Carter."

"I never thought of that," Phoebe said.

"We also found a gun. It was in her purse."

"So that's why it was so heavy and made a loud noise when she dropped the purse in the barn. Was it the gun that killed him?" Phoebe asked.

"No, it's a .22 pistol, a small piece with a six-inch barrel. Not a .38."

Phoebe decided not to tell him about the bullets she'd found. She didn't think admitting to a police officer that she had done some investigating on her own was a good idea.

"I guess that's good news for her. And I don't think she had a motive either. She was distraught about his death, though I never thought they were particularly close. At least not in public," she said.

"What were they like together?" Magly asked.

"He was jolly and blustering, and she was kind of sullen, like she wasn't happy to be here. But he got drunk once and insulted a guest and Jayne made sure it didn't happen again. So she wasn't as passive as she acted. They also used to take their car and go places for a day and sometimes overnight. I don't know, it's hard to judge a marriage from the outside."

Steve gave a shy smile.

"You're still coming to Nora's and my wedding next month, aren't you?"

"I wouldn't miss it," said Phoebe.

"Bring Virgil too, if you like."

"Oh. Well, sure. Thanks," said Phoebe, and then changed the subject.

"I have to go back to my office, thanks for coming over. I hope this gets cleared up soon."

"We'll do our best," said Magly.

Phoebe left her *casa* early the next morning to get coffee in the lodge, and before she reached the tiled pathway she saw Jayne Carter heading toward her car, looking right and left as she walked. Phoebe stepped quickly behind one of the tall cacti by her fence so she wouldn't be seen and watched Jayne get into her Buick and back slowly and silently out of its space.

Phoebe turned and ran back to the *casa*, grabbing her purse and car keys. The Nash was in its accustomed place behind the house, and she started the engine and rolled toward the ranch driveway. She could see Jayne's car ahead of her and stayed as far back as possible so she wouldn't be spotted.

Jayne turned onto the highway and headed toward town. As she drove, Phoebe wondered if she'd overreacted. Maybe Jayne just wanted to do some shopping, or go for a drive to clear her head? But then why had she looked so furtive when she left? As these thoughts went through her head, Phoebe watched Jayne go through town, drive for a few more minutes and then turn onto Old Caballo Road. Phoebe now knew where she was going, and she drove with purpose in the same direction.

To the Desert Grande Guest Ranch.

26

PHOEBE WATCHED JAYNE park her car in the Desert Grande's lot and hurry toward the ranch's massive front door. She maneuvered the Nash into a space that was surrounded by other cars far from the entrance and got out, still watching Jayne. Once she was inside, Phoebe walked up to the building and stood on the porch for a few minutes before pushing the door open.

The lobby was quiet, though she heard a gentle murmuring coming from the bar. No one was at the registration desk, and after looking around to make sure she was alone, Phoebe tiptoed toward Thelma's private office in the back of the lobby. Even before she got close to the door, she heard loud voices, and recognized both Thelma Powell and Jayne Carter. She couldn't tell what they were saying, so she reached for the doorknob. *Unlocked.*

She turned it and slowly cracked open the door. Not enough to see into the room, but she could now make out some of the conversation. Argument, really. And just as she heard Jayne say, "I don't care what happens to me…" the door flew out of Phoebe's hand and she stumbled into the office. Regaining her balance, she looked up to see Thelma Powell...*with a gun in her hand.*

"Get in here," she said, motioning with the barrel of her weapon. She closed and locked the door, and motioned for Phoebe to stand by a massive mahogany desk next to Jayne, who was rubbing her left wrist.

Phoebe asked Jayne if she was okay.

"She got my gun away from me."

"Shut up, both of you," said Thelma.

"I know what you're doing," said Phoebe.

"I don't think you do."

"You're trying to drive the H Double Bar out of business. The accidents, the fire, the cattle, those were your doing. Mary knows it was you."

Something else suddenly became clear. Phoebe looked at Jayne.

"And the two of you were in on it. You made it all happen. Just to close us down?" She looked at Thelma. "Were you going to buy up the ranch when it went under and open up another Desert Grande? Why would you do that?"

Jayne started to laugh.

"I knew you were stupid. Of course, it's about money, but it's about cleaning up dirty Las Vegas money."

"Shut your mouth, Jayne," said Thelma.

Jayne pointed at Thelma explaining, "She works for a big casino in Las Vegas, and it's owned by mobsters. They needed an outside investment to look legitimate where they could funnel the profits from their crooked gambling business, and the brothels they own. So they decided to take over a few dude ranches. They started with yours because it was the most successful. Then once it failed, they would slowly do the same to all the others. Everyone comes to the dude ranches around here. They're respectable. Nobody would look twice at someone opening new ranches, or taking over old ones. And she had Glenn killed, because he didn't want to help her anymore."

Phoebe stared at Jayne, and then at Thelma.

"So, what are you going to do, kill us both? How are you going to get away with that?"

Thelma said, "You both broke into my office. You threatened me with a gun, there was a struggle and it went off. 'It was self-defense, officer,'" she said with a little girl voice.

While she spoke, Jayne had been moving toward her, and before Thelma took her attention away from Phoebe, Jayne lunged at her, reaching for the gun.

Thelma stepped back, aimed the revolver at Jayne, and fired.

She screamed and fell to the ground with her hands around her leg. Thelma moved over to Jayne, ready to fire again.

Still standing by the desk, Phoebe noticed a set of bronze bookends shaped like horse heads. She grabbed the nearest one and threw it in Thelma's direction. She saw it coming and tried to get out of the way, but tripped on the rug, dropping the gun.

Both women dove toward it, but Thelma got there first. Phoebe saw her grab the barrel and turn the pistol around to get at the grip, and then she saw something shiny on the floor.

Jayne's longhorn pin.

She grabbed the pin in her palm and reached toward Thelma as she raised the revolver. Phoebe scraped and stabbed the sharp horn into the back of Thelma's hand, leaving a line of red that deepened and then dripped as Thelma howled and dropped the pistol.

Phoebe picked it up, pointed it at Thelma, and then went over to Jayne. She was now unconscious, and the pool of blood under her got wider as Phoebe watched. She leaned over and said to her, "Jayne, it's okay, I'm going to call for help."

She heard a noise just then, saw the office door fly open, and watched Thelma run out.

Phoebe kept the gun aimed at the door and picked up the phone on the desk just as people started coming into the office. She got the police dispatcher, and she was relieved to hear that someone had already called in a report of gunfire, and that officers were on their way. She asked him to call an ambulance, hung up, and turned to the growing crowd. Raising her voice, she said that there was an injured person in the room and everyone had to leave. There weren't any cowboys or other hands among the gawkers.

She noticed the office's private bathroom, and went in to get some towels. She wrapped them tightly around Jayne's leg, and then called to the people still lingering outside the door to bring more. The young woman who was usually at the front desk came in a minute later, white-faced, bearing a handful of various-sized linens.

"What…what happened?"

"I can't tell you right now, just please go out and look for the police and the ambulance. Tell them to come in here."

Jayne's blood continued to soak through the towels, but seemed to be slowing. Phoebe replaced them with clean ones and kept pressure on the wound, though she had no idea how bad it was.

"Glenn...." Jayne's eyes were now wide open and filled with pain.

"Don't say anything, help is almost here, just stay quiet and calm."

"Phoebe...he didn't...."

Jayne passed out again, and at that moment the room filled with people. This time it was two ambulance attendants with a stretcher, and three police officers, including Steve Magly.

Phoebe looked at him with relief but was startled to see him looking serious and almost angry. She stood up to let the medics work on Jayne.

"Steve, thank god," she began.

"Don't say anything, Phoebe," he said. "Please give me the gun and come with me."

"What? Oh, okay. Let me wash first."

She handed him the pistol, walked into the bathroom, and ran her shaking hands under hot water, scrubbing them with soap until they looked clean. She had used all the towels on Jayne's leg, so she let the water drip off her fingers as she followed Magly out of the office. She stopped when she saw Thelma Powell standing by the front desk with a bandage around her hand. Thelma turned and looked at Magly with a weak smile.

"Oh, thank you for catching her, Officer," she said.

Phoebe gaped at her.

"Miss Powell, you have made a serious accusation against Miss Kelley. I need to take you both down to the station for questioning. Phoebe, you will go in Officer Middleton's car, and I will take Miss Powell."

"But Steve..." Phoebe began.

He gestured to Middleton and said, "Take her now, Archie."

Phoebe was so stunned she didn't think of

resisting, and let him take her elbow, lead her to his patrol car, and help her in. As they drove away, she looked out the back window and saw Thelma getting into Steve's car. She then sat in silence as Middleton gunned the engine.

The Tribulation police station was in a new concrete building, constructed two years earlier to replace the worn-out wooden structure which had served the force for nearly thirty years. Phoebe and her driver arrived first and after they went in, he led her toward an enclosed area with a glass window like a bank teller's booth. Behind it was a young officer with bad acne, who asked her to empty her pockets and give him any personal items. She only had her car keys, and she handed them over with as much ill grace as possible.

Middleton then took her to the largest of two interrogation rooms, which officers and staff used for meetings as well as questioning suspects. It was equipped with a table, metal folding chairs, and slightly warped shelving which held documents, books, and an assortment of cups. The air smelled of stale coffee and cigarettes. The walls were a pale grayish-green.

Phoebe drummed her fingers on the table and after about twenty minutes she was just about to get up and ask what was going on when the door opened and Steve Magly came in. With him was the police chief, Bob Cramer. She'd met him once and liked him, but he didn't look friendly now.

"Miss Kelley, we are here to question you about the shooting of Mrs. Jayne Carter and the wounding of Miss Thelma Powell," he said.

"Wounding? I barely scraped her…"

Steve sighed impatiently. "Phoebe, please don't speak until we ask you a question."

Cramer continued, "Miss Kelley, please tell us how the shooting of Mrs. Carter occurred."

Phoebe told him how she followed Jayne to the Desert Grande, and her suspicions about Thelma Powell's role in the accidents at the H Double Bar. How she listened at the door and was caught by Thelma, who held a pistol on her and Jayne, until Jayne tried to get it away from her.

"She shot Jayne in the leg and was about to shoot her again, so I threw the bookend to distract her and she dropped the gun. She got to it before I did, but I saw Mrs. Carter's pin on the floor, and used it on her so she couldn't hold onto the gun. She let it go and I picked it up. Then she ran out of the room."

"Miss Powell tells a different story," said Cramer.

"I'll bet she does," Phoebe said with a smirk. "What did she say?"

"That Mrs. Carter threatened her with the pistol she kept in her purse, that you showed up to help her, and when Miss Powell tried to grab for the gun it went off and hit Mrs. Carter. You stabbed Powell with the pin, took away the gun, and threatened her with it until she ran."

"That's pure baloney and you know it, Steve," said Phoebe, looking at Magly.

"I'm questioning you, Miss Kelley," said Cramer. "This is a serious matter."

"I know that. You can ask Jayne, she'll tell you what happened."

"Mrs. Carter is undergoing surgery and her condition is not good," said Cramer.

Phoebe sat back in her chair.

Cramer pulled a pad of paper from the leather portfolio he'd brought with him, and took a pen out of his shirt pocket. He put both on the table in front of Phoebe.

"Please write down everything you just told us, include as much detail as possible, and sign your statement. You will need to remain here until further notice."

The two men got up and left the room.

Feeling sick, Phoebe picked up the pen and began to write.

"Phoebe. Phoebe, wake up."

She raised her head from the table and rubbed her eyes. Her heart fell as she recognized the chairs and the bilious walls. She glanced at her watch and was startled to see that it was nearly one.

Steve Magly was gently rubbing her shoulder, a concerned look on his face. He handed her a glass of water.

"Now what?" she asked, taking the glass and starting to drink.

"You can go home," he said.

"Why? I mean, what's happened?"

"We've arrested Thelma Powell."

"You did? For shooting Jayne? You believe me?"

"Yes, but I can't tell you anything more right now. Mary is here to take you back to the ranch."

Trying not to show how relieved she was, Phoebe got up and followed Magly out into the hallway and toward the front office. Mary was pacing by the door, and when she saw Phoebe she ran and threw her arms around her, with a glare at Magly.

"Come on, honey. Let's go."

"My car, it's still at the Desert Grande."

"Steve gave me your keys, I'll have Sam go out and drive it back later."

The women left, saying nothing to Magly or any of the other officers. Phoebe was quiet and Mary said nothing as she drove the station wagon.

After parking the car, Mary said, "Honey, why don't you go back to your house and take a bath or something and rest up. I'll have Carrie bring you some lunch. And you don't need to come to supper, she can bring that to you later."

"No, I want to be out among people, and I definitely need some time in the saloon. But can you call the hospital and check on Jayne? Did Steve tell you what happened to her?"

"Yes he did, and I'll check with the hospital, don't worry. I'll see you later."

After Mary left, Phoebe took her advice and soaked in her tub for a long time. She felt both numb and anxious. Thelma had been arrested. But Cramer hadn't believed Phoebe's story. Did he still suspect her? And Jayne...Phoebe was concerned about her condition, but then anger boiled when she thought about how the Carters had tried to close the ranch down.

I hope she'll be okay. Because I have a lot of questions that she needs to answer..

27

PHOEBE PUT ON her favorite red sweater and black slacks, and slid her feet into her second-best loafers. Her only jewelry was the turquoise roadrunner earrings. She felt presentable, which was all she could manage, because she was too tired to think about looking sharp for cocktails.

She was still thinking about Jayne as she walked toward the saloon and didn't see the man standing by the door until she was almost there.

Virgil.

An unbidden bubble of joy filled her, and she walked more quickly toward him. He smiled.

"Hi, Phoebe."

"Hi, Virgil. I guess Mary called you."

"Yes, she did. Can we take a walk or something?"

"Sure."

They strode away from the saloon and as soon as they had passed a few guests on their way to cocktails and were alone, Virgil spoke.

"I'm sorry about our quarrel."

"I am, too."

"I had no right to criticize you or your actions. I was just worried. I don't want anything to happen to you."

"Well, after what I went through today, you had a right to wonder about me."

"Mary told me a little bit about what went on over there. Are you okay?"

"Yes, I think so. I still don't know what the police are thinking, or what they arrested Thelma Powell for. I hope Magly or someone will tell us."

"I'm sure he will."

"Hey, I really need a drink. Let's go back to the saloon. Are you staying over tonight?"

"Yes, Mary offered me one of the empty cabins. She really has to stop doing that, she'll never be able to make a profit."

Phoebe laughed.

"She knows the difference between business and friendship. Did she tell you Jayne Carter and her husband tried to put us out of business?"

"Yes. They were in cahoots with that Powell woman, weren't they?"

"They were. I'm still so angry about that, but this afternoon I realized that I don't have to be. They could never have ruined the business. Mary and Sam have made something solid and sure here. Nobody can wreck that."

"You're right. Come on, let's go get that drink."

Mary had obviously given guests the latest news about Jayne, because Phoebe was swarmed when she and Virgil walked into the saloon. Being questioned by the police in an interrogation room gave Phoebe a status she hadn't expected, and she almost laughed at how people hung on the description of her ordeal. By the time the supper bell rang, she was feeling much better, and she took Virgil's arm as they walked up to the lodge.

Helen had made Phoebe's favorite chocolate cake with White Mountain frosting for that night's dessert, and Phoebe went into the kitchen to thank her.

"You needed something to forget what those stupid policemen put you through," she said.

Phoebe invited Virgil to her *casa* after supper, and when they settled on her couch with coffee, she gave him more details about Jayne and Glenn, Thelma, and the shooting at the Desert Grande.

"I wonder what happened to Jayne's pin," Phoebe said once she'd finished her story.

"The police probably have it," said Virgil.

"Well, it will certainly prove that I was trying to defend myself."

"Only you would use jewelry as a weapon," said Virgil with a smile.

"I'm glad I wasn't wearing the hair comb you gave me," said Phoebe. "I might have lost it like Ellender lost hers, and I would hate that."

Virgil was quiet, and stared into his cup of coffee.

"Oh, Virgil, I'm sorry, I didn't mean to remind you of what happened to her. I know it still hurts."

"Phoebe, I don't feel that pain anymore. I lost Ellender forty years ago. She's a memory of happiness, of my youth, but her loss doesn't haunt me."

"I'm glad. I know the feeling. Jack is just someone I knew, that I happened to be married to, and he's gone."

Virgil took a breath. "Phoebe, I'll just say this once and then I'll leave, but I need to tell you something. I love you, Phoebe. I've loved you since the day you gave me Ellender's diary. I came on so strong about keeping you safe because I can't bear the thought of losing you. I know I have nothing to offer but an old man's love, and that isn't good enough. But I wanted you to know. To know that you are loved, and I will always be out there if you need me."

He finished his coffee and got up, facing her from where he stood.

"Thank you for listening. Please keep in touch, please let me know how you are, and about your life in San Francisco. You mean everything to me. You always will."

Phoebe watched him reach for his coat on the back of the couch and walk toward the door. For a moment she couldn't breathe, and then breath and warmth filled her.

"Virgil, wait."

She moved toward him and he turned to her.

She put her hands on either side of his face and said, "Kiss me, you silly old man."

Phoebe and Virgil sat close together at breakfast the next morning, and just as they finished, Mary came into the lodge and sat down next to them.

"Steve Magly just called, he wants to talk to all of us."

"Oh no, not again," said Phoebe.

"I don't think he's coming to arrest you," said Mary. "He'll be here at ten. Come up to the house, that's where we're meeting."

"Okay," said Phoebe. "Oh, have you heard anything about Jayne's condition?"

"No, the hospital wouldn't tell me anything. I even tracked down Dr. Calhoun and he's tight-lipped," said Mary.

"Well, maybe Steve will know something."

"I'll ask him, that's for sure. Well, I have to go, see you later." Mary gave the two of them a sharp glance, and then left.

"Will you come too?" Phoebe asked Virgil.

"Of course." He gently squeezed her hand under the table.

Phoebe had some office work to do, and Virgil went back to his cabin, and at nine fifty-five they met behind the lodge and walked along the path to Mary and Sam's house, holding hands until they got to the front door. Mary let them in, served up coffee, and Phoebe and Virgil sat together on the leather sofa. Two minutes later Steve Magly arrived. He took the largest chair in the living room, refused a cup of coffee, and waited for Mary and Sam to take the other two chairs before he spoke.

"First, I wanted you to know that Mrs. Carter will be fine. The bullet just missed the big artery in her thigh, and though she lost a lot of blood, it could have been worse if you hadn't stopped the bleeding, Phoebe."

"I'm so glad," she said.

"And there will be no charges filed against you."

"Of course there won't," Mary interrupted. "It's ridiculous that you even considered that Phoebe would deliberately shoot someone."

"I didn't," said Magly.

"What?" Phoebe said.

"I had to go through the motions of questioning you for the record, but Cramer and I knew you weren't involved. Well, I knew you weren't, and I managed to convince the chief. We kept you busy and under our jurisdiction while we waited for a search warrant."

"For what?" Mary asked.

"Thelma Powell's office. We called the Las Vegas police after we brought both of you in, and they told us they have been suspicious of Powell's activities outside of Vegas for months. They were sure she was acting for some casino owners, but they didn't have anything on her. We told them what you said about the accidents around the H Double Bar, and then we told Judge Holt in Phoenix. He gave us the warrant."

"What did you find?" Phoebe asked.

"The gun that killed Glenn Carter," said Magly.

"She killed him?" Sam asked.

"I don't think so," Magly said. "She had at least one wrangler on her personal payroll, a guy named Bill Jordan. He's disappeared, but we'll find him. Anyway, the Carters were also part of her plan, she put them here to stage everything that happened. Cutting the cinch on his own saddle was brilliant, because no one would suspect that Glenn would do that to himself. He knocked down the fence and let your cattle out. Jordan set the fire. And put the rattlesnake in your guest's cabin."

"Why would Glenn do that?" asked Phoebe.

"Blackmail," said Magly. "Carter had thousands of dollars of gambling debts at the casino Powell worked for. She said he could wipe them out by helping her put you out of business."

"Then she would swoop in, take over the ranch, and start building her empire, is that right?" asked Mary.

"That's what Jayne said. Dude ranches were the perfect business to hide gambling profits, which they got by cheating, I guess. And their houses of prostitution," Phoebe told them.

Sam asked, "Why did Jayne go along with it?"

Mary spoke up before Magly could answer.

"She loved him. I'm right, aren't I?"

"Yes," said Magly. "She hoped they could just do what Powell said and then be done with her and go back to their life. But they didn't count on her ruthlessness. And no blackmailer ever lets a victim off the hook."

"What's going to happen to the Desert Grande now?" asked Sam.

"Well, it's in the process of being closed down. The guests have a few days before they need to leave. I don't know how they will get any of their money back, because the casino owner who financed it has also been arrested. The staff might receive some back wages, but it will be a while. It's almost empty already."

He looked at his watch.

"Well, I have to go. Jayne will be discharged in a couple of days. But we will be arresting her for her part in the scheme."

"Not if I don't press charges," said Mary.

Magly stared at her. Sam just smiled.

"What are you talking about?" Magly asked.

"I will not be pressing charges against her. You can throw the book at Powell and that cowboy of hers when you find him. But Jayne Carter only acted under duress, she didn't cause any of the incidents herself, and I will not be responsible for putting her in jail. Phoebe, what do you think?"

"I absolutely agree. She was a victim, too."

Magly almost rolled his eyes, but then said, "All right. She will still have to come into the station when she's out of the hospital and give her formal statement."

"And then we'll bring her home," said Mary.

After Magly left, they all talked for a while, and then Phoebe and Virgil went back to her *casa*.

Virgil kissed Phoebe as they sat together on the sofa, and then said, "I need to go home today. But I'll come back and see you soon. When are you returning to San Francisco?"

"I don't know. The ranch doesn't close for another five weeks, and I haven't decided about anything.

I haven't got a publisher waiting for my next book. But I don't want to go back to California and leave you here."

Virgil stroked her hair and ran his hand over the silver and turquoise comb.

"And I don't want you to go. Let's not worry about it for now, okay? Write to me, call me, and we will figure something out."

"I love you, Virgil. You've made me so happy."

"Are you going to tell Mary and Sam about us?"

"Yes, but in my own way. You know how she is. She'll want to plan our future."

Many minutes later, they walked out of the *casa* and before passing the wire fence which led to the walkway, Virgil reached out and pulled Phoebe to him. She disappeared into his arms and into a kiss that closed the door forever on the memory of all other kisses.

"Well, it's about time."

They broke apart to see a grinning Mary standing by the fence.

"I came by to see how you were. I guess I shouldn't have worried. Took you two long enough."

And with that, she chuckled, turned on her heel, and left them.

The couple watched Mary stride away and then broke into laughter themselves. Phoebe took Virgil's hand as they went to his cabin, where he picked up his suitcase and battered cowboy hat. She walked him to his car, which was parked by the registration office, and gave him a hug and a quick kiss, knowing that Mary was watching. He put his hand on her shoulder, as he had always done with his goodbyes, and drove off.

Phoebe watched him go down the drive and then went into the office.

"Go ahead, say it," she said to Mary.

"Okay, I will. I told you so," she said. And then got out of her chair to give Phoebe a squeeze.

"I've never seen you look so happy," Mary said.

"I don't know that I've been this happy."

"So, which one of you finally broke the ice and said how you felt?" Mary asked.

Phoebe smiled. "He did. He said he had to speak after I almost got killed again. And it turns out we were at cross purposes. I thought he was still mourning Ellender, he thought I never got over Jack. He thought he was too old for me, and I thought he wouldn't be interested in someone who wasn't his age."

"Oh, Phoebe, all men like younger women."

"I guess so, but that's not what it is."

"I know."

"I didn't realize how I felt about him until we quarreled, and until he told me he loved me. It was like the sun coming up after a long night."

"I'm so glad for you, honey. He's a good man. He's one of the best I've ever met."

"He is."

"I won't ask if you have any plans, because I know you don't. I hope he'll be coming back soon."

"Yes, and I told him he could stay here."

"Well, of course he can. He's family."

28

JAYNE WAS RELEASED from the hospital three days later. Steve Magly picked her up and took her to the station, where she spent two hours giving him the details of the arrangement with Thelma Powell, and what happened with Phoebe in the office. Magly was quietly relieved that her account matched Phoebe's exactly.

He then called Mary, and she and Phoebe drove to police headquarters. When Jayne walked into the front office Mary gathered her into one of her bear hugs, and Phoebe gave Jayne a smile. On their way back to the ranch, she tried to simultaneously explain, apologize, and thank Mary for keeping her out of jail.

"Nonsense," Mary said. "You are not to blame for your husband's problems, or for wanting to stay with him. You didn't do any lasting harm. And you lost your husband. That's punishment enough."

Jayne began to cry, and the other women kept quiet while she mopped up her tears. After parking the station wagon Mary told Jayne to come up to her house that evening for supper and that Phoebe would join them. She knew Jayne had more to say, and wanted her to have the privacy to do it.

With a grateful nod, Jayne got out of the car and went to her cabin.

Phoebe knocked on Jayne's door after cocktails to go with her up to the Watts house.

"How are you doing?" she asked.

"I'm fine. Phoebe, I want to say something to you before we go. What I said…that day, about riding, about you not being tough, about your career. I'm sorry. I didn't mean it. I was just worried about Glenn. I should have known better. You were so brave with Thelma, and you saved my life. I can never repay you for that. I can only tell you that nothing I said about you is true. I wish I was more like you."

Phoebe felt tears beginning but smiled to keep them at bay.

"I understand, I really do. I said some terrible things to Mary a couple of years ago when I was deeply hurt and upset. She knew I didn't mean it, either."

"Thank you. And one more thing."

Jayne walked over to the dresser, opened the top drawer, and pulled out a small box.

"I want you to have this."

Phoebe opened the box to find the longhorn pin. One of the horns was a little bent at the end.

"I can't ever wear this again," Jayne said. "But maybe you can, or at least keep it to remember what you did for me."

Phoebe wasn't sure she could wear it either, but she was touched.

"Thank you, Jayne. Come with me, let's go up to Mary's house."

Supper was simple, delicious, and nobody talked about Jayne's ordeal until Joe went to his room to do homework. Mary served drinks, and they sat in the living room. Sam had opened one of the windows to let in the brisk but not too cold night air. It smelled sweet and clean.

"I don't want to take up too much of your time," Jayne began. "But I do want to tell you about Glenn."

"We're listening," said Mary.

"It's true what the police officer told you. Glenn had debts in Las Vegas. Lots of them. And we didn't know what to do. Then Thelma approached us in Carson City, and made us a deal: we would help her with the plan to put dude ranches out of business in exchange for wiping out the IOUs that Glenn had signed.

"We didn't like it, but we didn't think we would have to do anything beyond some simple sabotage. We booked our stay over a few months so that whatever we did wouldn't look suspicious. That is, if things happened too often the police might investigate, and Thelma didn't want that. We thought if people saw the ranch being run poorly, they would stop coming, they would tell their friends to stay away.

"We didn't count on how popular your ranch is, and how well you managed your guests, even when things went wrong. Thelma told us to make something happen at the dudeo, but you all watched over things too closely. She then told Glenn to do something to that horse, Berry-Wise. He didn't like that Japanese girl, but he refused to harm a horse. Thelma was livid. She said if he wouldn't hurt an animal, he'd have to injure one of the guests. Then they would sue the ranch and you'd definitely have to close down."

Mary's face grew hard for a moment, but she let Jayne's story continue.

"Glenn absolutely refused to hurt anyone. So, she sent her trained cowboy, Bill Jordan, to set the fire. He thought someone might get burned or inhale too much smoke or something. But your men kept things from getting out of control. Glenn hoped it would be enough to scare people, but it wasn't. Thelma was crazy. She wanted someone to die. So, I went over there one day to plead with her."

"I saw you," said Phoebe. "You had a terrible look on your face and you walked right past me."

"You never told me that," said Mary.

"I didn't know what it meant, so I didn't want to say anything," said Phoebe.

"I was so angry that day," said Jayne. "Thelma wouldn't see reason. She wouldn't see that we'd done enough. So, she...had Glenn killed."

"Are you sure?" asked Mary. "Maybe that Jordan guy did it on his own, or someone from Las Vegas?"

"He did it, but she told him to. Jordan lured Glenn out of our cabin, marched him into the desert, and shot him. She told me that just before you came into the office, Phoebe."

Jayne looked around the room.

"Please don't think badly of Glenn," she said. "He was a wonderful man, and a good husband. He was a happier person than I am, but he had this…this devil inside him. He couldn't stop gambling. Those overnight trips we took were to illegal games in Phoenix. I hated it, but I couldn't let him go by himself. Then Thelma heard about it, and told him to quit or she would do something to me. It's the only thing that stopped him.

"I miss him so much."

"I know, and we're so sorry," said Mary. "But

that's in the past and it's time for you to move on. And I have a question."

"What is it?"

"Where did you learn to ride?"

Jayne smiled and said, "At home in Nevada, where I grew up. I lived on horses when I was a kid, and I still ride now and then."

"Why didn't you go on more trail rides?"

"I couldn't let anyone know I was experienced. We had to look like real dudes while we were here."

"Well, you sure did," said Mary. "What are you going to do now?"

"I will have to come back to Arizona to testify at Thelma's trial, but I'm going home to Carson City. I'm going to open a secretarial school. Glenn had a life insurance policy and I'll get a little money out of that. And I'm going to buy a horse."

Mary smiled her approval.

Jayne stayed at the ranch for another three days, even showing up to cocktails and meals. There were only two couples staying at the ranch, and they knew nothing about what had happened.

Jayne checked out on a beautiful mid-March day, and Phoebe came to the registration office to join Mary in saying goodbye. As Jayne loaded her suitcases into the Buick she turned to the two women and said, "I think I'll offer a stay at the H Double Bar to the top student at my secretarial school."

Phoebe and Mary smiled and waved as she drove down the long drive.

One more couple checked in on the day that Jayne left, and Mary was chatting with them at cocktails when Phoebe arrived that evening. They finished their conversation and Mary joined Phoebe at the bar.

"Have you heard from Virgil?" she asked.

"You know I have, you saw his letter come in," said Phoebe.

"And?"

"He wants to get here on Friday the first, so he can come with us to Steve and Nora's wedding on Saturday."

"I'm glad he's coming, that will be fun."

"It was nice of them to invite him. I guess I should also start thinking about what I'll do when you close next month. I don't want to go back to San Francisco for another six months, leave him behind, and then come back here in the fall. You do want me back, don't you?"

"Silly, of course, I do. But don't worry about that right now."

Two days later Phoebe got a letter postmarked New York with *Holiday Magazine* in the return address. Thinking it was about her subscription she didn't open it until she got to her office after lunch to work on *Trail Notes*. Putting aside her typed pages, she absently opened the envelope and took out a letter.

March 14, 1955

Miss Phoebe Kelley
H Double Bar Dude Ranch
Tribulation, Arizona

Dear Miss Kelley:

Your publisher, Mr. Arthur Mackenzie, gave me your name and address. I am looking for a writer to contribute to a column on dude ranching that we plan to start in Holiday *next spring. We want someone to visit the dude ranches in Montana, Wyoming, and Colorado this summer and to write profiles for our readers as they make their 1956 vacation plans.*

Mr. Mackenzie recommended you very highly, and I was impressed with your book, Lady in the Desert. *I would like to speak with you about this opportunity if you are interested. Please write or call at your earliest convenience and let me know.*

Yours very sincerely,

Nancy Blake (Miss)
Features Editor

With the letter in her hand, Phoebe tore out of the lodge to look for Mary. She wasn't at the front desk, so Phoebe went to the barn and found her there, watching Joe saddle Buster. He wanted to join that afternoon's trail ride, and with Lorraine in charge, Mary was sure he would do fine. Meaning that Lorraine would keep him from heading off the trail on his own.

Once the ride began, Phoebe gestured to Mary and then handed her the letter.

"Look at this, I got it today," she said.

Mary read quickly and then said, "You're going to do it, aren't you?"

"Well, I sure want to. I don't know what the pay or other details are, though. I'm going to call Miss Blake tomorrow morning. Good old Mr. Mackenzie, I guess he still had faith in me after all."

"All of us do, honey. I hope you're still not doubting yourself after what Jayne said."

"Not really, and I've been busy so I haven't been

thinking about what to do with my writing. I've just been thinking about Virgil."

"As you should. You will have to see how he feels about this."

"Yes, and his opinion is important. But he knows that writing is part of who I am, and I can't put it aside."

"You know him better than I do, but I don't think he would ask you to do that."

"Me, neither."

Phoebe called Miss Blake early the following morning, and after a short conversation, she accepted the magazine's offer. Three days later she received the letter with full details about the job and a contract. She showed the paperwork to Mary and Sam, who told her to sign and return the contract right away.

Eden had urged Phoebe to spend time with her new horse, so Phoebe rode Lark on many of the trail rides over the next two weeks. Lark wasn't a plodder like Applesauce, and was just spirited enough to keep Phoebe on her toes, and firmly in the saddle.

The day Virgil was due to arrive Phoebe waited impatiently near the parking lot, and he pulled in just before four. They hugged each other briefly as he got out and then Phoebe gave him the key Mary had left on the registration desk.

"I have so much to tell you," Phoebe said as they walked to his cabin.

"Good stuff, I hope?" he replied.

"Oh, yes. Come down to my place after supper."

They postponed talking for a while after the cabin door closed.

29

LATER THAT EVENING Virgil and Phoebe sat together on her couch with bourbon-laced coffee.

"I feel like we have been doing this forever," she said with a comfortable sigh.

"So do I." Virgil leaned over to kiss her. "Now, what's this news you have for me?"

Phoebe took a breath and told him about her book being turned down, and her publisher then recommending her to an editor at *Holiday* magazine. She gave him a description of the columns Miss Blake wanted her to write, and then got to the heart of the matter.

"They will pay my travel to seven dude ranches over the summer, and a monthly stipend. Then I have to write up detailed descriptions of what it's like to take a vacation at each of the ranches, what activities they offer, that kind of thing. If they like what I give them, they will do the same thing for the Southwestern ranches, and send me around Arizona, New Mexico, and southern California during the winter. This could turn into something very big for me."

Virgil was beaming.

"It sounds perfect for you, Phoebe."

"Yes, but I'd be away from you all summer. I don't want to turn it down, but I don't like the thought of not seeing you for months."

"Well, maybe you're overlooking something."

"What do you mean?"

"I could come with you."

"Oh, Virgil, that would be wonderful! The magazine wouldn't pay your train fare, or for an extra room at the ranch, but we can do that, can't we?"

"We can pay the train fare. But I know a way we wouldn't have to pay for an extra room."

"How?"

Virgil reached into his pants pocket and pulled out a small box.

"This is how."

He opened it to reveal a thin silver ring topped with a small diamond and two deep turquoise stones.

"Phoebe, will you be my wife?"

He took the ring out of the box and looked into her eyes.

She looked at the ring and then at him and said, "Yes. Oh, yes!"

He put the ring on her finger and watched her gaze at it before she wrapped her arms around his neck and kissed him with a tenderness equal to the passion they had already shown to each other.

Holding up her left hand she said, "Did you design this?"

"Yes, and I hope you don't mind, but the diamond and the band were Ellender's. It had been in her family for years, and it was the ring she wore when she was married to Daniel. Then I had it reset when we married. I couldn't bury it with her, and I didn't know why. But now I do. It was meant for you."

Phoebe had started crying as soon as Virgil mentioned Ellender.

"I don't mind, of course I don't mind, it's perfect."

"I know this seems sudden, but at my age I don't have time to waste on the niceties."

"I don't want to wait either. Besides, you need to come with me on my dude ranch trips, and I don't think they'd let us room together if we were living in sin."

They both giggled, and then Phoebe said, "Let's tell Mary and Sam first thing tomorrow before we go to the wedding. She'd be furious if I showed up in public wearing an engagement ring and she didn't know about it first."

Mary nearly jumped up and down when Phoebe and Virgil showed up at the Watts house early the next morning to give her and Sam the news. She hugged them both, Sam shook Virgil's hand, and Joe smiled but his mind was on Buster.

"Virgil is coming with me when I go to the dude ranches this summer to write for the magazine. But they might want me to travel in the winter, too. So, I might not be able to help you next season," said Phoebe.

"We won't think about that now. You need to do this, it's what you've been wanting," said Mary.

"I have everything I want," said Phoebe.

Nora and Steve's wedding was simple but beautiful, held in Tribulation's seventy-five-year-old

Presbyterian church. Barbara Burington and her friend Celeste motioned Phoebe and Virgil over when they walked in and gave them a seat. Barbara pointed at the ring on Phoebe's finger as soon as they sat down, Phoebe nodded and smiled and Barbara whispered, "Congratulations!" Mary, Sam, and Joe sat with Jim and Laura Stevenson, and the church soon filled up with nearly the entire town. Police officers in full uniform took up the back pews.

The reception was held in town hall, and when the dancing started, Virgil pulled Phoebe onto the floor with a skill she hadn't expected.

"Where did you learn to dance so well?"

"My mother," he said with a grin.

The celebration went on all afternoon, and Mary and Sam said their goodbyes just before five. Steve and Nora knew they had guests at the ranch who needed them, and Phoebe and Virgil decided to go along to help with the cocktail hour. They all said goodbye and good wishes to the newly-married couple.

The saloon was lively that night. There had been an unexpected rush of guests, and Mary was tickled to know that many of them had been at the Desert Grande before it closed, or had planned to go there. The same thing happened at the other ranches.

"I knew Powell wouldn't make a success of that place," Mary said to Phoebe and Virgil. "People want the real thing, not a flashy, fake guest ranch."

"She might have gotten away with it if it wasn't for you and Jayne," Virgil said, looking at Phoebe.

"True, but I'm with Mary on this. She would have been found out eventually."

"Well, enough about her. What are you two planning for your wedding?" asked Mary.

"All we know is that we want to have it here before we leave for the magazine assignment in June," said Phoebe. "Is that okay with you? When do the last guests check out?"

"Oh honey, of course it is. Everyone will be gone by April eleventh, that's a Monday. We aren't due to leave for Wyoming until the thirtieth. That's not a lot of time to plan a wedding, though."

"We don't want plans, we just want to invite the ranch staff, and a few friends, and just have a simple ceremony and some of Helen's good food."

"All right, consider it done. We'll look at the calendar tomorrow."

After supper that night and some time alone together in her *casa*, Virgil said good night to Phoebe and went back to his cabin. Phoebe wrote a short letter to Eden, telling her about the engagement to Virgil, and the offer from *Holiday Magazine*.

Then she walked over to her telephone table and dialed Katie's number.

"I have a lot to tell you," she said.

She started with the events at the Desert Grande, and then told her about Virgil, and their engagement.

"Well, I'm thrilled, I knew it had to happen sometime. Congratulations!"

"It seems my friends knew about Virgil and me before I did. Anyway, we're planning a simple wedding here at the H Double Bar sometime before the end of April. Will you be able to get away and come? We'll have a cabin for you, and will pick you up at the train station."

"You bet I'll be there. I'll tell the history department dean I have a family emergency. He's afraid of me, he won't say no."

"Oh Katie, I'm so glad, I wouldn't want to have a wedding without you."

"I'm excited to finally see the place. But there's one thing that worries me."

"What?"

"If I stay at the ranch, will I have to ride a horse?"

"Don't worry," said Phoebe. "I'll teach you."

Acknowledgments

When I finished writing *Dudes Rush In*, I hoped I had another novel in me. For a while, I didn't think I did, and then my characters clamored to go back to the H Double Bar dude ranch. So did many of my friends and relatives. Heartfelt thanks to all of you, because you helped make this book happen.

Additional thanks go to my early readers: Patti Elkin, Cari Lyn Stanton, and Mark Yateman. My cheerleading posse also kept me going: Jennifer Gunn, Jill Hunting, Rachel Santino, and Jeff Spielberg.

I am especially grateful to Annette Chaudet of Pronghorn Press, my publisher, editor, and friend. Her skills and her encouragement make me a better novelist.

I also wish to thank my friend, Hiromi Horie, who helped me choose historically accurate names for my Japanese and Japanese-American characters.

Trick rider Eden Williams came from a very personal place. Throughout my childhood my father told stories about what happened to many of his high school friends at the start of World War II. He went to Analy High School in Sebastopol, California—a rural, agricultural town in Sonoma County where Japanese-American families had lived and worked for generations. Their kids who were my father's age went to Analy and many of them were his friends.

They were also American citizens.

In May of 1942 Dad went to school one day and they were gone.

President Franklin Roosevelt signed Executive Order 9066 in February of 1942, which meant that anyone of Japanese descent had to leave their lives behind, get on specially-chartered trains, and relocate to internment camps set up all over the U.S. Sonoma County citizens were sent to Camp Amache, outside of Granada, Colorado, that May. And there they lived until the fall of 1945.

My father spoke bitterly of this injustice his whole life. He also made sure my sister and I knew about it, as well as the story of the Japanese-American men who joined the 442nd Regimental Combat Team, the most decorated military unit of its size in American history.

Eden Williams showed up one day as I thought about creating a trick-riding character for my book. I knew I wanted this person to have a past which causes some of the conflict in the story, and there she was.

Eden lives because my father wanted me to remember his friends.

This book is for him, and for them.

About the Author

Lynn Downey is a native Californian and self-described dudine. She grew up around her uncle's horses and her rodeo cowboy cousins in the San Francisco Bay Area, but instead of spending her childhood on horseback, she ended up as a historian and novelist of the West.

She read about the culture of dude ranching while working as the company Historian for Levi Strauss & Co., and spent her first dude ranch vacation in Wickenburg, Arizona. She became fascinated with this unique American institution and made it the setting for her award-winning debut novel, *Dudes Rush In*, the first book in her H Double Bar Dude Ranch series.

Lynn has written about Western history for over thirty years, and her books include *American Dude Ranch: A Touch of the Cowboy and the Thrill of the West; Levi Strauss: The Man Who Gave Blue Jeans to the World*;

Arequipa Sanatorium: Life in California's Lung Resort for Women; Arizona's Vulture Mine and Vulture City; Wickenburg: Images of America; and *A Short History of Sonoma.*

Her books have won many accolades: the Will Rogers Medallion Award, New Mexico-Arizona Book Award, the WILLA award from Women Writing the West, and the INDIE award from Foreword Reviews.

She shares her home in Sonoma, California with a collection of very entertaining cats and occasionally makes wine from the Pinot Noir vineyard in her backyard.

You can find Lynn on Instagram at lynn.downey.historian. Her website is at lynndowney.com, and she also writes the blog *Tumblereads: A New Twist on the Old West:* tumblereadsblog.

Milton Keynes UK
Ingram Content Group UK Ltd.
UKHW051807161023
430697UK00021B/987